D1440805

"FIND THE DANGER, THALE!"
The psipsych put her arm around the tele-path, stroked him, coaxed him. "Tell us about Royd. Was he telling the truth?" The phan-tom image of the *Nightflyer*'s captain stared at them with no reaction to the mention of his name.

Thale shrugged off the woman's support and sat upright. "My head hurts. . . ." He looked at Royd's ghost with terrified eyes. "He's—"

Then his skull exploded.

"WE KNOW YOUR TRUE NAME," THE FROG SAID.
It didn't help Mr. Slippery to know that the frog was only a high-resolution EEG simula-tion of the implacable government agent. It was for the moment real enough, and so was its implied threat.

He was a powerful warlock in this ana-logue-world inside the planetwide computer network—but, back in the dimly remembered realtime, his mortal body slept defenselessly. The one thing that had kept him safe from a vengeful, frightened government was ano-nymity—and now that was gone.

BINARY STAR BOOKS PUBLISHED BY DELL SF:

BINARY STAR #1:
Destiny Times Three by Fitz Lieber
Riding the Torch by Norman Spinrad
Illustrated by Freff

BINARY STAR #2:
The Twilight River by Gordon Eklund
The Tery by F. Paul Wilson
Illustrated by Stephen Fabian

BINARY STAR #3:
Dr. Scofflaw by Ron Goulart
Outerworld by Isidore Haiblum
Illustrated by James Odbert

BINARY STAR #4:
Legacy by Joan D. Vinge
The Janus Equation by Steven G. Spruill
Illustrated by Jack Gaughan

BINARY STAR NO.5

NIGHTFLYERS
George R. R. Martin

TRUE NAMES
Vernor Vinge

A DELL BOOK

Published by
Dell Publishing Co., Inc.
1 Dag Hammarskjold Plaza
New York, New York 10017

Dell ® TM 681510, Dell Publishing Co., Inc.

ISBN: 0-440-10757-1

Printed in Canada

First printing—February 1981

INTRODUCTION

James R. Frenkel, SERIES EDITOR

Each Binary Star volume has contained a pair of novellas, and in each case the novellas have complemented each other. In this volume, however, the complementary process goes a step further. Both stories owe their plots to computers. Without giving away anything that might spoil your enjoyment, I can tell you that both tales feature crimes, both take place in the future, and both are suspenseful, exciting pieces.

And at this point, George Martin and Vernor Vinge part company. Each approaches computers with his own, unique point of view. Martin, the Hugo- and Nebula-winning author of such stories as "A Song for Lya" and the recent "Sandkings," uses computers (actually, a single computer) as a foil for human characters involved in a locked-spaceship multiple murder mystery. Vernor Vinge, himself a mathematician and something of an experienced hand at computers, sets his entire story in the unique ambience created by a group of people whose computer machinations mesh . . . fantastically.

George Martin has little background in computers; yet he has set his piece in a future where computers are vital to the smooth function of spacecraft. When

I asked George Martin if he'd like to do a Binary Star novella, I didn't say, "Well, George, you can do what you like, but it'd better have computers in it." I merely asked him for a novella, without specifying topic or setting. Yet it's perfectly natural that he should have come up with a story which included computers. A sign of the times.

It wasn't always so. Older readers will have no difficulty remembering the days before computers became essential to our lives. Forty years ago, computers were just getting started, little more than oversized calculators, with lots of moving parts and with virtually nothing like the sophistication and flexibility of later models. For decades, computers have been an increasingly important tool in industry, government, business . . . and now they are finally having an impact directly in people's homes.

If you think I've wandered from the point, be assured that I'm only talking about what was considered science fiction a mere twenty years ago. We stand at the beginning of the new computer age. Home computers have been available for a little over five years, and several hundred thousand units are actually working—monitoring people's phone messages, paying bills, keeping track of energy consumption, communicating with banks and other financial institutions for their owners, working in tandem with cable television to act as communications links with electronic media—to make our lives run more smoothly.

These machines are a powerful agent of social change. Soon an increasing number of families will acquire home computers, and the ways in which we interact will change radically. Especially when coupled with cable television, home computers are making it possible—even practical—for people to do at home most things that would've required a trip outside several years ago. Shopping can now be done via cable

TV catalogues, with payment accomplished by credit transfer through a home computer. Many clerical tasks can be done at home by use of a word processor computer. Copies can be made on your printer—your computer printer. (By the bye, *True Names* was produced on a word processor.) There are almost endless possibilities inherent in the use of computers, and many of the possibilities lead toward the increasing physical isolation of people in cities, and in suburban areas.

Since World War II, population has become increasingly decentralized; since the advent of television, people have tended to stay at home for entertainment. Cable TV and home computers are making it even easier for people to stay at home. Not just for entertainment, either, but also for the more basic needs; in addition to shopping, and clerical tasks, many other vocational and survival needs can be met by home computers. It may not seem so right now, but once the price of home units begins to drop seriously, as consumer demand increases, the number of people with home computers will increase geometrically.

So what, you ask, is the big deal? The big deal is that nobody knows how such a social change will affect other aspects of our lives. Nobody—thirty years later —knows what television does to us; and yet, though we know the effects are not necessarily good, the population of the United States watches an average of more than six hours of TV each day. Computers are not like television; they don't rot your brain. But there are unanswered questions: what will happen when people no longer physically have to share space with other people? Is physical contact necessary to the maintenance of a real society?

These questions will become more important as home computers take hold. But computers are already with us, as witnessed by the settings of the two tales in this book. Let them be food for thought, and perhaps these science fiction entertainments will take on greater meaning in your life.

Nightflyers and *True Names* are illustrated by Jack Gaughan. Jack has been illustrating science fiction for over twenty years, and his technique and skill continue to develop. The work he's done in *True Names* is most unusual and effective, due in part to a special tool—printed-circuit boards. Jack felt that the unique setting of the story deserved a treatment that would mirror the reality of the plane on which the story's action occurs. It's exciting to see Jack's illustrations capture the essence of these stories as he did in *Binary Star #4*. A talented artist will adapt his creations to their context, and Jack continues to demonstrate his award-winning talent in a variety of works. Another fine collection of his black-and-white interpretations appears in Alfred Bester's new novel, *Golem¹⁰⁰*.

George R.R. Martin hasn't been writing science fiction for as long as Jack Gaughan has been illustrating it, but Martin is into his second decade and beginning to hit his stride. The Nebula Award for "Sandkings" is not his first award. "A Song for Lya" won the Hugo Award for best novelette a few years ago. Though nominated for the John W. Campbell Award for best new writer in 1973, he didn't win. He did, however, become the editor of *New Voices,* a series of anthologies featuring original works by Campbell Award nominees. With three volumes published, and more on the way, *New Voices* is starting to gain a larger audience than it first enjoyed.

His first novel, *Dying of the Light,* was well received, and *Windhaven,* a novel written in collaboration with Lisa Tuttle, will be published soon. After teaching for several years at Dubuque, Iowa, George recently gave up the great plains and moved to Santa Fe, New Mexico.

Vernor Vinge is also in his second decade of science fiction writing, but with a difference. He made a pretty big splash in the late sixties with a batch of stories published mostly in *Analog* magazine. His first novel, *Grimm's World,* was published in 1969, and its appearance marked him as a formidable talent. A second novel, *The Witling,* appeared in 1976, but since then nothing new has issued forth, until *True Names.* His work as professor of mathematics at San Diego State University has kept him busy, but not so busy that he couldn't reenter the science fiction world. He's currently working on a new novel, and other work is forthcoming. Originally from Michigan, he's lived in San Diego for some time.

Both George and Vernor have more to say, but you'd better read the novellas first. I'm told that they really mean their Afterwords to be read *after* each other's stories. My own feeling is that *Binary Star #5* is the best book in the series thus far. You'll have to decide for yourself.

—James R. Frenkel
New York City, July 1980

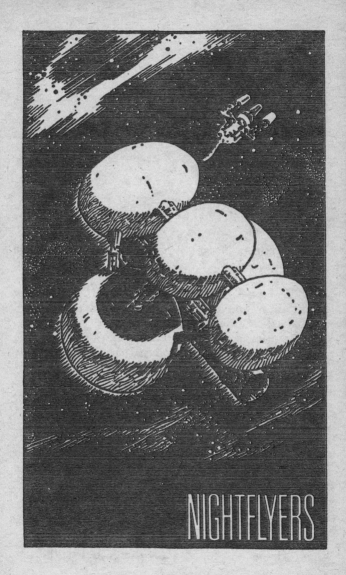

NIGHTFLYERS

When Jesus of Nazareth hung dying on his cross, the *volcryn* passed within a year of his agony, headed outward.

When the Fire Wars raged on Earth, the *volcryn* sailed near Old Poseidon, where the seas were still unnamed and unfished. By the time the stardrive had transformed the Federated Nations of Earth into the Federal Empire, the *volcryn* had moved into the fringes of Hrangan space. The Hrangans never knew it. Like us, they were children of the small bright worlds that circled their scattered suns, with little interest in and less knowledge of the things that moved in the gulfs between.

War flamed for a thousand years and the *volcryn* passed through it, unknowing and untouched, safe in a place where no fires could ever burn. Afterward the Federal Empire was shattered and gone, and the Hrangans vanished in the dark of the Collapse, but it was no darker for the *volcryn*.

When Kleronomas took his survey ship out from Avalon, the *volcryn* came within ten light years of him. Kleronomas found many things, but he did not

find the *volcryn*. Not then and not on his return to
Avalon a lifetime later.

When I was a child of three, Kleronomas was dust,
as distant and dead as Jesus of Nazareth, and the
volcryn passed close to Daronne. That season all the
Crey sensitives grew strange and sat staring at the
stars with luminous, flickering eyes.

When I was grown, the *volcryn* had sailed beyond
Tara, past the range of even the Crey, still head-
ing outward.

And now I am old and growing older and the
volcryn will soon pierce the Tempter's Veil where it
hangs like a black mist between the stars. And we
follow, we follow. Through the dark gulfs where no
one goes, through the emptiness, through the silence
that goes on and on, my *Nightflyer* and I give chase.

They made their way slowly down the length of the
transparent tube that linked the orbital docks to the
waiting starship ahead, pulling themselves hand over
hand through weightlessness.

Melantha Jhirl, the only one among them who did
not seem clumsy and ill at ease in free-fall, paused
briefly to look at the dappled globe of Avalon below, a stately vastness in jade and amber. She smiled
and moved swiftly down the tube, passing her com-
panions with an easy grace. They had boarded starships before, all of them, but never like this. Most
ships docked flush against the station, but the craft
that Karoly d'Branin had chartered for his mission
was too large, and of too singular a design. It loomed
ahead; three small eggs side by side, two larger spheres
beneath and at right angles, the cylinder of the driveroom between, lengths of tube connecting it all. The
ship was white and austere.

Melantha Jhirl was the first one through the airlock. The others straggled up one by one until they
had all boarded; five women and four men, each an

Academy scholar, their backgrounds as diverse as their fields of study. The frail young telepath, Thale Lasamer, was the last to enter. He glanced about nervously as the others chatted and waited for the entry procedure to be completed. "We're being watched," he said.

The outer door was closed behind them, the tube had fallen away; now the inner door slid open. "Welcome to my *Nightflyer*," said a mellow voice from within.

But there was no one there.

Melantha Jhirl stepped into the corridor. "Hello," she said, looking about quizzically. Karoly d'Branin followed her.

"Hello," the mellow voice replied. It was coming from a communicator grill beneath a darkened viewscreen. "This is Royd Eris, master of the *Nightflyer*. I'm pleased to see you again, Karoly, and pleased to welcome the rest of you."

"Where are you?" someone demanded.

"In my quarters, which occupy half of this life-support sphere," the voice of Royd Eris replied amiably. "The other half is comprised of a lounge-library-kitchen, two sanitary stations, one double cabin, and a rather small single. The rest of you will have to rig sleepwebs in the cargo spheres, I'm afraid. The *Nightflyer* was designed as a trader, not a passenger vessel. However, I've opened all the appropriate passageways and locks, so the holds have air and heat and water. I thought you'd find it more comfortable that way. Your equipment and computer system have been stowed in the holds, but there is still plenty of space, I assure you. I suggest you settle in, and then meet in the lounge for a meal."

"Will you join us?" asked the psipsych, a querulous, hatchet-faced woman named Agatha Marij-Black.

"In a fashion," Royd Eris said, "in a fashion."

* * *

The ghost appeared at the banquet.

They found the lounge easily enough, after they had rigged their sleepwebs and arranged their personal belongings around their sleeping quarters. It was the largest room in this section of the ship. One end of it was a fully equipped kitchen, well stocked with provisions. The opposite end offered several comfortable chairs, two readers, a holotank, and a wall of books and tapes and crystal chips. In the center was a long table with places set for ten.

A light meal was hot and waiting. The academicians helped themselves and took seats at the table, laughing and talking to each other, more at ease now than when they had boarded. The ship's gravity grid was on, which went a long way toward making them more comfortable; the queasy awkwardness of their weightless transit was soon forgotten.

Finally all the seats were occupied except for one at the head of the table.

The ghost materialized there.

All conversation stopped.

"Hello," said the specter, the bright shade of a lithe, pale-eyed young man with white hair. He was dressed in clothing twenty years out of date: a loose blue pastel shirt that ballooned at his wrists; clinging white trousers with built-in boots. They could see through him, and his own eyes did not see them at all.

"A holograph," said Alys Northwind, the short, stout xenotech.

"Royd, Royd, I do not understand," said Karoly d'Branin, staring at the ghost. "What is this? Why do you send us a projection? Will you not join us in person?"

The ghost smiled faintly and lifted an arm. "My quarters are on the other side of that wall," he said. "I'm afraid there is no door or lock between the two halves of the sphere. I spend most of my time by myself, and I value my privacy. I hope you will all understand, and respect my wishes. I will be a gracious host nonetheless. Here in the lounge my projection can join you. Elsewhere, if you have anything you need, if you want to talk to me, just use a communicator. Now please resume your meal, and your conversations. I'll gladly listen. It's been a long time since I had passengers."

They tried. But the ghost at the head of the table cast a long shadow, and the meal was strained and hurried.

From the hour the *Nightflyer* slipped into stardrive, Royd Eris watched his passengers.

Within a few days most of the academicians had grown accustomed to the disembodied voice from the communicators and the holographic specter in the lounge, but only Melantha Jhirl and Karoly d'Branin ever seemed really comfortable in his presence. The others would have been even more uncomfortable if they had known that Royd was always with them. Always and everywhere, he watched. Even in the sanitary stations, Royd had eyes and ears.

He watched them work, eat, sleep, copulate; he listened untiringly to their talk. Within a week he knew them, all nine, and had begun to ferret out their tawdry little secrets.

The cyberneticist, Lommie Thorne, talked to her computers and seemed to prefer their company to that of humans. She was bright and quick, with a mobile, expressive face and a small hard boyish body; most of the others found her attractive, but she did not like to be touched. She sexed only once, with Melantha Jhirl. Lommie Thorne wore shirts of softly woven metal and had an implant in her left wrist that let her interface directly with her computers.

The xenobiologist, Rojan Christopheris, was a surly, argumentative man, a cynic whose contempt

for his colleagues was barely kept in check, a solitary
drinker. He was tall and stooped and ugly.

The two linguists, Dannel and Lindran, were lovers in public, constantly holding hands and supporting each other. In private they quarreled bitterly.
Lindran had a mordant wit and liked to wound Dannel where it hurt the most, with jokes about his professional competence. They sexed often, both of them,
but not with each other.

Agatha Marij-Black, the psipsych, was a hypochon-
driac given to black depressions which worsened in
the close confines of the *Nightflyer.*

Xenotech Alys Northwind ate constantly and never
washed. Her stubby fingernails were always caked
with black dirt, and she wore the same jumpsuit for
the first two weeks of the voyage, taking it off only
for sex, and then only briefly.

Telepath Thale Lasamer was nervous and temper-
amental, afraid of everyone around him, yet given to
bouts of arrogance in which he taunted his com-
panions with thoughts he had snatched from their
minds.

Royd Eris watched them all, studied them, lived
with them and through them. He neglected none, not
even the ones he found the most distasteful. But by
the time the *Nightflyer* had been lost in the roiling
flux of stardrive for two weeks, two of his riders had
come to engage the bulk of his attention.

"Most of all, I want to know the *why* of them,"
Karoly d'Branin told him one false night the second
week out from Avalon.

Royd's luminescent ghost sat close to d'Branin in
the darkened lounge, watching him drink bittersweet
chocolate. The others were all asleep. Night and day
are meaningless on a starship, but the *Nightflyer* kept
the usual cycles and most of the passengers followed
them. Old d'Branin, administrator, generalist, and

mission leader, was the exception; he kept his own hours, preferred work to sleep, and liked nothing better than to talk about his pet obsession, the *volcryn* he hunted.

"The *if* of them is important as well, Karoly," Royd answered. "Can you truly be certain these aliens of yours exist?"

"*I* can be certain," Karoly d'Branin said, with a broad wink. He was a compact man, short and slender, iron-gray hair carefully styled and tunic almost fussily neat, but the expansiveness of his gestures and the giddy enthusiasms to which he was prone belied his sober appearance. "That is enough. If everyone else were certain as well, we would have a fleet of research ships instead of your little *Nightflyer*." He sipped at his chocolate and sighed with satisfaction. "Do you know the Nor T'alush, Royd?"

The name was strange, but it took Royd only a moment to consult his library computer. "An alien race on the other side of human space, past the Fyndii worlds and the Damoosh. Possibly legendary."

D'Branin chuckled. "No, no, no! Your library is out of date, my friend, you must supplement it the next time you visit Avalon. Not legends, no; real enough, though far away. We have little information about the Nor T'alush, but we are sure they exist, though you and I may never meet one. They were the start of it all."

"Tell me," Royd said. "I am interested in your work, Karoly."

"I was coding some information into the Academy computers, a packet newly arrived from Dam Tullian after twenty standard years in transit. Part of it was Nor T'alush folklore. I had no idea how long that had taken to get to Dam Tullian, or by what route it had come, but it did not matter—folklore is timeless anyway, and this was fascinating material. Did you know that my first degree was in xenomythology?"

"I did not. Please continue."

"The *volcryn* story was among the Nor T'alush myths. It awed me; a race of sentients moving out from some mysterious origin in the core of the galaxy, sailing toward the galactic edge and, it was alleged, eventually bound for intergalactic space itself, meanwhile always keeping to the interstellar depths, no planetfalls, seldom coming within a light-year of a star." D'Branin's gray eyes sparkled, and as he spoke, his hands swept enthusiastically to either side as if they could encompass the galaxy. "And doing it all *without a stardrive,* Royd, that is the real wonder! Doing it in ships moving only a fraction of the speed of light! That was the detail that obsessed me! How different they must be, my *volcryn*—wise and patient, long-lived and long-viewed, with none of the terrible haste and passion that consume the lesser races. Think how *old* they must be, those *volcryn* ships!"

"Old," Royd agreed. "Karoly, you said *ships.* More than one?"

"Oh, yes," d'Branin said. "According to the Nor T'alush, one or two appeared first, on the innermost edges of their trading sphere, but others followed. Hundreds of them, each solitary, moving by itself, bound outward, always outward. The direction was always the same. For fifteen thousand standard years they moved among the Nor T'alush stars, and then they began to pass out from among them. The myth said that the last *volcryn* ship was gone three thousand years ago."

"Eighteen thousand years," Royd said, adding. "Are the Nor T'alush that old?"

"Not as star-travelers, no," d'Branin said, smiling. "According to their own histories, the Nor T'alush have only been civilized for about half that long. That bothered me for a while. It seemed to make the *volcryn* story clearly a legend. A wonderful legend, true, but nothing more.

"Ultimately, however, I could not let it alone. In my spare time I investigated, cross-checking with other alien cosmologies to see whether this particular myth was shared by any races other than the Nor T'alush. I thought perhaps I could get a thesis out of it. It seemed a fruitful line of inquiry.

"I was startled by what I found. Nothing from the Hrangans, or the Hrangan slaveraces, but that made sense, you see. They were *out* from human space; the *volcryn* would not reach them until after they had passed through our own sphere. When I looked *in*, however, the *volcryn* story was everywhere." D'Branin leaned forward eagerly, "Ah, Royd, the stories, the *stories!*"

"Tell me," Royd said.

"The Fyndii call them *iy-wivii*, which translates to something like void-horde or dark-horde. Each Fyndii horde tells the same story; only the mindmutes disbelieve. The ships are said to be vast, much larger than any known in their history or ours. Warships, they say. There is a story of a lost Fyndii horde, three hundred ships under *rala-fyn*, all destroyed utterly when they encountered an *iy-wivii*. This was many thousands of years ago, of course, so the details are unclear.

"The Damoosh have a different story, but they accept it as literal truth—and the Damoosh, you know, are the oldest race we've yet encountered. The people of the gulf, they call my *volcryn*. Lovely stories, Royd, lovely! Ships like great dark cities, still and silent, moving at a slower pace than the universe around them. Damoosh legends say the *volcryn* are refugees from some unimaginable war deep in the core of the galaxy, at the very beginning of time. They abandoned the worlds and stars on which they had evolved, sought true peace in the emptiness between.

"The gethsoids of Aath have a similar story, but in

their tale that war destroyed all life in our galaxy, and the *volcryn* are gods of a sort, reseeding the worlds as they pass. Other races see them as God's messengers, or shadows out of hell warning us all to flee some terror soon to emerge from the core."

"Your stories contradict each other, Karoly."

"Yes, yes, of course, but they all agree on the essentials—the *volcryn* sailing out, passing through our short-lived empires and transient glories in their ancient eternal sublight ships. *That* is what matters! The rest is frippery, ornamentation; we will soon know the truth of it. I checked what little was known about the races said to flourish further in still, beyond even the Nor T'alush—civilizations and peoples half-legendary themselves, like the Dan'lai and the Ullish and the Rohenna'kh—and where I could find anything at all, I found the *volcryn* story once again."

"The legend of the legends," Royd suggested. The specter's wide mouth turned up in a smile.

"Exactly, exactly," d'Branin agreed. "At that point I called in the experts, specialists from the Institute for the Study of Non-Human Intelligence. We researched for two years. It was all there, in the libraries and memories and matrices of the Academy. No one had ever looked before, or bothered to put it together.

"The *volcryn* have been moving through the man-realm for most of human history, since before the dawn of spaceflight. While we twist the fabric of space itself to cheat relativity, they have been sailing their great ships right through the heart of our alleged civilization, past our most populous worlds, at stately slow sublight speeds, bound for the Fringe and the dark between the galaxies. Marvelous, Royd, marvelous!"

"Marvelous," Royd agreed.

Karoly d'Branin drained his chocolate cup with a

swig and reached out to catch Royd's arm, but his hand passed through empty light. He seemed disconcerted for a moment, before he began to laugh at himself. "Ah, my *volcryn*. I grow overenthused, Royd. I am so close now. They have preyed on my mind for a dozen years, and within the month I will have them, will behold their splendor with my own weary eyes. Then, *then*, if only I can open communication, if only my people can reach ones so great and strange as they, so different from us—I have hopes, Royd, hopes that at last I will know the *why* of it!"

The ghost of Royd Eris smiled for him, and looked on through calm transparent eyes.

Passengers soon grow restless on a starship under drive, sooner on one as small and spare as the *Nightflyer*. Late in the second week the speculation began in deadly earnest.

"Who is this Royd Eris, really?" the xenobiologist, Rojan Christopheris, complained one night when four of them were playing cards. "Why doesn't he come out? What's the purpose of keeping himself sealed off from the rest of us?"

"Ask him," suggested Dannel, the male linguist.

"What if he's a criminal of some sort?" Christopheris said. "Do we know anything about him? No, of course not. D'Branin engaged him, and d'Branin is a senile old fool, we all know that."

"It's your play," Lommie Thorne said.

Christopheris snapped down a card. "Setback," he declared, "you'll have to draw again." He grinned. "As for this Eris, who knows that he isn't planning to kill us all."

"For our vast wealth, no doubt," said Lindran, the female linguist. She played a card on top of the one Christopheris had laid down. "Ricochet," she called softly. She smiled.

So did Royd Eris, watching.

* * *

Melantha Jhirl was good to watch.

Young, healthy, active, Melantha Jhirl had a vibrancy about her the others could not match. She was big in every way; a head taller than anyone else on board, large-framed, large-breasted, long-legged, strong muscles moving fluidly beneath shiny coal-black skin. Her appetites were big as well. She ate twice as much as any of her colleagues, drank heavily without ever seeming drunk, exercised for hours every day on equipment she had brought with her and set up in one of the cargo holds. By the third week out she had sexed with all four of the men on board and two of the other women. Even in bed she was always active, exhausting most of her partners. Royd watched her with consuming interest.

"I am an improved model," she told him once as she worked out on her parallel bars, sweat glistening on her bare skin, her long black hair confined in a net.

"Improved?" Royd said. He could not send his projection down to the holds, but Melantha had summoned him with the communicator to talk while she exercised, not knowing he would have been there anyway.

She paused in her routine, holding her body straight and aloft with the strength of her arms and her back. "Altered, captain," she said. She had taken to calling him captain. "Born on Prometheus among the elite, child of two genetic wizards. Improved, captain. I require twice the energy you do, but I use it all. A more efficient metabolism, a stronger and more durable body, an expected life span half again the normal human's. My people have made some terrible mistakes when they try to radically redesign humanity, but the small improvements they do well."

She resumed her exercises, moving quickly and easily, silent until she had finished. When she was done, she vaulted away from the bars and stood breathing heavily for a moment, then crossed her arms and cocked her head and grinned. "Now you know my life story, captain," she said. She pulled off the net to shake free her hair.

"Surely there is more," said the voice from the communicator.

Melantha Jhirl laughed. "Surely," she said. "Do you want to hear about my defection to Avalon, the whys and wherefores of it, the trouble it caused my family on Prometheus? Or are you more interested in my extraordinary work in cultural xenology? Do you want to hear about that?"

"Perhaps some other time," Royd said politely. "What is that crystal you wear?"

It hung between her breasts, ordinarily; she had removed it when she stripped for her exercises. She picked it up again and slipped it over her head; a small green gem laced with traceries of black, on a silver chain. When it touched her, Melantha closed her eyes briefly, then opened them again, grinning. "It's alive," she said. "Haven't you ever seen one? A whisperjewel, captain. Resonant crystal, etched psionically to hold a memory, a sensation. The touch brings it back, for a time."

"I am familiar with the principle," Royd said, "but not this use. Yours contains some treasured memory, then? Of your family, perhaps?"

Melantha Jhirl snatched up a towel and began to dry the sweat from her body. "Mine contains the sensations of a particularly satisfying session in bed, captain. It arouses me. Or it did. Whisperjewels fade in time, and this isn't as potent as it once was. But sometimes—often when I've come from lovemaking or strenuous exercise—it comes alive on me again, like it did just then."

"Oh," said Royd's voice. "It has made you aroused, then? Are you going off to copulate now?"

Melantha grinned. "I know what part of my life *you* want to hear about, captain—my tumultuous and passionate love life. Well, you won't have it. Not until I hear your life story, anyway. Among my modest attributes is an insatiable curiosity. Who are you, captain? Really?"

"One as improved as you," Royd replied, "should certainly be able to guess."

Melantha laughed and tossed her towel at the communicator grill.

Lommie Thorne spent most of her days in the cargo hold they had designated the computer room, setting up the system they would use to analyze the *volcryn*. As often as not, the xenotech Alys Northwind came with her to lend a hand. The cyberneticist whistled as she worked; Northwind obeyed her orders in a sullen silence. Occasionally they talked.

"Eris isn't human," Lommie Thorne said one day as she supervised the installation of a display viewscreen.

Alys Northwind grunted. "What?" A frown broke across her square, flat features. Christopheris and his talk had made her nervous about Eris. She clicked another component into position and turned.

"He talks to us, but he can't be seen," the cyberneticist said. "This ship is uncrewed, seemingly all automated except for him. Why not entirely automated, then? I'd wager this Royd Eris is a fairly sophisticated computer system, perhaps a genuine Artificial Intelligence. Even a modest program can carry on a blind conversation indistinguishable from a human's. This one could fool you, I'd bet, once it's up and running."

The xenotech grunted and turned back to her work. "Why fake being human, then?"

"Because," said Lommie Thorne, "most legal systems give AIs no rights. A ship can't own itself, even on Avalon. The *Nightflyer* is probably afraid of being seized and disconnected." She whistled. "Death, Alys, the end of self-awareness and conscious thought."

"I work with machines every day," Alys Northwind said stubbornly. "Turn them off, turn them on, makes no difference. They don't mind. Why should this machine care?"

Lommie Thorne smiled. "A computer is different, Alys," she said. "Mind, thought, life, the big systems have all of that." Her right hand curled around her left wrist, and her thumb began idly rubbing the nubs of her implant. "Sensation, too. I know. No one wants the end of sensation. They are not so different from you and I, really."

The xenotech glanced back and shook her head. "Really," she repeated, in a flat, disbelieving voice.

Royd Eris listened and watched, unsmiling.

Thale Lasamer was a frail young thing; nervous, sensitive, with limp flaxen hair that fell to his shoulders, and watery blue eyes. Normally he dressed like a peacock, favoring the lacy V-neck shirts and codpieces that were still the fashion among the lower classes of his homeworld. But on the day he sought out Karoly d'Branin in his cramped, private cabin, Lasamer was dressed almost somberly, in an austere gray jumpsuit.

"I feel it," he said, clutching d'Branin by the arm, his long fingernails digging in painfully. "Something is wrong, Karoly, something is very wrong. I'm beginning to get frightened."

The telepath's nails bit, and d'Branin pulled away hard. "You are hurting me," he protested. "My friend, what is it? Frightened? Of what, of who? I do not understand. What could there be to fear?"

Lasamer raised pale hands to his face. "I don't know, I don't *know*," he wailed. "Yet it's *there*; I feel it. Karoly, I'm picking up something. You know I'm

good. I am, that's why you picked me. Just a moment
ago, when my nails dug into you, I felt it. I can read
you now, in flashes. You're thinking I'm too excit-
able, that it's the confinement, that I've got to be
calmed down." The young man laughed a thin hysterical laugh that died as quickly as it had begun.
"No, you see, I am good. Class one, tested, and I tell
you I'm afraid. I sense it. Feel it. Dream of it. I felt
it even as we were boarding, and it's gotten worse.
Something dangerous. Something volatile. And alien,
Karoly, *alien!*"

"The *volcryn?*" d'Branin said.

"No, impossible. We're in drive, they're light-years
away." The edgy laughter sounded again. "I'm not
that good, Karoly. I've heard your Crey story, but
I'm only a human. No, this is close. On the ship."

"One of us?"

"Maybe," Lasamer said. He rubbed his cheek absently. "I can't sort it out."

D'Branin put a fatherly hand on his shoulder.
"Thale, this feeling of yours—could it be that you
are just tired? All of us have been under strain. Inac-
tivity can be taxing."

"Get your hand off me," Lasamer snapped.

D'Branin drew back his hand quickly.

"This is *real,*" the telepath insisted, "and I don't
need you thinking that maybe you shouldn't have
taken me, all that crap. I'm as stable as anyone on
this . . . this . . . how *dare* you think I'm unstable.
You ought to look inside some of these others—
Christopheris with his bottle and his dirty little fantasies, Dannel half-sick with fear, Lommie and her
machines, with her it's all metal and lights and cool
circuits, sick, I tell you, and Jhirl's arrogant and
Agatha whines even in her head to herself all the
time, and Alys is empty, like a cow. You, you don't
touch them, see into them, what do you know of
stable? Losers, d'Branin, they've given you a bunch of

losers, and I'm one of your best, so don't you go thinking that I'm not stable, not sane, you hear." His blue eyes were fevered. "Do you *hear?*"

"Easy," d'Branin said. "Easy, Thale, you're getting excited."

The telepath blinked, and suddenly the wildness was gone. "Excited?" he said. "Yes." He looked around guiltily. "It's hard, Karoly, but listen to me. You must; I'm warning you. We're in danger."

"I will listen," d'Branin said, "but I cannot act without more definite information. You must use your talent and get it for me, yes? You can do that."

Lasamer nodded. "Yes," he said. "Yes." They talked quietly for more than an hour, and finally the telepath left peacefully.

Afterward d'Branin went straight to the psipsych, who was lying in her sleepweb surrounded by medicines, complaining bitterly of aches. "Interesting," she said when d'Branin told her. "I've felt something, too, a sense of threat, very vague, diffuse. I thought it was me, the confinement, the boredom, the way I feel. My moods betray me at times. Did he say anything more specific?"

"No."

"I'll make an effort to move around, read him, read the others, see what I can pick up. Although, if this is real, he should know it first. He's a one, I'm only a three."

D'Branin nodded. "He seems very receptive," he said. "He told me all kinds of things about the others."

"Means nothing. Sometimes, when a telepath insists he is picking up everything, what it means is that he's picking up nothing at all. He imagines feelings, readings, to make up for those that will not come. I'll keep careful watch on him, d'Branin. Sometimes a talent can crack, slip into a kind of hysteria, and begin to broadcast instead of receive. In a closed environment that's very dangerous."

Karoly d'Branin nodded. "Of course, of course."

In another part of the ship, Royd Eris frowned.

"Have you noticed the clothing on that holograph he sends us?" Rojan Christopheris asked Alys Northwind. They were alone in one of the holds, reclining on a mat, trying to avoid the wet spot. The xenobiologist had lit a joystick. He offered it to his companion, but Northwind waved it away. "A decade out of style, maybe more. My father wore shirts like that when he was a boy on Old Poseidon."

"Eris has old-fashioned taste," Alys Northwind said. "So? I don't care what he wears. Me, I like my jumpsuits. They're comfortable. Don't care what people think."

"You don't, do you?" Christopheris said, wrinkling his huge nose. She did not see the gesture. "Well, you miss the point. What if that isn't really Eris? A projection can be anything, can be made up out of whole cloth. I don't think he really looks like that."

"No?" Now her voice was curious. She rolled over and curled up beneath his arm, her heavy white breasts against his chest.

"What if he's sick, deformed, ashamed to be seen the way he really looks?" Christopheris said. "Perhaps he has some disease. The Slow Plague can waste a person terribly, but it takes decades to kill, and there are other contagions——manthrax, new leprosy, the melt, Langamen's Disease, lots of them. Could be that Royd's self-imposed quarantine is just that. A quarantine. Think about it."

Alys Northwind frowned. "All this talk of Eris," she said, "is making me edgy."

The xenobiologist sucked on his joystick and laughed. "Welcome to the *Nightflyer,* then. The rest of us are already there."

In the fifth week out Melantha Jhirl pushed her pawn to the sixth rank and Royd saw that it was unstoppable and resigned. It was his eighth straight defeat at her hands in as many days. She was sitting cross-legged on the floor of the lounge, the chessmen spread out before her in front of a darkened viewscreen. Laughing, she swept them all away. "Don't feel bad, Royd," she told him. "I'm an improved model. Always three moves ahead."

"I should tie in my computer," he replied. "You'd never know." His holographic ghost materialized suddenly, standing in front of the viewscreen, and smiled at her.

"I'd know within three moves," Melantha Jhirl said. "Try it."

They were the last victims of a chess fever that had swept the *Nightflyer* for more than a week. Initially it had been Christopheris who produced the set and urged people to play, but the others had lost interest quickly when Thale Lasamer sat down and beat them all, one by one. Everyone was certain that he'd done it by reading their minds, but the telepath was in a volatile, nasty mood, and no one dared voice the accusation. Melantha, however, had been able to defeat Lasamer without very much trouble. "He isn't that good a player," she told Royd afterward, "and if he's trying to lift ideas from me, he's getting gibberish. The improved model knows certain mental disciplines. I can shield myself well enough, thank you." Christopheris and a few of the others then tried a game or two against Melantha and were routed for their troubles. Finally Royd asked if he might play. Only Melantha and Karoly were willing to sit down with him over the board, and since Karoly could barely recall how the pieces moved from one moment to the next, that left Melantha and Royd as regular opponents. They both seemed to thrive on the games, though Melantha always won.

Melantha stood up and walked to the kitchen, stepping right through Royd's ghostly form, which she steadfastly refused to pretend was real. "The rest of them walk around me," Royd complained.

She shrugged and found a bulb of beer in a storage compartment. "When are you going to break down and let me behind your wall for a visit, captain?" she asked. "Don't you get lonely back there? Sexually frustrated? Claustrophobic?"

"I have flown the *Nightflyer* all my life, Melantha," Royd said. His projection, ignored, winked out. "If I were subject to claustrophobia, sexual frustration, or loneliness, such a life would have been impossible. Surely that should be obvious to you, being as improved a model as you are?"

She took a squeeze of her beer and laughed her mellow, musical laugh at him. "I'll solve you yet, captain," she warned.

"Meanwhile," he said, "tell me some more lies about your life."

"Have you ever heard of Jupiter?" the xenotech demanded of the others. She was drunk, lolling in her sleepweb in the cargo hold.

"Something to do with Earth," said Lindran. "The same myth system originated both names, I believe."

"Jupiter," the xenotech announced loudly, "is a gas giant in the same solar system as Old Earth. Didn't know that, did you?"

"I've got more important things to occupy my mind than such trivia, Alys," Lindran said.

Alys Northwind smiled down smugly. "Listen, I'm talking to you. They were on the verge of exploring this Jupiter when the stardrive was discovered, oh, way back. After that, course, no one bothered with gas giants. Just slip into drive and find the habitable worlds, settle them, ignore the comets and the rocks and the gas giants—there's another star just a few light-years away, and it has *more* habitable planets. But there were people who thought those Jupiters might have life, you know. Do you see?"

"I see that you're blind drunk," Lindran said.

Christopheris looked annoyed. "If there is intelligent life on the gas giants, it shows no interest in leaving them," he snapped. "All of the sentient species we have met up to now have originated on worlds similar to Earth, and most of them are oxygen breathers. Unless you're suggesting that the *volcryn* are from a gas giant?"

The xenotech pushed up to a sitting position and smiled conspiratorially. "Not the *volcryn*," she said. "Royd Eris. Crack that forward bulkhead in the lounge, and watch the methane and ammonia come smoking out." Her hand made a sensuous waving motion through the air, and she convulsed with giddy laughter.

The system was up and running. Cyberneticist Lommie Thorne sat at the master console, a featureless black plastic plate upon which the phantom images of a hundred keyboard configurations came and went in holographic display, vanishing and shifting even as she used them. Around her rose crystalline data grids, ranks of viewscreens and readout panels upon which columns of figures marched and geometric shapes did stately whirling dances, dark columns of seamless metal that contained the mind and soul of her system. She sat in the semi-darkness happily, whistling as she ran the computer through several simple routines, her fingers moving across the flickering keys with blind speed and quickening tempo. "Ah," she said once, smiling. Later, only, "Good."

Then it was time for the final run-through. Lommie Thorne slid back the metallic fabric of her left sleeve, pushed her wrist beneath the console, found the prongs, jacked herself in. Interface.

Ecstasy.

Inkblot shapes in a dozen glowing colors twisted and melded and broke apart on the readout screens.

In an instant it was over.

Lommie Thorne pulled free her wrist. The smile on her face was shy and satisfied, but across it lay another expression, the merest hint of puzzlement. She touched her thumb to the holes of her wrist jack and found them warm to the touch, tingling. Lommie shivered.

The system was running perfectly, hardware in good condition, all software systems functioning according to plan, interface meshing well. It had been a delight, as it always was. When she joined with the system, she was wise beyond her years, and powerful, and full of light and electricity and the stuff of life, cool and clean and exciting to touch, and never alone, never small or weak. That was what it was always like when she interfaced and let herself expand.

But this time something had been different. Something cold had touched her, only for a moment. Something very cold and very frightening, and together she and the system had seen it cleanly for a brief moment, and then it had been gone again.

The cyberneticist shook her head and drove the nonsense out. She went back to work. After a time she began to whistle.

During the sixth week Alys Northwind cut herself badly while preparing a snack. She was standing in the kitchen, slicing a spiced meatstick with a long knife, when suddenly she screamed.

Dannel and Lindran rushed to her and found her staring down in horror at the chopping block in front of her. The knife had taken off the first joint of the index finger on her left hand, and the blood was spreading in ragged spurts. "The ship lurched," Alys said numbly, staring up at Dannel. "Didn't you feel it jerk? It pushed the knife to the side."

"Get something to stop the bleeding," Lindran said. Dannel looked around in panic.

"Oh, I'll do it myself," Lindran finally said, and she did.

The psipsych, Agatha Marij-Black, gave North-wind a tranquilizer, then looked at the two linguists. "Did you see it happen?"

"She did it herself, with the knife," Dannel said.

From somewhere down the corridor there came the sound of wild, hysterical laughter.

"I dampened him," Marij-Black reported to Karoly d'Branin later the same day. "Psionine-4. It will blunt his receptivity for several days, and I have more if he needs it."

D'Branin wore a stricken look. "We talked several times, and I could see that Thale was becoming ever more fearful, but he could never tell me the why of it. Did you have to shut him off?"

The psipsych shrugged. "He was edging into the irrational. Given his level of talent, if he'd gone over the edge, he might have taken us all with him. You should never have taken a class-one telepath, d'Branin. Too unstable."

"We must communicate with an alien race. I remind you that is no easy task. The *volcryn* will be more alien than any sentients we have yet encountered. We needed class-one skills if we were to have any hope of reaching them. And they have so much to teach us, my friend!"

"Glib," she said, "but you might have no working skills at all, given the condition of your class one. Half the time he's curled up into the fetal position in his sleepweb, half the time he's strutting and crowing and half-mad with fear. He insists we're all in real physical danger, but he doesn't know why or from what. The worst of it is that I can't tell if he's really sensing something or simply having an acute attack of paranoia. He certainly displays some classic paranoid symptoms. Among other things he insists that he's being watched. Perhaps his condition is completely unrelated to us, the *volcryn,* and his talent. I can't be sure."

"What of your own talent?" d'Branin said. "You are an empath, are you not?"

"Don't tell me my job," she said sharply. "I sexed with him last week. You don't get more proximity or better rapport for esping than that. Even under those conditions I couldn't be sure of anything. His mind is a chaos, and his fear is so rank it stank up the sheets. I don't read anything from the others either, besides the ordinary tensions and frustrations. But I'm only a three, so that doesn't mean much. My abilities are limited. You know I haven't been feeling well, d'Branin. I can barely breathe on this ship. The air seems thick and heavy to me; my head throbs. Ought to stay in bed."

"Yes, of course," d'Branin said hastily. "I did not mean to criticize. You have been doing all you can under difficult circumstances. How long will it be until Thale is with us again?"

The psipsych rubbed her temple wearily. "I'm recommending we keep him dampened until the mission is over, d'Branin. I warn you, an insane or hysterical telepath is dangerous. That business with Northwind and the knife might have been his doing, you know. He started screaming not long after, remember. Maybe he'd touched her, for just an instant —oh, it's a wild idea, but it's possible. The point is, we don't take chances. I have enough psionine-4 to keep him numb and functional until we're back on Avalon."

"*But*—Royd will take us out of drive soon, and we

will make contact with the *volcryn*. We will need Thale—his mind, his talent. Is it vital to keep him dampened? Is there no other way?"

Marij-Black grimaced. "My other option was an injection of esperon. It would have opened him up completely, increased his psionic receptivity tenfold for a few hours. Then, I'd hope, he could focus in on this danger he's feeling. Exorcise it if it's false, deal with it if it's real. But psionine-4 is a lot safer. Esperon is a hell of a drug, with devastating side effects. It raises the blood pressure dramatically, sometimes brings on hyperventilation or seizures, has even been known to stop the heart. Lasamer is young enough so that I'm not worried about that, but I don't think he has the emotional stability to deal with that kind of power. The psionine should tell us something. If his paranoia persists, I'll know it has nothing to do with his telepathy."

"And if it does not persist?" Karoly d'Branin said.

Agatha Marij-Black smiled wickedly at him. "If Lasamer becomes quiescent and stops babbling about danger? Why, that would mean he was no longer picking up anything, wouldn't it? And *that* would mean there had been something to pick up, that he'd been right all along."

At dinner that night Thale Lasamer was quiet and distracted, eating in a rhythmic, mechanical sort of way, with a cloudy look in his blue eyes. Afterward he excused himself and went straight to bed, falling into exhausted slumber almost immediately.

"What did you do to him?" Lommie Thorne asked Marij-Black.

"I shut off that prying mind of his," she replied.

"You should have done it two weeks ago," Lindran said. "Docile, he's a lot easier to take."

Karoly d'Branin hardly touched his food.

* * *

False night came, and Royd's wraith materialized while Karoly d'Branin sat brooding over his chocolate. "Karoly," the apparition said, "would it be possible to tie in the computer your team brought on board with my shipboard system? Your *volcryn* stories fascinate me, and I would like to be able to study them further at my leisure. I assume the details of your investigation are in storage."

"Certainly," d'Branin replied in an offhand, distracted manner. "Our system is up now. Patching it into the *Nightflyer* should present no problem. I will tell Lommie to attend to it tomorrow."

Silence hung in the room heavily. Karoly d'Branin sipped at his chocolate and stared off into the darkness, almost unaware of Royd.

"You are troubled," Royd said after a time.

"Eh? Oh, yes." D'Branin looked up. "Forgive me, my friend. I have much on my mind."

"It concerns Thale Lasamer, does it not?"

Karoly d'Branin looked at the pale, luminescent figure across from him for a long time before he finally managed a stiff nod. "Yes. Might I ask how you knew that?"

"I know everything that occurs on the *Nightflyer*," Royd said.

"You have been watching us," d'Branin said gravely, accusation in his tone. "Then it is so, what Thale says, about us being watched. Royd, how could you? Spying is beneath you."

The ghost's transparent eyes had no life in them, did not see. "Do not tell the others," Royd warned. "Karoly, my friend—if I may call you my friend—I have my own reasons for watching, reasons it would not profit you to know. I mean you no harm. Believe that. You have hired me to take you safely to the *volcryn* and safely back, and I mean to do just that."

"You are being evasive, Royd," d'Branin said.

"Why do you spy on us? Do you watch everything? Are you a voyeur, some enemy—is that why you do not mix with us? Is watching all you intend to do?"

"Your suspicions hurt me, Karoly."

"Your deception hurts me. Will you not answer me?"

"I have eyes and ears everywhere," Royd said. "There is no place to hide from me on the *Nightflyer*. Do I see everything? No, not always. I am only human, no matter what your colleagues might think. I sleep. The monitors remain on, but there is no one to observe them. I can only pay attention to one or two scenes or inputs at once. Sometimes I grow distracted, unobservant. I watch everything, Karoly, but I do not see everything."

"*Why?*" D'Branin poured himself a fresh cup of chocolate, steadying his hand with an effort.

"I do not have to answer that question. The *Nightflyer* is my ship."

D'Branin sipped chocolate, blinked, nodded to himself. "You grieve me, my friend. You give me no choice. Thale said we were being watched, and he was right, I now learn. He says also that we are in danger. Something alien, he says. You?"

The projection was still and silent.

D'Branin clucked. "You do not answer. Ah, Royd, what am I to do? I must believe him, then. We are in danger, perhaps from you. I must abort our mission, then. Return us to Avalon, Royd. That is my decision."

The ghost smiled wanly. "So close, Karoly? Soon now we will be dropping out of drive."

Karoly d'Branin made a small, sad noise deep in his throat. "My *volcryn*," he said, sighing. "So close—ah, it pains me to desert them. But I cannot do otherwise, I cannot."

"You can," said the voice of Royd Eris. "Trust me. That is all I ask, Karoly. Believe me when I tell you that I have no sinister intentions. Thale Lasamer may speak of danger, but no one has been harmed so far, have they?"

"No," admitted d'Branin. "No, unless you count Alys, cutting herself this afternoon."

"What?" Royd hesitated briefly. "Cutting herself? I did not see, Karoly. When did this happen?"

"Oh, early—just before Lasamer began to scream and rant, I believe."

"I see." Royd's voice was thoughtful. "I was watching Melantha go through her exercises," he said finally, "and talking to her. I did not notice. Tell me how it happened."

D'Branin told him.

"Listen to me," Royd said. "Trust me, Karoly, and I will give you your *volcryn*. Calm your people. Assure them that I am no threat. And keep Lasamer drugged and quiescent, do you understand? That is very important. He is the problem."

"Agatha advises much the same thing."

"I know," said Royd. "I agree with her. Will you do as I ask?"

"I do not know," d'Branin said. "You make it hard for me. I do not understand what is going wrong, my friend. Will you not tell me more?"

Royd Eris did not answer. His ghost waited.

"Well," d'Branin said at last, "you do not talk. How difficult you make it. How soon, Royd? How soon will we see my *volcryn?*"

"Quite soon," Royd replied. "We will drop out of drive in approximately seventy hours."

"Seventy hours," d'Branin said. "Such a short time. Going back would gain us nothing." He moistened his lips, lifted his cup, found it empty. "Go on, then. I will do as you bid. I will trust you, keep Lasamer drugged; I will not tell the others of your spying. Is that enough, then? Give me my *volcryn*. I have waited so long!"

"I know," said Royd Eris. "I know."

Then the ghost was gone, and Karoly d'Branin sat alone in the darkened lounge. He tried to refill his cup, but his hand began to tremble unaccountably, and he poured the chocolate over his fingers and dropped the cup, swearing, wondering, hurting.

The next day was a day of rising tensions and a hundred small irritations. Lindran and Dannel had a "private" argument that could be overheard through half the ship. A three-handed war game in the lounge ended in disaster when Christopheris accused Melantha Jhirl of cheating. Lommie Thorne complained of unusual difficulties in tying her system into the shipboard computers. Alys Northwind sat in the lounge for hours, staring at her bandaged finger with a look of sullen hatred on her face. Agatha Marij-Black prowled through the corridors, complaining that the ship was too hot, that her joints throbbed, that the air was thick and full of smoke, that the ship was too cold. Even Karoly d'Branin was despondent and on edge.

Only the telepath seemed content. Shot full of psionine-4, Thale Lasamer was often sluggish and lethargic, but at least he no longer flinched at shadows.

Royd Eris made no appearance, either by voice or holographic projection.

He was still absent at dinner. The academicians ate uneasily, expecting him to materialize at any moment, take his accustomed place, and join in the mealtime conversation. Their expectations were still unfulfilled when the afterdinner pots of chocolate and spiced tea and coffee were set on the table.

"Our captain seems to be occupied," Melantha Jhirl observed, leaning back in her chair and swirling a snifter of brandy.

"We will be shifting out of drive soon," Karoly

d'Branin said. "Undoubtedly there are preparations to make." Secretly he fretted over Royd's absence and wondered if they were being watched even now.

Rojan Christopheris cleared his throat. "Since we're all here and he's not, perhaps this is a good time to discuss certain things. I'm not concerned about him missing dinner. He doesn't eat. He's a damned holograph. What does it matter? Maybe it's just as well; we need to talk about this. Karoly, a lot of us have been getting uneasy about Royd Eris. What do you know about this mystery man, anyway?"

"Know, my friend?" D'Branin refilled his cup with the thick bittersweet chocolate and sipped at it slowly, trying to give himself a moment to think. "What is there to know?"

"Surely you've noticed that he never comes out to play with us," Lindran said dryly. "Before you engaged his ship, did anyone remark on this quirk of his?"

"I'd like to know the answer to that one, too," said Dannel, the other linguist. "A lot of traffic comes and goes through Avalon. How did you come to choose Eris? What were you told about him?"

"Told about him? Very little, I must admit. I spoke to a few port officials and charter companies, but none of them was acquainted with Royd. He had not traded out of Avalon originally, you see."

"How convenient," said Lindran.

"How suspicious," added Dannel.

"Where *is* he from, then?" Lindran demanded. "Dannel and I have listened to him pretty carefully. He speaks standard very flatly, with no discernible accent, no idiosyncrasies to betray his origins."

"Sometimes he sounds a bit archaic," Dannel put in, "and from time to time one of his constructions will give me an association, Only it's a different one each time. He's traveled a lot."

"Such a deduction," Lindran said, patting his hand. "Traders frequently do, love. Comes of owning a starship."

Dannel glared at her, but Lindran just went on. "Seriously, though, do you know anything about him? Where did this nightflyer of ours come from?"

"I do not know," d'Branin admitted. "I—I never thought to ask."

The members of his research team glanced at each other incredulously. "You never thought to *ask?*" Christopheris said. "How did you come to select this ship?"

"It was available. The administrative council approved my project and assigned me personnel, but they could not spare an Academy ship. There were budgetary constraints as well."

Agatha Marij-Black laughed sourly. "What d'Branin is telling those of you who haven't figured it out is that the Academy was pleased with his studies in xenomyth, with the discovery of the *volcryn* legend, but less than enthusiastic about his plan to seek them out. So they gave him a small budget to keep him happy and productive, assuming this little mission would be fruitless, and they assigned him people who wouldn't be missed back on Avalon." She looked around. "Look at the lot of you. None of us had worked with d'Branin in the early stages, but we were all available for this jaunt. And not a one of us is a first-rate scholar."

"Speak for yourself," Melantha Jhirl said. "I volunteered for this mission."

"I won't argue the point," the psipsych said. "The crux is that the choice of the *Nightflyer* is no large enigma. You just engaged the cheapest charter you could find, didn't you, d'Branin?"

"Some of the available ships would not consider my proposition," d'Branin said. "The sound of it is odd, we must admit. And many shipmasters have an almost superstitious fear of dropping out of drive in interstellar space, without a planet near. Of those who would agree to the conditions, Royd Eris offered the best terms, and he was able to leave at once."

"And we *had* to leave at once," said Lindran. "Otherwise the *volcryn* might get away. They've only been passing through this region for ten thousand years, give or take a few thousand."

Someone laughed. D'Branin was nonplussed. "Friends, no doubt I could have postponed departure. I admit I was eager to meet my *volcryn*, to see their great ships and ask them all the questions that have haunted me, to discover the why of them. But I admit also that a delay would have been no great hardship. But why? Royd has been a gracious host, a good pilot. We have been treated well."

"Did you meet him?" Alys Northwind asked. "When you were making your arrangements, did you ever see him?"

"We spoke many times, but I was on Avalon, and Royd in orbit. I saw his face on my viewscreen."

"A projection, a computer simulation, could be anything," Lommie Thorne said. "I can have my system conjure up all sorts of faces for your viewscreen, Karoly."

"No one has ever seen this Royd Eris," Christopheris said. "He has made himself a cipher from the start."

"Our host wishes his privacy to remain inviolate," d'Branin said.

"Evasions," Lindran said. "What is he hiding?"

Melantha Jhirl laughed. When all eyes had moved to her, she grinned and shook her head. "Captain Royd is perfect—a strange man for a strange mission. Don't any of you love a mystery? Here we are flying light-years to intercept a hypothetical alien starship from the core of the galaxy, that has been outward bound for longer than humanity has been having wars, and all of you are upset because you can't count the warts on Royd's nose." She leaned across the table to refill her brandy snifter. "My mother was right," she said lightly. "Normals are subnormal."

"Maybe we should listen to Melantha," Lommie Thorne said thoughtfully. "Royd's foibles and neuroses are his business, if he does not impose them on us."

"It makes me uncomfortable," Dannel complained weakly.

"For all we know," said Alys Northwind, "we might be traveling with a criminal or an alien."

"Jupiter," someone muttered. The xenotech flushed red and there was sniggering around the long table.

But Thale Lasamer looked up furtively from his plate and giggled. "An *alien,*" he said. His blue eyes flicked back and forth in his skull as if seeking escape. They were bright and wild.

Marij-Black swore. "The drug is wearing off," she said quickly to d'Branin. "I'll have to go back to my cabin to get some more."

"What drug?" Lommie Thorne demanded. D'Branin had been careful not to tell the others too much about Lasamer's ravings, for fear of inflaming the shipboard tensions. "What's going on?"

"Danger," Lasamer said. He turned to Lommie, sitting next to him, and grasped her forearm hard, his long painted fingernails clawing at the silvery metal of her shirt. "We're in danger, I tell you, I'm reading it. Something *alien.* It means us ill. Blood, I see blood." He laughed. "Can you taste it, Agatha? I can almost taste the blood. *It* can, too."

Marij-Black rose. "He's not well," she announced to the others. "I've been dampening him with psionine, trying to hold his delusions in check. I'll get some more." She started toward the door.

"Dampening him?" Christopheris said, horrified.

"He's warning us of something. Don't you hear him? I want to know what it *is*."

"Not psionine," said Melantha Jhirl. "Try esperon."

"Don't tell me my job, woman!"

"Sorry," Melantha said. She gave a modest shrug. "I'm one step ahead of you, though. Esperon might exorcise his delusions, no?"

"Yes, but—"

"And it might help him focus on this threat he claims to detect, correct?"

"I know the characteristics of esperon quite well," the psipsych said testily.

Melantha smiled over the rim of her brandy glass. "I'm sure you do. Now listen to me. All of you are anxious about Royd, it seems. You can't stand not knowing whatever it is he's concealing. Rojan has been making up stories for weeks, and he's ready to believe any of them. Alys is so nervous she cut her finger off. We're squabbling constantly. Fears like that won't help us work together as a team. Let's end them. Easy enough." She pointed to Thale. "Here sits a class-one telepath. Boost his power with esperon and he'll be able to recite our captain's life history to us until we're all suitably bored with it. Meanwhile he'll also be vanquishing his personal demons."

"He's watching us," the telepath said in a low, urgent voice.

"No," said Karoly d'Branin, "we must keep Thale dampened."

"Karoly," Christopheris said, "this has gone too far. Several of us are nervous, and this boy is terrified. I believe we all need an end to the mystery of Royd Eris. For once Melantha is right."

"We have no right," d'Branin said.

"We have the need," said Lommie Thorne. "I agree with Melantha."

"Yes," echoed Alys Northwind. The two linguists were nodding.

D'Branin thought regretfully of his promise to Royd. They were not giving him any choice. His eyes met those of the psipsych and he sighed. "Do it, then," he said. "Get him the esperon."

"*He's going to kill me!*" Thale Lasamer screamed. He leaped to his feet, and when Lommie Thorne tried to calm him with a hand on his arm, he seized a cup of coffee, and threw it square in her face. It took three of them to hold him down.

"Hurry," Christopheris barked as the telepath struggled.

Marij-Black shuddered and left the lounge.

When she returned, the others had lifted Lasamer to the table and forced him down, pulling aside his long pale hair to bare the arteries in his neck.

Marij-Black moved to his side.

"Stop that," Royd said. "There is no need."

His ghost shimmered into being in its empty chair at the head of the long dinner table. The psipsych froze in the act of slipping an ampule of esperon into her injection gun, and Alys Northwind started visibly and released one of Lasamer's arms. The captive did not pull free. He lay on the table, breathing heavily, his pale blue eyes fixed glassily on Royd's projection, transfixed by the vision of his sudden materialization.

Melantha Jhirl lifted her brandy glass in salute. "Boo," she said. "You've missed dinner, captain."

"Royd," said Karoly d'Branin, "I am sorry."

The ghost stared unseeing at the far wall. "Release him," said the voice from the communicators. "I will tell you my great secrets, if my privacy intimidates you so."

"He *has* been watching us," Dannel said.

"We're listening," Northwind said suspiciously. "What are you?"

"I liked your guess about the gas giants," Royd

said. "Sadly, the truth is less dramatic. I am an ordinary *Homo sapiens* in middle age. Sixty-eight standard, if you require precision. The holograph you see before you is the real Royd Eris, or was so some years ago. I am somewhat older now, but I use computer simulation to project a more youthful appearance to my guests."

"Oh?" Lommie Thorne's face was red where the coffee had scalded her. "Then why the secrecy?"

"I will begin the tale with my mother," Royd replied. "The *Nightflyer* was her ship originally, custom-built to her design in the Newholme spaceyards. My mother was a freetrader, a notably successful one. She was born trash on a world called Vess, which is a very long way from here, although perhaps some of you have heard of it. She worked her way up, position by position, until she won her own command. She soon made a fortune through a willingness to accept the unusual consignment, fly off the major trade routes, take her cargo a month or a year or two years beyond where it was customarily transferred. Such practices are riskier but more profitable than flying the mail runs. My mother did not worry about how often she and her crews returned home. Her ships were her home. She forgot about Vess as soon as she left it, and seldom visited the same world twice if she could avoid it."

"Adventurous," Melantha Jhirl said.

"No," said Royd. "Sociopathic. My mother did not like people, you see. Not at all. Her crews had no love for her, nor she for them. Her one great dream was to free herself from the necessity of crew altogether. When she grew rich enough, she had it done. The *Nightflyer* was the result. After she boarded it at Newholme, she never touched a human being again, or walked a planet's surface. She did all her business from the compartments that are now mine, by viewscreen or lasercom. You would call her insane. You would be right." The ghost smiled faintly. "She did have an interesting life, though, even after her isolation. The worlds she saw, Karoly! The things she might have told you would break your heart, but you'll never hear them. She destroyed most of her records for fear that other people might get some use or pleasure from her experiences after her death. She was like that."

"And you?" asked Alys Northwind.

"She must have touched at least *one* other human being," Lindran put in, with a smile.

"I should not call her my mother," Royd said. "I am her cross-sex clone. After thirty years of flying this ship alone, she was bored. I was to be her companion and lover. She could shape me to be a perfect diversion. She had no patience with children, however, and no desire to raise me herself. After she had done the cloning, I was sealed in a nurturant tank, an embryo linked into her computer. It was my teacher. Before birth and after. I had no birth, really. Long after the time a normal child would have been born, I remained in the tank, growing, learning, on slow-time, blind and dreaming and living through tubes. I was to be released when I had attained the age of puberty, at which time she guessed I would be fit company."

"How horrible," Karoly d'Branin said. "Royd, my friend, I did not know."

"I'm sorry, captain," Melantha Jhirl said. "You were robbed of your childhood."

"I never missed it," Royd said. "Nor her. Her plans were all futile, you see. She died a few months after the cloning, when I was still a fetus in the tank. She had programmed the ship for such an eventuality, however. It dropped out of drive and shut down, drifted in interstellar space for eleven standard years while the computer made me—" He stopped, smiling. "I was going to say *while the computer made me a human being.* Well. While the computer made me whatever I am, then. That was how I inherited the *Nightflyer.* When I was born, it took me some months to acquaint myself with the operation of the ship and my own origins."

"Fascinating," said Karoly d'Branin.

"Yes," said the linguist Lindran, "but it doesn't explain why you keep yourself in isolation."

"Ah, but it does," Melantha Jhirl said. "Captain, perhaps you should explain further for the less improved models?"

"My mother hated planets," Royd said. "She hated stinks and dirt and bacteria, the irregularity of the weather, the sight of other people. She engineered for us a flawless environment, as sterile as she could possibly make it. She disliked gravity as well. She was accustomed to weightlessness from years of service on ancient freetraders that could not afford gravity grids, and she preferred it. These were the conditions under which I was born and raised.

"My body has no immune systems, no natural resistance to anything. Contact with any of you would probably kill me, and would certainly make me very sick. My muscles are feeble, in a sense atrophied. The gravity the *Nightflyer* is now generating is for your comfort, not mine. To me it is agony. At this moment the real me is seated in a floating chair that supports my weight. I still hurt, and my internal organs may be suffering damage. It is one reason I do not often take on passengers."

"You share your mother's opinion of the run of humanity?" asked Marij-Black.

"I do not. I like people. I accept what I am, but I did not choose it. I experience human life in the only way I can—vicariously. I am a voracious consumer of books, tapes, holoplays, fictions and drama and histories of all sorts. I have experimented with dreamdust. And infrequently, when I dare, I carry passengers. At those times I drink in as much of their lives as I can."

"If you kept your ship under weightlessness at all times, you could take on more riders," suggested Lommie Thorne.

"True," Royd said politely. "I have found, however, that most planet-born are as uncomfortable weightless as I am under gravity. A ship master who does not have artificial gravity, or elects not to use it, attracts few riders. The exceptions often spend much of the voyage sick or drugged. No. I could also mingle with my passengers, I know, if I kept to my chair and wore a sealed environwear suit. I have done so. I find it lessens my participation instead of increasing it. I become a freak, a maimed thing, one who must be treated differently and kept at a distance. These things do not suit my purpose. I prefer isolation. As often as I dare, I study the aliens I take on as riders."

"Aliens?" Northwind's voice was confused.

"You are all aliens to me," Royd answered.

Silence filled the *Nightflyer*'s lounge.

"I am sorry this has happened, my friend," Karoly d'Branin said. "We ought not have intruded on your personal affairs."

"Sorry," muttered Agatha Marij-Black. She frowned and pushed the ampule of esperon into the injection chamber. "Well, it's glib enough, but is it the truth? We still have no proof, just a new bedtime story. The holograph could have claimed it was a creature from Jupiter, a computer, or a diseased war criminal just as easily. We have no way of verifying anything that he's said. No—we have *one* way, rather." She took two quick steps forward to where Thale Lasamer lay on the table. "He still needs treatment and we still need confirmation, and I don't see any sense in stopping now after we've gone this far. Why should we live with all this anxiety if we can end it all now?" Her hand pushed the telepath's unresisting head to one side. She found the artery and pressed the gun to it.

"Agatha," said Karoly d'Branin. "Don't you think . . . perhaps we should forego this, now that Royd . . . ?"

"*No*," Royd said. "Stop. I order it. This is my ship. Stop, or . . ."

". . . or what?" The gun hissed loudly, and there was a red mark on the telepath's neck when she lifted it away.

Lasamer raised himself to a half-sitting position, supported by his elbows, and Marij-Black moved close to him. "Thale," she said in her best professional tones, "focus on Royd. You can do it; we all know how good you are. Wait just a moment. The esperon will open it all up for you."

His pale blue eyes were clouded. "Not close enough," he muttered. "One, I'm one, tested. Good, you know I'm good, but I got to be *close*." He trembled.

The psipsych put an arm around him, stroked him, coaxed him. "The esperon will give you range, Thale," she said. "Feel it, feel yourself grow stronger. Can you feel it? Everything's getting clear, isn't it?" Her voice was a reassuring drone. "You can hear what I'm thinking, I know you can, but never mind that. The others, too, push them aside, all that chatter, thoughts, desires, fear. Push it all aside. Remember the danger now? Remember? Go find it, Thale, go find the danger. Look beyond the wall there, tell us what it's like beyond the wall. Tell us about Royd. Was he telling the truth? Tell us. You're good, we all know that, you can tell us." The phrases were almost an incantation.

He shrugged off her support and sat upright by himself. "I can feel it," he said. His eyes were suddenly clearer. "Something—my head hurts—I'm *afraid!*"

"Don't be afraid," said Marij-Black. "The esperon

won't make your head hurt; it just makes you better. We're all here with you. Nothing to fear." She stroked his brow. "Tell us what you see."

Thale Lasamer looked at Royd's ghost with terrified little-boy eyes, and his tongue flicked across his lower lips. "He's—"

Then his skull exploded.

Hysteria and confusion.

The telepath's head had burst with awful force, splattering them all with blood and bits of bone and flesh. His body thrashed madly on the tabletop for a long instant, blood spurting from the arteries in his neck in a crimson stream, his limbs twitching in a macabre dance. His head had simply ceased to exist, but he would not be still.

Agatha Marij-Black, who had been standing closest to him, dropped her injection gun and stood slack-mouthed. She was drenched with his blood, covered with pieces of flesh and brain. Beneath her right eye a long sliver of bone had penetrated her skin, and her own blood was mingling with his. She did not seem to notice.

Rojan Christopheris fell over backward, scrambled to his feet, and pressed himself hard against the wall.

Dannel screamed, and screamed, and screamed, until Lindran slapped him hard across a blood-smeared cheek and told him to be quiet.

Alys Northwind dropped to her knees and began to mumble a prayer in a strange tongue.

Karoly d'Branin sat very still, staring, blinking, his chocolate cup forgotten in his hand.

"Do something," Lommie Thorne moaned. "Somebody *do* something." One of Lasamer's arms moved feebly and brushed against her. She shrieked and pulled away.

Melantha Jhirl pushed aside her brandy snifter.

"Control yourself," she snapped. "He's dead; he can't hurt you."

They all looked at her, but for d'Branin and Marij-Black, both of whom seemed frozen in shock. Royd's projection had vanished at some point, Melantha realized suddenly. She began to give orders. "Dannel, Lindran, Rojan—find a sheet or something to wrap him in, and get him out of here. Alys, you and Lommie get some water and sponges. We've got to clean up." Melantha moved to d'Branin's side as the others rushed to do as she had told them. "Karoly," she said, putting a gentle hand on his shoulder, "are you all right, Karoly?"

He looked up at her, gray eyes blinking. "I—yes, yes, I am—I told her not to go ahead, Melantha. I told her."

"Yes, you did," Melantha Jhirl said. She gave him a reassuring pat and moved around the table to Agatha Marij-Black. "Agatha," she called. But the psipsych did not respond, not even when Melantha shook her bodily by the shoulders. Her eyes were empty. "She's in shock," Melantha announced. She frowned at the silver of bone protruding from Marij-Black's cheek. Sponging off her face with a napkin, she carefully removed the splinter.

"What do we do with the body?" asked Lindran. They had found a sheet and wrapped it up. It had finally stopped twitching, although blood continued to seep out, turning the concealing sheet red.

"Put it in a cargo hold," suggested Christopheris.

"No," Melantha said, "not sanitary. It will rot." She thought for a moment. "Suit up and take it down to the driveroom. Cycle it through and lash it in place somehow. Tear up the sheet if you have to. That section of the ship is vacuum. It will be best there."

Christopheris nodded, and the three of them moved

off, the dead weight of Lasamer's corpse supported between them. Melantha turned back to Marij-Black, but only for an instant. Lommie Thorne, who was mopping the blood from the tabletop with a piece of cloth, suddenly began to retch violently. Melantha swore. "Someone help her," she snapped.

Karoly d'Branin finally seemed to stir. He rose and took the blood-soaked cloth from Lommie's hand and led her away back to his cabin.

"I can't do this alone," whined Alys Northwind, turning away in disgust.

"Help me, then," Melantha said. Together she and Northwind half-led and half-carried the psipsych from the lounge, cleaned her and undressed her, and put her to sleep with a shot of one of her own drugs. Afterward Melantha took the injection gun and made the rounds. Northwind and Lommie Thorne required mild tranquilizers, Dannel a somewhat stronger one.

It was three hours before they met again.

The survivors assembled in the largest of the cargo holds, where three of them hung their sleepwebs. Seven of eight attended. Agatha Marij-Black was still unconscious, sleeping or in a coma or deep shock; none of them was sure. The rest seemed to have recovered, though their faces were pale and drawn. All of them had changed clothes, even Alys Northwind, who had slipped into a new jumpsuit identical to the old one.

"I do not understand," Karoly d'Branin said. "I do not understand what . . ."

"Royd killed him, is all," Northwind said bitterly. "His secret was endangered, so he just—just blew him apart. We all saw it."

"I cannot believe that," Karoly d'Branin said in an anguished voice. "I cannot. Royd and I, we have talked, talked many a night when the rest of you were sleeping. He is gentle, inquisitive, sensitive. A dreamer. He understands about the *volcryn*. He would not do such a thing, could not."

"His projection certainly winked out quick enough when it happened," Lindran said. "And you'll notice he hasn't had much to say since."

"The rest of us haven't been unusually talkative either," said Melantha Jhirl. "I don't know what to think, but my impulse is to side with Karoly. We have no proof that the captain was responsible for Thale's death. There's something here none of us understands yet."

Alys Northwind grunted. "Proof," she said disdainfully.

"In fact," Melantha continued unperturbed, "I'm not even sure *anyone* is responsible. Nothing happened until he was given the esperon. Could the drug be at fault?"

"Hell of a side effect," Lindran muttered.

Rojan Christopheris frowned. "This is not my field, but I would think no. Esperon is extremely potent, with both physical and psionic side effects verging on the extreme, but not *that* extreme."

"What, then?" said Lommie Thorne. "What killed him?"

"The instrument of death was probably his own talent," the xenobiologist said, "undoubtedly augmented by his drug. Besides boosting his principal power, his telepathic sensitivity, esperon would also tend to bring out other psi-talents that might have been latent in him."

"Such as?" Lommie demanded.

"Biocontrol. Telekinesis."

Melantha Jhirl was way ahead of him. "Esperon shoots blood pressure way up anyway. Increase the pressure in his skull even more by rushing all the blood in his body to his brain. Decrease the air pressure around his head simultaneously, using teke to induce a short-lived vacuum. Think about it."

They thought about it, and none of them liked it.

"Who could do such a thing?" Karoly d'Branin said. "It could only have been self-induced, his own talent wild out of control."

"Or turned against him by a greater talent," Alys Northwind said stubbornly.

"No human telepath has talent on that order, to seize control of someone else, body and mind and soul, even for an instant."

"Exactly," the stout xenotech replied. "No *human* telepath."

"Gas-giant people?" Lommie Thorne's tone was mocking.

Alys Northwind stared her down. "I could talk about Crey sensitives or *githyanki* soulsucks, name a half-dozen others off the top of my head, but I don't need to. I'll only name one. A Hrangan Mind."

That was a disquieting thought. All of them fell silent and stirred uneasily, thinking of the vast, inimicable power of a Hrangan Mind hidden in the command chambers of the *Nightflyer*, until Melantha Jhirl broke the spell with a short, derisive laugh. "You're frightening yourself with shadows, Alys," she said. "What you're saying is ridiculous if you stop to think about it. I hope that isn't too much to ask. You're supposed to be xenologists, the lot of you, experts in alien languages, psychology, biology, technology. You don't act the part. We warred with Old Hranga for a thousand years, but we *never* communicated successfully with a Hrangan Mind. If Royd Eris is a Hrangan, they've improved their conversational skills markedly in the centuries since the Collapse."

Alys Northwind flushed. "You're right," she said. "I'm jumpy."

"Friends," said Karoly d'Branin, "we must not let our actions be dictated by panic or hysteria. A terrible thing has happened. One of our colleagues is dead, and we do not know why. Until we do, we can only go on. This is no time for rash actions against the innocent. Perhaps, when we return to Avalon, an investigation will tell us what happened. The body is safe for examination, is it not?"

"We cycled it through the airlock into the drive-room," Dannel said. "It'll keep."

"And it can be studied closely on our return," d'Branin said.

"Which should be immediate," said Northwind. "Tell Eris to turn this ship around!"

D'Branin looked stricken. "But the *volcryn!* A week more and we shall know them, if my figures are correct. To return would take us six weeks. Surely it is worth one additional week to know that they exist? Thale would not have wanted his death to be for nothing."

"Before he died, Thale was raving about aliens, about danger," Northwind insisted. "We're rushing to meet some aliens. What if they're the danger? Maybe these *volcryn* are even more potent than a Hrangan Mind, and maybe they don't want to be met, or investigated, or observed. What about that, Karoly? You ever think about that? Those stories of yours—don't some of them talk about terrible things happening to the races that meet the *volcryn?*"

"Legends," d'Branin said. "Superstition."

"A whole Fyndii horde vanishes in one legend," Rojan Christopheris put in.

"We cannot put credence in these fears of others," d'Branin argued.

"Perhaps there's nothing to the stories," Northwind said, "but do you care to risk it? *I* don't. For what? Your sources may be fictional or exaggerated or wrong, your interpretations and computations may be in error, or they may have changed course—the *volcryn* may not even be within light-years of where we'll drop out."

"Ah," Melantha Jhirl said, "I understand. Then we shouldn't go on because they won't be there, and besides, they might be dangerous."

D'Branin smiled and Lindran laughed. "Not funny," protested Alys Northwind, but she argued no further.

"No," Melantha continued, "any danger we are in will not increase significantly in the time it will take us to drop out of drive and look about for *volcryn*. We have to drop out anyway, to reprogram for the shunt home. Besides, we've come a long way for these *volcryn*, and I admit to being curious." She looked at each of them in turn, but no one spoke. "We continue, then."

"And Royd?" demanded Christopheris. "What do we do about him?"

"What *can* we do?" said Dannel.

"Treat the captain as before," Melantha said decisively. "We should open lines to him and talk. Maybe now we can clear up some of the mysteries that are bothering us, if Royd is willing to discuss things frankly."

"He is probably as shocked and dismayed as we are, my friends," said d'Branin. "Possibly he is fearful that we will blame him, try to hurt him."

"I think we should cut through to his section of the ship and drag him out kicking and screaming," Christopheris said. "We have the tools. That would write a quick end to all our fears."

"It could kill Royd," Melantha said. "Then he'd be justified in anything he did to stop us. He controls this ship. He could do a great deal, if he decided we were his enemies." She shook her head vehemently. "No, Rojan, we can't attack Royd. We've got to reassure him. I'll do it, if no one else wants to talk to him." There were no volunteers. "All right.

But I don't want any of you trying any foolish schemes. Go about your business. Act normally."

Karoly d'Branin was nodding agreement. "Let us put Royd and poor Thale from our minds, and concern ourselves with our work, with our preparations. Our sensory instruments must be ready for deployment as soon as we shift out of drive and reenter normal space, so we can find our quarry quickly. We must review everything we know of the *volcryn*." He turned to the linguists and began discussing some of the preliminaries he expected of them, and in a short time the talk had turned to the *volcryn*, and bit by bit the fear drained out of the group.

Lommie Thorne sat listening quietly, her thumb absently rubbing her wrist implant, but no one noticed the thoughtful look in her eyes.

Not even Royd Eris, watching.

Melantha Jhirl returned to the lounge alone.

Someone had turned out the lights. "Captain?" she said softly.

He appeared to her; pale, glowing softly, with eyes that did not see. His clothes, filmy and out of date, were all shades of white and faded blue. "Hello, Melantha," the mellow voice said from the communicators as the ghost silently mouthed the same words.

"Did you hear, captain?"

"Yes," he said, his voice vaguely tinged by surprise. "I hear and I see everything on my *Nightflyer*, Melantha. Not only in the lounge, and not only when the communicators and viewscreens are on. How long have you known?"

"Known?" She smiled. "Since you praised Alys's gas-giant solution to the Roydian mystery. The communicators were not on that night. You had no way of knowing. Unless . . ."

"I have never made a mistake before," Royd said.

"I told Karoly, but that was deliberate. I am sorry. I have been under stress."

"I believe you, captain," she said. "No matter. I'm the improved model, remember? I'd guessed weeks ago."

For a time Royd said nothing. Then: "When do you begin to reassure me?"

"I'm doing so right now. Don't you feel reassured yet?"

The apparition gave a ghostly shrug. "I am pleased that you and Karoly do not think I murdered that man. Otherwise, I am frightened. Things are getting out of control, Melantha. Why didn't she listen to me? I told Karoly to keep him dampened. I told Agatha not to give him that injection. I warned them."

"They were afraid, too," Melantha said. "Afraid that you were only trying to frighten them off, to protect some awful plan. I don't know. It was my fault, in a sense. I was the one who suggested esperon. I thought it would put Thale at ease and tell us something about you. I was curious." She frowned. "A deadly curiosity. Now I have blood on my hands."

Melantha's eyes were adjusting to the darkness in the lounge. By the faint light of the holograph, she could see the table where it had happened, dark streaks of drying blood across its surface among the plates and cups and cold pots of tea and chocolate. She heard a faint dripping as well and could not tell if it was blood or coffee. She shivered. "I don't like it in here."

"If you would like to leave, I can be with you wherever you go."

"No," she said. "I'll stay. Royd, I think it might be better if you were *not* with us wherever we go. If you kept silent and out of sight, so to speak. If I asked you to, would you shut off your monitors throughout the ship? Except for the lounge, perhaps. It would make the others feel better, I'm sure."

"They don't know."

"They will. You made that remark about gas giants in everyone's hearing. Some of them have probably figured it out by now."

"If I told you I had cut myself off, you would have no way of knowing whether it was the truth."

"I could trust you," Melantha Jhirl said.

Silence. The specter stared at her. "As you wish," Royd's voice said finally. "Everything off. Now I see and hear only in here. Now, Melantha, you must promise to control them. No secret schemes or attempts to breach my quarters. Can you do that?"

"I think so," she said.

"Did you believe my story?" Royd asked.

"Ah," she said. "A strange and wondrous story, captain. If it's a lie, I'll swap lies with you anytime. You do it well. If it's true, then you are a strange and wondrous man."

"It's true," the ghost said quietly. "Melantha . . ."

"Yes?"

"Does it bother you that I have . . . watched you? Watched you when you were not aware?"

"A little," she said, "but I think I can understand it."

"I watched you copulating."

She smiled. "Ah," she said, "I'm good at it."

"I wouldn't know," Royd said. "You're good to watch."

Silence. She tried not to hear the steady, faint dripping off to her right. "Yes," she said after a long hesitation.

"Yes? What?"

"Yes, Royd," she said, "I would probably sex with you if it were possible."

"*How did you know what I was thinking?*" Royd's

voice was suddenly frightened, full of anxiety and something close to fear.

"Easy," Melantha said, startled. "I'm an improved model. It wasn't so difficult to figure out. I told you, remember? I'm three moves ahead of you."

"You're not a telepath, are you?"

"No," Melantha said. "No."

Royd considered that for a long time. "I believe I'm reassured," he said at last.

"Good," she said.

"Melantha," he added, "one thing. Sometimes it is not wise to be too many moves ahead. Do you understand?"

"Oh? No, not really. You frighten me. Now reassure me. Your turn, Captain Royd."

"Of what?"

"What happened in here? Really?"

Royd said nothing.

"I think you know something," Melantha said. "You gave up your secret to stop us from injecting Lasamer with esperon. Even after your secret was forfeit, you ordered us not to go ahead. Why?"

"Esperon is a dangerous drug," Royd said.

"More than that, captain," Melantha said. "You're evading. What killed Thale Lasamer? Or is it *who?*"

"*I* didn't."

"One of us? The *volcryn?*"

Royd said nothing.

"Is there an alien aboard your ship, captain?"

Silence.

"Are we in danger? Am *I* in danger, captain? I'm not afraid. Does that make me a fool?"

"I like people," Royd said at last. "When I can stand it, I like to have passengers. I watch them, yes. It's not so terrible. I like you and Karoly especially. I won't let anything happen to you."

"What might happen?"

Royd said nothing.

"And what about the others, Royd? Christopheris and Northwind, Dannel and Lindran, Lommie Thorne? Are you taking care of them, too? Or only Karoly and me?"

No reply.

"You're not very talkative tonight," Melantha observed.

"I'm under strain," his voice replied. "And certain things you ask are safer not to know. Go to bed, Melantha Jhirl. We've talked long enough."

"All right, captain," she said. She smiled at the ghost and lifted her hand. His own rose to meet it. Warm dark flesh and pale radiance brushed, melded, were one. Melantha Jhirl turned to go. It was not until she was out in the corridor, safe in the light once more, that she began to tremble.

False midnight.

The talks had broken up, and one by one the academicians had gone to bed. Even Karoly d'Branin had retired, his appetite for chocolate quelled by his memories of the lounge.

The linguists had made violent, noisy love before giving themselves up to sleep, as if to reaffirm their life in the face of Thale Lasamer's grisly death. Rojan Christopheris had listened to music. But now they were all still.

The *Nightflyer* was filled with silence.

In the darkness of the largest cargo hold, three sleepwebs hung side by side. Melantha Jhirl twisted occasionally in her sleep, her face feverish, as if in the grip of some nightmare. Alys Northwind lay flat on her back, snoring loudly, a reassuring wheeze of noise from her solid, meaty chest.

Lommie Thorne lay awake, thinking.

Finally she rose and dropped to the floor, nude, quiet, light and careful as a cat. She pulled on a tight pair of pants, slipped a wide-sleeved shirt of black metallic cloth over her head, belted it with a silver chain, shook out her short hair. She did not don her boots. Barefoot was quieter. Her feet were small and soft, with no trace of callous.

She moved to the middle sleepweb and shook Alys Northwind by her shoulder. The snoring stopped abruptly. "Huh?" the xenotech said. She grunted in annoyance.

"Come," whispered Lommie Thorne. She beckoned.

Northwind got heavily to her feet, blinking, and followed the cyberneticist through the door and out into the corridor. She'd been sleeping in her jumpsuit, its seam open nearly to her crotch. She frowned and sealed it. "What the hell," she muttered. She was disarrayed and unhappy.

"There's a way to find out if Royd's story was true," Lommie Thorne said carefully. "Melantha won't like it, though. Are you game to try?"

"What?" Northwind asked. Her face betrayed her interest.

"Come," the cyberneticist said.

They moved silently through the ship to the computer room. The system was up, but dormant. They entered quietly; all empty. Currents of light ran silkily down crystalline channels in the data grids, meeting, joining, splitting apart again; rivers of wan, multihued radiance crisscrossing a black landscape. The chamber was dim, the only noise a buzz at the edge of human hearing, until Lommie Thorne moved through it, touching keys, tripping switches, directing the silent, luminescent currents. Bit by bit the machine woke.

"What are you *doing?*" Alys Northwind said.

"Karoly told me to tie in our system with the ship," Lommie Thorne replied as she worked. "I was told Royd wanted to study the *volcryn* data. Fine, I did it.

Do you understand what that means?" Her shirt whispered in soft metallic tones when she moved.

Eagerness broke across the flat features of xenotech Alys Northwind. "The two systems are tied together!"

"Exactly. So Royd can find out about the *volcryn*, and we can find out about Royd." She frowned. "I wish I knew more about the *Nightflyer*'s hardware, but I think I can feel my way through. This is a pretty sophisticated system d'Branin requisitioned."

"Can you take over from Eris?"

"Take over?" Lommie sounded puzzled. "You been drinking again, Alys?"

"No, I'm serious. Use your system to break into the ship's control, overwhelm Eris, countermand his orders, make the *Nightflyer* respond to us, down here. Wouldn't you feel safer if we were in control?"

"Maybe," the cyberneticist said doubtfully. "I could try, but why do that?"

"Just in case. We don't have to use the capacity. Just so we have it, if an emergency arises."

Lommie Thorne shrugged. "Emergencies and gas giants. I only want to put my mind at rest about Royd, whether he had anything to do with killing Lasamer." She moved over to a readout panel, where a half-dozen meter-square viewscreens curved around a console, and brought one of them to life. Long fingers ghosted through holographic keys that appeared and disappeared as she used them, the keyboard changing shape again and yet again. The cyberneticist's pretty face grew thoughtful and serious. "We're in," she said. Characters began to flow across a viewscreen, red flickerings in glassy black depths. On a second screen a schematic of the *Nightflyer* appeared, revolved, halved; its spheres shifted size and perspective at the whim of Lommie's fingers, and a line of numerals below gave the specifications. The cyberneticist watched, and finally froze both screens.

"Here," she said, "here's my answer about the hardware. You can dismiss your takeover idea, unless those gas-giant people of yours are going to help. The *Nightflyer*'s bigger and smarter than our little system here. Makes sense, when you stop to think about it. Ship's all automated, except for Royd."

Her hands moved again, and two more display screens stirred. Lommie Thorne whistled and coaxed her search program with soft words of encouragement. "It looks as though there *is* a Royd, though. Configurations are all wrong for a robot ship. Damn, I would have bet anything." The characters began to flow again, Lommie watching the figures as they drifted by. "Here's life-support specs, might tell us something." A finger jabbed, and one screen froze yet again.

"Nothing unusual," Alys Northwind said in disappointment.

"Standard waste disposal. Water recycling. Food processor, with protein and vitamin supplements in stores." She began to whistle. "Tanks of Renny's moss and neograss to eat up the CO_2. Oxygen cycle, then. No methane or ammonia. Sorry about that."

"Go sex with a computer!"

The cyberneticist smiled. "Ever tried it?" Her fingers moved again. "What else should I look for? You're the tech—what would be a giveaway? Give me some ideas."

"Check the specs for nurturant tanks, cloning equipment, that sort of thing," the xenotech said. "That would tell us whether he was lying."

"I don't know," Lommie Thorne said. "Long time ago. He might have junked that stuff. No use for it."

"Find Royd's life history," Northwind said. "His mother's. Get a readout on the business they've done, all this alleged trading. They must have records. Account books, profit and loss, cargo invoices, that kind

of thing." Her voice grew excited, and she gripped
the cyberneticist from behind by her shoulders. "A
log, a ship's log! There's got to be a log. Find it!"

"All right." Lommie Thorne whistled, happy, at
ease with her system, riding the data winds, curious,
in control. Then the screen in front of her turned a
bright red and began to blink. She smiled, touched a
ghost key, and the keyboard melted away and re-
formed under her. She tried another tack. Three more
screens turned red and began to blink. Her smile
faded.

"What is it?"

"Security," said Lommie Thorne. "I'll get through
it in a second. Hold on." She changed the keyboard
yet again, entered another search program, attached
a rider in case it was blocked. Another screen flashed
red. She had her machine chew the data she'd gathered, sent out another feeler. More red. Flashing.
Blinking. Bright enough to hurt the eyes. All the
screens were red now. "A good security program,"
she said with admiration. "The log is well protected."

Alys Northwind grunted. "Are we blocked?"

"Response time is too slow," Lommie Thorne said,
chewing on her lower lip as she thought. "There's a
way to fix that." She smiled and rolled back the soft
black metal of her sleeve.

"What are you doing?"

"Watch," she said. She slid her arm under the
console, found the prongs, jacked in.

"Ah," she said, low in her throat. The flashing red
blocks vanished from her readout screens, one after
the other, as she sent her mind coursing into the
Nightflyer's system, easing through all the blocks.
"Nothing like slipping past another system's security.
Like slipping onto a man." Log entries were flickering past them in a whirling, blurring rush, too fast
for Alys Northwind to read. But Lommie read them.

Then she stiffened. "Oh," she said. It was almost a

whimper. "Cold," she said. She shook her head and it was gone, but there was a sound in her ears, a terrible whooping sound. "Damn," she said, "that'll wake everyone." She glanced up when she felt Alys's fingers dig painfully into her shoulder, squeezing, hurting.

A gray steel panel slid almost silently across the access to the corridor, cutting off the whooping cry of the alarm. "What?" Lommie Thorne said.

"That's an emergency airseal," said Alys Northwind in a dead voice. She knew starships. "It closes where they're about to load or unload cargo in vacuum."

Their eyes went to the huge curving outer airlock above their heads. The inner lock was almost completely open, and as they watched, it clicked into place, and the seal on the outer door cracked, and now it was open half a meter, sliding, and beyond was twisted nothingness so burning-bright it seared the eyes.

"Oh," said Lommie Thorne, as the cold coursed up her arm. She had stopped whistling.

Alarms were hooting everywhere. The passengers began to stir. Melantha Jhirl tumbled from her sleep-web and darted into the corridor, nude, frantic, alert. Karoly d'Branin sat up drowsily. The psipsych muttered fitfully in drug-induced sleep. Rojan Christopheris cried out in alarm.

Far away, metal crunched and tore, and a violent shudder ran through the ship, throwing the linguists out of their sleepwebs, knocking Melantha from her feet.

In the command quarters of the *Nightflyer* was a spherical room with featureless white walls, a lesser sphere—a suspended control console—floating in its center. The walls were always blank when the ship was in drive; the warped and glaring underside of spacetime was painful to behold.

But now darkness woke in the room, a holoscape coming to life, cold black and stars everywhere, points of icy unwinking brilliance, no up and no down and no direction, the floating control sphere the only feaure in the simulated sea of night.

The *Nightflyer* had shifted out of drive.

Melantha Jhirl found her feet again and thumbed on a communicator. The alarms were still hooting, and it was hard to hear. "Captain," she shouted, "what's happening?"

"I don't know," Royd's voice replied. "I'm trying to find out. Wait."

Melantha waited. Karoly d'Branin came staggering out into the corridor, blinking and rubbing his eyes. Rojan Christopheris was not long behind him. "What is it? What's wrong?" he demanded, but Melantha just shook her head. Lindran and Dannel soon appeared as well. There was no sign of Marij-Black, Alys Northwind, or Lommie Thorne. The academicians looked uneasily at the seal that blocked cargo hold three. Finally Melantha told Christopheris to go look. He returned a few minutes later. "Agatha is still unconscious," he said, talking at the top of his voice to be heard over the alarms. "The drugs still have her. She's moving around, though. Crying out."

"Alys and Lommie?"

Christopheris shrugged. "I can't find them. Ask your friend Royd."

The communicator came back to life as the alarms died. "We have returned to normal space," Royd's voice said, "but the ship is damaged. Hold three, your computer room, was breached while we were under drive. It was ripped apart by the flux. The computer dropped us out of drive automatically, fortunately for us, or the drive forces might have torn my entire ship apart."

"Royd," said Melantha, "Northwind and Thorne are missing."

"It appears your computer was in use when the hold was breached," Royd said carefully. "I would presume them dead, although I cannot say that with certainty. At Melantha's request, I have deactivated most of my monitors, retaining only the lounge input. I do not know what transpired. But this is a small ship, and if they are not with you, we must assume the worst." He paused briefly. "If it is any consolation, they died swiftly and painlessly."

"You killed them," Christopheris said, his face red and angry. He started to say more, but Melantha slipped her hand firmly over his mouth. The two linguists exchanged a long, meaningful look.

"Do we know how it happened, captain?" Melantha asked.

"Yes," he said reluctantly.

The xenobiologist had taken the hint, and Melantha took away her hand to let him breathe. "Royd?" she prompted.

"It sounds insane, Melantha," his voice replied, "but it appears your colleagues opened the hold's loading lock. I doubt they did so deliberately, of course. They were using the system interface to gain entry to the *Nightflyer*'s data storage and controls, and they shunted aside all the safeties."

"I see," Melantha said. "A terrible tragedy."

"Yes. Perhaps more terrible than you think. I have yet to discover the extent of damage to my ship."

"We should not keep you if you have duties to perform," Melantha said. "All of us are shocked, and it is difficult to talk now. Investigate the condition of your ship, and we'll continue our discussion at a more opportune time. Agreed?"

"Yes," said Royd.

Melantha turned off the communicator. Now, in

theory, the device was dead; Royd could neither see nor hear them.

"Do you believe him?" Christopheris snapped.

"I don't know," Melantha Jhirl said, "but I do know that the other three cargo holds can all be flushed just as hold three was. I'm moving my sleep-web into a cabin. I suggest that those of you who are living in hold two do the same."

"Clever," Lindran said with a sharp nod of her head. "We can crowd in. It won't be comfortable, but I doubt that I'd sleep the sleep of angels in the holds after this."

"We should also get our suits out of storage in four," Dannel suggested. "Keep them close at hand. Just in case."

"If you wish," Melantha said. "It's possible that all the locks might pop open simultaneously. Royd can't fault us for taking precautions." She flashed a grim smile. "After today we've earned the right to act irrationally."

"This is no time for your damned jokes, Melantha," Christopheris said. He was still red-faced, and his tone was full of fear and anger. "Three people are dead, Agatha is perhaps deranged or catatonic, the rest of us are endangered—"

"Yes. And we still have no idea what is happening," Melantha pointed out.

"*Royd Eris is killing us!*" Christopheris shrieked. "I don't know who or what he is and I don't know if that story he gave us is true and I don't *care*. Maybe he's a Hrangan Mind or the avenging angel of the *volcryn* or the second coming of Jesus Christ. What the hell difference does it make? He's *killing* us!" He looked at each of them in turn. "Any one of us could be next," he added. "Any one of us. Unless . . . we've got to make plans, *do* something, put a stop to this once and for all."

"You realize," Melantha said gently, "that we cannot actually know whether the good captain has turned off his sensory inputs down here. He could be watching and listening to us right now. He isn't, of course. He said he wouldn't and I believe him. But we have only his word on that. Now, Rojan, you don't appear to trust Royd. If that's so, you can hardly put any faith in his promises. It follows, therefore, that from your own point of view, it might not be wise to say the things that you're saying." She smiled slyly. "Do you understand the implications of what I'm saying?"

Christopheris opened his mouth and closed it again, looking very like a tall, ugly fish. He said nothing, but his eyes moved furtively and his flush deepened.

Lindran smiled thinly. "I think he's got it," she said.

"The computer is gone, then," Karoly d'Branin said suddenly in a low voice.

Melantha looked at him. "I'm afraid so, Karoly."

D'Branin ran his fingers through his hair as if half-aware of how untidy he looked. "The *volcryn*," he muttered. "How will we work without the computer?" He nodded to himself. "I have a small unit in my cabin, a wrist model, perhaps it will suffice. It *must* suffice; it must. I will get the figures from Royd, learn where we have dropped out. Excuse me, my friends. Pardon, I must go." He wandered away in a distracted haze, talking to himself.

"He hasn't heard a word we've said," Dannel said, incredulous.

"Think how distraught he'd be if *all* of us were dead," added Lindran. "Then he'd have no one to help him look for *volcryn*."

"Let him go," Melantha said. "He is as hurt as any of us, maybe more so. He wears it differently. His obsessions are his defense."

"Ah. And what is *our* defense?"

"Patience, maybe," said Melantha Jhirl. "All of the dead were trying to breach Royd's secret when they died. We haven't tried. Here we are discussing their deaths."

"You don't find that suspicious?" asked Lindran.

"Very," Melantha said. "I even have a method of testing my suspicions. One of us can make yet another attempt to find out whether our captain told us the truth. If he or she dies, we'll know." She shrugged. "Forgive me, however, if I'm not the one who tries. But don't let me stop you if you have the urge. I'll note the results with interest. Until then, I'm going to move out of the cargo hold and get some sleep." She turned and strode off, leaving the others to stare at each other.

"Arrogant bitch," Dannel observed almost conversationally after Melantha had left.

"Do you really think he can hear us?" Christopheris whispered to the two linguists.

"Every pithy word," Lindran said. She smiled at his discomfiture. "Come, Dannel, let's get to a safe area and back to bed."

He nodded.

"But," said Christopheris, "we have to *do* something. Make plans. Defenses."

Lindran gave him a final withering look and pulled Dannel off behind her down the corridor.

"Melantha? Karoly?"

She woke quickly, alert at the mere whisper of her name, fully awake almost at once, and sat up in the narrow single bed. Squeezed in beside her, Karoly d'Branin groaned and rolled over, yawning.

"Royd?" she asked. "Is it morning?"

"We are drifting in interstellar space three light-years from the nearest star, Melantha," replied the soft voice from the walls. "In such a context, the term *morning* has no meaning. But, yes, it is morning."

Melantha laughed. "*Drifting,* you said? How bad is the damage?"

"Serious, but not dangerous. Hold three is a complete ruin, hanging from my ship like half of a broken egg, but the damage was confined. The drives themselves are intact, and the *Nightflyer*'s computers did not seem to suffer from your system's destruction. I feared they might. I have heard of phenomena like electronic death traumas."

D'Branin said, "Eh? Royd?"

Melantha stroked him affectionately. "I'll tell you later, Karoly," she said. "Go back to sleep. Royd, you sound serious. Is there more?"

"I am worried about our return flight, Melantha," Royd said. "When I take the *Nightflyer* back into drive, the flux will be playing directly on portions of the ship that were never engineered to withstand it. Our configurations are askew now. I can show you the mathematics of it, but the question of the flux forces is the vital one. The airseal across the access to hold three is a particular concern. I've run some simulations, and I don't know if it can take the stress. If it bursts, my whole ship will split apart in the middle. My engines will go shunting off by themselves, and the rest— Even if the life-support sphere remains intact, we will all soon be dead."

"I see. Is there anything we can do?"

"Yes. The exposed areas would be easy enough to reinforce. The outer hull is armored to withstand the warping forces, of course. We could mount it in place—a crude shield, but according to my projections, it would suffice. If we do it correctly, it will help correct our configurations as well. Large portions of the hull were torn loose when the locks opened, but they are still out there, most within a kilometer or two, and could be used."

At some point Karoly d'Branin had finally come awake. "My team has four vacuum sleds," he said. "We can retrieve those pieces for you, my friend."

"Fine, Karoly, but that is not my primary concern. My ship is self-repairing within certain limits, but this exceeds those limits by an order of magnitude. I will have to do this myself."

"You?" D'Branin was startled. "Royd, you said—that is, your muscles, your weakness—this work will be too much for you. Surely we can do this for you!"

Royd's reply was tolerant. "I am only a cripple in a gravity field, Karoly. Weightless, I am in my element, and I will be killing the *Nightflyer*'s gravity grid momentarily, to try to gather my own strength for the repair work. No, you misunderstand. I am capable of the work. I have the tools, including my own heavy-duty sled."

"I think I know what you are concerned about, captain," Melantha said.

"I'm glad," Royd said. "Perhaps then you can answer my question. If I emerge from the safety of my chambers to do this work, can you keep your colleagues from harming me?"

Karoly d'Branin was shocked. "Oh, Royd, Royd, how could you think such a thing? We are scholars, scientists, not—not criminals, or soldiers, or—or animals. We are human—how can you believe we would threaten you or do you harm?"

"Human," Royd repeated, "but alien to me, suspicious of me. Give me no false assurances, Karoly."

He sputtered. Melantha took him by the hand and bid him be quiet. "Royd," she said, "I won't lie to you. You'd be in some danger. But I'd hope that, by coming out, you'd make our friends joyously happy. They'd be able to see that you told the truth, see that you were only human." She smiled. "They *would* see that, wouldn't they?"

"They would," Royd said, "but would it be enough

to offset their suspicions? They believe I am responsible for the deaths of the other three, do they not?"

"*Believe* is too strong a word. They suspect it, they fear it. They are frightened, captain, and with good cause. *I* am frightened."

"No more than I."

"I would be less frightened if I knew what *did* happen. Will you tell me?"

Silence.

"Royd, if—"

"I have made mistakes, Melantha," Royd said gravely. "But I am not alone in that. I did my best to stop the esperon injection, and I failed. I might have saved Alys and Lommie if I had seen them, heard them, known what they were about. But you made me turn off my monitors, Melantha. I cannot help what I cannot see. Why? If you saw three moves ahead, did you calculate these results?"

Melantha Jhirl felt briefly guilty. "Mea culpa, captain; I share the blame. I know that. Believe me, I know that. It is hard to see three moves ahead when you do not know the rules, however. Tell me the rules."

"I am blind and deaf," Royd said, ignoring her. "It is frustrating. I cannot help if I am blind and deaf. I am going to turn on the monitors again, Melantha. I am sorry if you do not approve. I want your approval, but I must do this with or without it. I have to *see*."

"Turn them on," Melantha said thoughtfully. "I was wrong, captain. I should never have asked you to blind yourself. I did not understand the situation, and I overestimated my own power to control the others. A failing of mine. Improved models too often think they can do anything." Her mind was racing, and she felt almost sick; she had miscalculated, misled, and there was more blood on her hands. "I think I understand better now."

"Understand what?" Karoly d'Branin said, baffled.

"You do *not* understand," Royd said sternly. "Don't pretend that you do, Melantha Jhirl. Don't! It is not wise or safe to be too many moves ahead." There was something disturbing in his tone.

Melantha understood that, too.

"What?" Karoly said. "I do not understand."

"Neither do I," Melantha said carefully. "Neither do I, Karoly." She kissed him lightly. "None of us understands, do we?"

"Good," said Royd.

She nodded and put a reassuring arm around Karoly. "Royd," she said, "to return to the question of repairs—it seems to me you must do this work, regardless of what promises we can give you. You won't risk your ship by slipping back into drive in your present condition, and the only other option is to drift out here until we all die. What choice do we have?"

"I have a choice," Royd said with deadly seriousness. "I could kill all of you, if that were the only way to save myself and my ship."

"You could try," Melantha said.

"Let us have no more talk of death," d'Branin said.

"You are right, Karoly," Royd said. "I do not wish to kill any of you. But I must be protected."

"You will be," Melantha said. "Karoly can set the others to chasing your hull fragments. I'll be your protection. I'll stay by your side. If anyone tries to attack you, they'll have to deal with me. They won't find that easy. And I can assist you. The work will be done three times as fast."

Royd was polite. "It is my experience that most planet-born are clumsy and easily tired in weightlessness. It would be more efficient if I worked alone, although I will gladly accept your services as a bodyguard."

"I remind you that I'm the improved model, captain," Melantha said. "Good in free-fall as well as in bed. I'll help."

"You are stubborn. As you will, then. In a few moments I shall depower the gravity grid. Karoly, go and prepare your people. Unship your vacuum sleds and suit up. I will exit the *Nightflyer* in three standard hours, after I have recovered from the pains of your gravity. I want all of you outside the ship before I leave. Is that condition understood?"

"Yes," said Karoly. "All except Agatha. She has not regained consciousness, friend; she will not be a problem."

"No," said Royd, "I meant *all* of you, including Agatha. Take her outside with you."

"But, Royd!" protested d'Branin.

"You're the captain," Melantha Jhirl said firmly. "It will be as you say; all of us outside. Including Agatha."

Outside. It was as though some vast animal had taken a bite out of the stars.

Melantha Jhirl waited on her sled close by the *Nightflyer* and looked at stars. It was not so very different out here in the depths of interstellar space. The stars were cold, frozen points of light; unwinking, austere, more chill and uncaring somehow than the same suns made to dance and twinkle by an atmosphere. Only the absence of a landmark primary reminded her of where she was: in the places between, where men and women and their ships do not stop, where the *volcryn* sail crafts impossibly ancient. She tried to pick out Avalon's sun, but she did not know where to search. The configurations were strange to her and she had no idea of how she was oriented. Behind her, before her, above, all around, the starfields stretched endlessly. She glanced down, or what seemed like down just then, beyond her feet and her sled and the *Nightflyer*, expecting still more alien stars. And the bite hit her with an almost physical force.

Melantha fought off a wave of vertigo. She was suspended above a pit, a yawning chasm in the universe, black, starless, vast.

Empty.

She remembered then: the Tempter's Veil. Just a cloud of dark gases, nothing really, galactic pollution that obscured the light from the stars of the Fringe. But this close at hand, it seemed immense, terrifying, and she had to break her gaze when she began to feel as if she were falling. It was a gulf beneath her and the frail silver-white shell of the *Nightflyer*, a gulf about to swallow them.

Melantha touched one of the controls on the sled's forked handle, swinging around so the Veil was to her side instead of beneath her. That seemed to help somehow. She concentrated on the *Nightflyer*, ignoring the looming wall of blackness beyond. It was the largest object in her universe, bright amid the darkness, ungainly, its shattered cargo sphere giving the whole craft an unbalanced cast.

She could see the other sleds as they angled through the black, tracking the missing pieces of hull, grappling with them, bringing them back. The linguistic team worked together, as always, sharing a sled. Rojan Christopheris was alone, working in a sullen silence. Melantha had to threaten him with physical violence before he agreed to join them. The xenobiologist was certain that it was all another plot, that once they were outside, the *Nightflyer* would slip into drive without them and leave them to lingering deaths. His suspicions were inflamed by drink, and there had been alcohol on his breath when Melantha and Karoly had finally forced him to suit up. Karoly had

a sled, too, and a silent passenger; Agatha Marij-
Black, freshly drugged and asleep in her vacuum
suit, safely locked into place.

While her colleagues labored, Melantha Jhirl waited
for Royd Eris, talking to the others occasionally
over the comm link. The two linguists, unaccustomed
to weightlessness, were complaining a good deal, and
bickering as well. Karoly tried to soothe them frequently. Christopheris said little, and his few comments were edged and biting. He was still angry.
Melantha watched him flit across her field of vision,
a stick figure in form-fitting black armor standing
erect at the controls of his sled.

Finally the circular airlock atop the foremost of
the *Nightflyer*'s major spheres dilated, and Royd
Eris emerged.

She watched him approach, curious, wondering
what he would look like. In her mind were a half-
dozen contradictory pictures. His genteel, cultured,
too-formal voice sometimes reminded her of the dark
aristocrats of her native Prometheus, the wizards who
toyed with human genes and played baroque status
games. At other times his naïveté made her imagine
him as an inexperienced youth. His ghost was a tired-
looking thin young man, and he was supposed to be
considerably older than that pale shadow, but Melantha found it difficult to hear an old man talking
when he spoke.

Melantha felt a nervous tingle as he neared. The
lines of his sled and his suit were different from theirs,
disturbingly so. Alien, she thought, and quickly
squelched the thought. Such differences meant nothing. Royd's sled was large, a long oval plate with
eight jointed grappling arms bristling from its underside like the legs of a metallic spider. A heavy-duty
cutting laser was mounted beneath the controls, its
snout jutting threateningly forward. His suit was far
more massive than the carefully engineered Academy

worksuits they wore, with a bulge between its shoulder blades that was probably a powerpack, and rakish radiant fins atop shoulders and helmet. It made him seem hulking; hunched and deformed.

But when he finally came near enough for Melantha to see his face, it was just a face.

White, very white, that was the predominant impression she got; white hair cropped very short, a white stubble around the sharply chiseled lines of his jaw, almost invisible eyebrows beneath which his eyes moved restlessly. His eyes were large and vividly blue, his best feature. His skin was pale and unlined, scarcely touched by time.

He looked wary, she thought. And perhaps a bit frightened.

Royd stopped his sled close to hers, amid the twisted ruin that had been cargo hold three, and surveyed the damage, the pieces of floating wreckage that had once been flesh, blood, glass, metal, plastic. Hard to distinguish now, all of them fused and burned and frozen together. "We have a good deal of work to do," he said. "Shall we begin?"

"First let's talk," she replied. She shifted her sled closer and reached out to him, but the distance was still too great, the width of the bases of the two vacuum sleds keeping them apart. Melantha backed off and turned herself over completely, so that Royd stood upside down in her world and she upside down in his. She moved to him again, positioning her sled directly over/under his. Their gloved hands met, brushed, parted. Melantha adjusted her altitude. Their helmets touched.

"Now I have touched you," Royd said, with a tremor in his voice. "I have never touched anyone before, or been touched."

"Oh, Royd. This isn't touching, not really. The suits are in the way. But I will touch you, *really* touch you. I promise you that."

"You can't. It's impossible."

"I'll find a way," she said firmly. "Now, turn off your comm. The sound will carry through our helmets."

He blinked and used his tongue controls and it was done.

"Now we can talk," she said. "Privately."

"I do not like this, Melantha," he said. "This is too obvious. This is dangerous."

"There is no other way. Royd, I *do* know."

"Yes," he said. "I knew you did. Three moves ahead, Melantha. I remember the way you play chess. But this is a more serious game, and you are safer if you feign ignorance."

"I understand that, captain. Other things I'm less sure about. Can we talk about them?"

"No. Don't ask me to. Just do as I tell you. You are in peril, all of you, but I can protect you. The less you know, the better I can protect you." Through the transparent faceplates, his expression was somber.

She stared into his upside-down eyes. "It might be a second crew member, someone else hidden in your quarters, but I don't believe that. It's the ship, isn't it? Your ship is killing us. Not you. It. Only that doesn't make sense. You command the *Nightflyer.* How can it act independently? And why? What motive? And how was Thale Lasamer killed? The business with Alys and Lommie, that was easy, but a psionic murder? A starship with psi? I can't accept that. It can't be the ship. Yet it can't be anything else. Help me, captain."

He blinked, anguish behind his eyes. "I should never have accepted Karoly's charter, not with a telepath among you. It was too risky. But I wanted to see the *volcryn,* and he spoke of them so movingly." He sighed. "You understand too much already, Melantha. I can't tell you more, or I would be powerless to protect you. The ship is malfunctioning; that is all you need to know. It is not safe to push too hard. As long as I am at the controls, I think I can keep you and the others from harm. Trust me."

"Trust is a two-way bond," Melantha said.

Royd lifted his hand and pushed her away, then tongued his communicator back to life. "Enough gossip," he announced. "We have work to do. Come. I want to see just how improved you actually are."

In the solitude of her helmet, Melantha Jhirl swore softly.

With an irregular twist of metal locked beneath him in his sled's magnetic grip, Rojan Christopheris sailed back toward the *Nightflyer*. He was watching from a distance when Royd Eris emerged on his oversized work sled. He was closer when Melantha Jhirl moved to him, inverted her sled, and pressed her faceplate to Royd's. Christopheris listened to their soft exchange, heard Melantha promise to touch him, Eris, the *thing*, the killer. He swallowed his rage. Then they cut him out, cut all of them out, went off the open circuit. But still she hung there, suspended by that cipher in the hunchbacked spacesuit, faces pressed together like two lovers kissing.

Christopheris swept in close, unlocked his captive plate so it would drift toward them. "Here," he announced. "I'm off to get another." He tongued off his own comm and swore, and his sled slid around the spheres and tubes of the *Nightflyer*.

Somehow they were all in it together, Royd and Melantha and possibly old d'Branin as well, he thought sourly. She had protected Eris from the first, stopped them when they might have taken action together, found out who or what he was. He did not trust her. His skin crawled when he remembered that they had been to bed together. She and Eris were the same, whatever they might be. And now poor Alys was dead, and that fool Thorne and even that damned telepath, but still Melantha was with *him,* against them. Rojan Christopheris was deeply afraid, and angry, and half-drunk.

The others were out of sight, off chasing spinning wedges of half-slagged metal. Royd and Melantha were engrossed in each other, the ship abandoned and vulnerable. This was his chance. No wonder Eris had insisted that all of them precede him into the void; outside, isolated from the controls of the *Nightflyer,* he was only a man. A weak one at that.

Smiling a thin hard smile, Christopheris brought his sled curling around the cargo spheres, hidden from sight, and vanished into the gaping maw of the driveroom. It was a long tunnel, everything open to vacuum, safe from the corrosion of an atmosphere. Like most starships, the *Nightflyer* had a triple propulsion system. the gravfield for landing and lifting, useless away from a gravity well, the nukes for deep space sublight maneuverings, and the great stardrives themselves. The lights of his sled flickered past the encircling ring of nukes and sent long bright streaks along the sides of the closed cylinders of the stardrives, the huge engines that bent the stuff of spacetime, encased in webs of metal and crystal.

At the end of the tunnel was a great circular door, reinforced metal, closed: the main airlock.

Christopheris set the sled down, dismounted—pulling his boots free of the sled's magnetic grip with an effort—and moved to the airlock. This was the hardest part, he thought. The headless body of Thale Lasamer was tethered loosely to a massive support strut by the lock, like a grisly guardian of the way. The xenobiologist had to stare at it while he waited for the lock to cycle. Whenever he glanced away, somehow he would find his eyes creeping back to it. The body looked almost natural, as if it had never had a head. Christopheris tried to remembered what Lasamer had looked like, but the features would not come to mind. He moved uncomfortably, but then the lock door slid open and he gratefully entered the chamber to cycle through.

He was alone in the *Nightflyer*.

A cautious man, Christopheris kept his suit on, though he collapsed the helmet and yanked loose the suddenly limp metallic fabric so it fell behind his back like a hood. He could snap it in place quickly enough if the need arose. In cargo hold four, where they had stored their equipment, the xenobiologist found what he was looking for: a portable cutting laser, charged and ready. Low power, but it would do.

Slow and clumsy in weightlessness, he pulled himself down the corridor into the darkened lounge.

It was chilly inside, the air cold on his cheeks. He tried not to notice. He braced himself at the door and pushed off across the width of the room, sailing above the furniture, which was all safely bolted into place. As he drifted toward his objective, something wet and cold touched his face. It startled him, but it was gone before he could quite make out what it was.

When it happened again, Christopheris snatched at it, caught it, and felt briefly sick. He had forgotten. No one had cleaned the lounge yet. The—the *remains* were still there, floating now, blood and flesh and bits of bone and brain. All around him.

He reached the far wall, stopped himself with his arms, pulled himself down to where he wanted to go. The bulkhead. The wall. No doorway was visible, but the metal couldn't be very thick. Beyond was the control room, the computer access, safety, power. Rojan Christopheris did not think of himself as a vindictive man. He did not intend to harm Royd Eris; that judgment was not his to make. He would take control of the *Nightflyer*, warn Eris away, make certain the man stayed sealed in his suit. He would take them all back without any more mysteries, any

more killings. The Academy arbiters could listen to the story, and probe Eris, and decide the right and wrong of it, guilt and innocence, what should be done.

The cutting laser emitted a thin pencil of scarlet light. Christopheris smiled and applied it to the bulkhead. It was slow work, but he had patience. They would not have missed him, quiet as he'd been, and if they did they would assume he was off sledding after some hunk of salvage. Eris's repairs would take hours, maybe days, to finish. The bright blade of the laser smoked where it touched the metal. Christopheris applied himself diligently.

Something moved on the periphery of his vision, just a little flicker, barely seen. A floating bit of brain, he thought. A sliver of bone. A bloody piece of flesh, hair still hanging from it. Horrible things, but nothing to worry about. He was a biologist; he was used to blood and brains and flesh. And worse, and worse; he had dissected many an alien in his day, cutting through chitin and mucus, pulsing stinking food sacs and poisonous spines; he had seen and touched it all.

Again the motion caught his eye, teased at it. Not wanting to, Christopheris found himself drawn to look. He could not *not* look, somehow, just as he had been unable to ignore the headless corpse near the airlock. He looked.

It was an eye.

Christopheris trembled and the laser slipped sharply off to one side, so he had to wrestle with it to bring it back to the channel he was cutting. His heart raced. He tried to calm himself. Nothing to be frightened of. No one was home, and if Royd should return, well, he had the laser as a weapon and he had his suit on if an airlock blew.

He looked at the eye again, willing away his fear. It was just an eye, Thale Lasamer's eye, pale blue,

bloody but intact, the same watery eye the boy had
when alive, nothing supernatural. A piece of dead
flesh, floating in the lounge amid other pieces of dead
flesh. Someone should have cleaned up the lounge,
Christopheris thought angrily. It was indecent to
leave it like this, it was uncivilized.

The eye did not move. The other grisly bits were
drifting on the air currents that flowed across the
room, but the eye was still. It neither bobbed nor
spun. It was fixed on him. Staring.

He cursed himself and concentrated on the laser,
on his cutting. He had burned an almost straight line
up the bulkhead for about a meter. He began another at right angles.

The eye watched dispassionately. Christopheris
suddenly found he could not stand it. One hand released its grip on the laser, reached out, caught the
eye, flung it across the room. The action made him
lose balance. He tumbled backward, the laser slipping from his grasp, his arms flapping like the wings
of some absurd heavy bird. Finally he caught an
edge of the table and stopped himself.

The laser hung in the center of the room, floating
amid coffee pots and pieces of human debris, still firing, turning slowly. That did not make sense. It
should have ceased fire when he released it. A mal-
function, Christopheris thought nervously. Smoke was
rising where the thin line of the laser traced a path
across the carpet.

With a shiver of fear, Christopheris realized that
the laser was turning toward him.

He raised himself, put both hands flat against the
table, pushed up out of the way, bobbing toward the
ceiling.

The laser was turning more swiftly now.

He pushed away from the ceiling hard, slammed
into a wall, grunted in pain, bounced off the floor,

kicked. The laser was spinning quickly, chasing him. Christopheris soared, braced himself for another ricochet off the ceiling. The beam swung around, but not fast enough. He'd get it while it was still firing off in the other direction.

He moved close, reached, and saw the eye.

It hung just above the laser. Staring.

Rojan Christopheris made a small whimpering sound low in his throat, and his hand hesitated—not long, but long enough—and the scarlet beam came up and around.

Its touch was a light, hot caress across his neck.

It was more than an hour later before they missed him. Karoly d'Branin noticed his absence first, called for him over the comm link, and got no answer. He discussed it with the others.

Royd Eris moved his sled back from the armor plate he had just mounted, and through his helmet Melantha Jhirl could see the lines around his mouth grow hard.

It was just then that the noises began.

A shrill bleat of pain and fear, followed by moans and sobbing. Terrible wet sounds, like a man choking on his own blood. They all heard. The sounds filled their helmets. And almost clear amid the anguish was something that sounded like a word; "Help."

"That's Christopheris," a woman's voice said. Lindran.

"He's hurt," Dannel added. "He's crying for help. Can't you hear it?"

"Where—?" someone started.

"The ship," Lindran said. "He must have returned to the ship."

Royd Eris said, "The fool. No. I warned—"

"We're going to check," Lindran announced.

Dannel cut free the hull fragment they had been bringing in, and it spun away, tumbling. Their sled angled down toward the *Nightflyer*.

"Stop," Royd said. "I'll return to my chambers and check from there, if you wish, but you may not enter the ship. Stay outside until I give you clearance."

The terrible sounds went on and on.

"Go to hell," Lindran snapped at him over the open circuit.

Karoly d'Branin had his sled in motion, too, hastening after the linguists, but he had been further out and it was a long way back to the ship. "Royd, what can you mean? We must help, don't you see? He is hurt—listen to him. Please, my friend."

"No," Royd said. "Karoly, stop! If Rojan went back to the ship alone, he is dead."

"How do you know that?" Dannel demanded. "Did you arrange it? Set traps in case we disobeyed you?"

"No," Royd said. "Listen to me. You can't help him now. Only I could have helped him, and he did not listen to me. Trust me. Stop." His voice was despairing.

In the distance d'Branin's sled slowed. The linguists' did not. "We've already listened to you too damn much, I'd say," Lindran said. She almost had to shout to be heard above the noises, the whimpers and moans, the awful wet sucking sounds, the distorted pleas for help. Agony filled their universe. "Melantha," Lindran continued, "keep Eris right where he is. We'll go carefully, find out what is happening inside, but I don't want him getting back to his controls. Understood?"

Melantha Jhirl hesitated. The sounds beat against her ears. It was hard to think.

Royd swung his sled around to face her, and she could feel the weight of his stare. "Stop them," he said. "Melantha, Karoly, order it. They will not listen to me. They do not know what they are doing." He was clearly in pain.

In his face Melantha found decision. "Go back inside quickly, Royd. Do what you can. I'm going to try to intercept them."

"Whose side are you on?" Lindran demanded.

Royd nodded to her across the gulf, but Melantha was already in motion. Her sled backed clear of the work area, congested with hull fragments and other debris, then accelerated briskly as she raced around the exterior of the *Nightflyer* toward the drive-room.

But even as she approached, she knew it was too late. The linguists were too close and already moving much faster than she was.

"*Don't,*" she said, authority in her tone. "Christopheris is dead."

"His ghost is crying for help, then," Lindran replied. "When they tinkered you together, they must have damaged the genes for hearing, bitch."

"The ship isn't safe."

"Bitch," was all the answer she got.

Karoly's sled pursued vainly. "Friends, you must stop, please, I beg it of you. Let us talk this out together."

The sounds were his only reply.

"I am your superior," he said. "I order you to wait outside. Do you hear me? I order it, I invoke the authority of the Academy of Human Knowledge. Please, my friends, please."

Melantha watched helplessly as Lindran and Dannel vanished down the long tunnel of the driveroom.

A moment later she halted her own sled near the waiting black mouth, debating whether she should follow them on into the *Nightflyer*. She might be able to catch them before the airlock opened.

Royd's voice, hoarse counterpoint to the sounds, answered her unvoiced question. "Stay, Melantha. Proceed no further."

She looked behind her. Royd's sled was approaching.

"What are you doing here? Royd, use your own lock. You have to get back inside!"

"Melantha," he said calmly, "I cannot. The ship will not respond to me. The lock will not dilate. The main lock in the driveroom is the only one with manual override. I am trapped outside. I don't want you or Karoly inside the ship until I can return to my console."

Melantha Jhirl looked down the shadowed barrel of the driveroom, where the linguists had vanished.

"What will—"

"Beg them to come back, Melantha. Plead with them. Perhaps there is still time."

She tried. Karoly d'Branin tried as well. The twisted symphony of pain and pleading went on and on, but they could not raise Dannel or Lindran at all.

"They've cut out their comm," Melantha said furiously. "They don't want to listen to us. Or that . . . that sound."

Royd's sled and d'Branin's reached her at the same time. "I do not understand," Karoly said. "Why can you not enter, Royd? What is happening?"

"It is simple, Karoly," Royd replied. "I am being kept outside until—until—"

"Yes?" prompted Melantha.

"—until mother is done with them."

The linguists left their vacuum sled next to the one that Christopheris had abandoned and cycled through the airlock in unseemly haste, with hardly a glance for the grim headless doorman.

Inside they paused briefly to collapse their helmets.

"I can still hear him," Dannel said. The sounds were faint inside the ship.

Lindran nodded. "It's coming from the lounge. Hurry."

They kicked and pulled their way down the corridor in less than a minute. The sounds grew steadily louder, nearer. "He's in there," Lindran said when they reached the doorway.

"Yes," Dannel said, "but is he alone? We need a weapon. What if . . . Royd had to be lying. There *is* someone else on board. We need to defend ourselves."

Lindran would not wait. "There are two of us," she said. "Come *on!*" She launched herself through the doorway, calling Christopheris by name.

It was dark inside. What little light there was spilled through the door from the corridor. Her eyes took a long moment to adjust. Everything was confused; walls and ceilings and floor were all the same, she had no sense of direction. "Rojan," she called, dizzily. "Where are you?" The lounge seemed empty, but maybe it was only the light, or her sense of unease.

"Follow the sound," Dannel suggested. He hung in the door, peering warily about for a minute, and then began to feel his way cautiously down a wall, groping with his hands.

As if in response to his comment, the sobbing sounds grew suddenly louder. But they seemed to come first from one corner of the room, then from another.

Lindran, impatient, propelled herself across the chamber, searching. She brushed against a wall in the kitchen area, and that made her think of weapons, and Dannel's fears. She knew where the utensils were stored. "Here," she said a moment later, turning toward him. "Here, I've got a knife, that should thrill you." She flourished it and brushed against a floating

bubble of liquid as big as her fist. It burst and re-
formed into a hundred smaller globules. One moved
past her face, close, and she tasted it. Blood.

But Lasamer had been dead a long time. His blood
ought to have dried by now, she thought.

"Oh, merciful god," said Dannel.

"What?" Lindran demanded. "Did you find him?"
Dannel was fumbling his way back toward the
door, creeping along the wall like an oversized insect,
back the way he had come. "Get out, Lindran," he
warned. *"Hurry!"*

"Why?" She trembled despite herself. "What's
wrong?"

"The screams," he said. "The wall, Lindran, the
wall. The sounds."

"You're not making sense," she snapped. "Get hold
of yourself."

He gibbered. "Don't you see? The sounds are coming from the *wall*. The communicator. Faked. Simulated." Dannel reached the door and dove through
it, sighing audibly. He did not wait for her. He bolted
down the corridor and was gone, pulling himself hand
over hand wildly, his feet thrashing and kicking behind him.

Lindran braced herself and moved to follow.

The sounds came from in front of her, from the
door. "Help me," it said, in Rojan Christopheris's
voice. She heard moaning and that terrible wet choking sound, and she stopped.

From her side came a wheezing ghastly death rattle. "Ahhhh," it moaned, loudly, building in a counterpoint to the other noise. "Help me."

"Help me, help me, help me," said Christopheris
from the darkness behind her.

Coughing and a weak groan sounded under her
feet.

"Help me," all the voices chorused, "help me, help
me, help me." Recordings, she thought, recordings be-

ing played back. "Help me, help me, help me, help me." All the voices rose higher and louder, and the words turned into a scream, and the scream ended in wet choking, in wheezes and gasps and death. Then the sounds stopped. Just like that; turned off.

Lindran kicked off, floated toward the door, knife in hand.

Something dark and silent crawled from beneath the dinner table and rose to block her path. She saw it clearly for a moment, as it emerged between her and the light. Rojan Christopheris, still in his vacuum suit, but with the helmet pulled off. He had something in his hand that he raised to point at her. It was a laser, Lindran saw, a simple cutting laser.

She was moving straight toward him, coasting, helpless. She flailed and tried to stop herself, but she could not.

When she got quite close, she saw that Rojan had a second mouth below his chin, a long blackened slash, and it was grinning at her, and little droplets of blood flew from it, wetly, as he moved.

Dannel rushed down the corridor in a frenzy of fear, bruising himself as he smashed off walls and doorways. Panic and weightlessness made him clumsy. He kept glancing over his shoulder as he fled, hoping to see Lindran coming after him, but terrified of what he might see in her stead. Every time he looked back, he lost his sense of balance and went tumbling again.

It took a long, *long* time for the airlock to open. As he waited, trembling, his pulse began to slow. The sounds had dwindled behind him, and there was no sign of pursuit. He steadied himself with an effort. Once inside the lock chamber, with the inner door sealed between him and the lounge, he began to feel safe.

Suddenly Dannel could barely remember why he had been so terrified.

And he was ashamed; he had run, abandoned Lindran. And for what? What had frightened him so? An empty lounge? Noises from the walls? A rational explanation for that forced itself on him all at once. It only meant that poor Christopheris was somewhere else in the ship, that's all, just somewhere else, alive and in pain, spilling his agony into a comm unit.

Dannel shook his head ruefully. He'd hear no end of this, he knew. Lindran liked to taunt him. She would never let him forget it. But at least he would return, and apologize. That would count for something. Resolute, he reached out and killed the cycle on the airlock, then reversed it. The air that had been partially sucked out came gusting back into the chamber.

As the inner door rolled back, Dannel felt his fear return briefly, an instant of stark terror when he wondered what might have emerged from the lounge to wait for him in the corridors of the *Nightflyer*. He faced the fear and willed it away. He felt strong.

When he stepped out, Lindran was waiting.

He could see neither anger nor disdain in her curiously calm features, but he pushed himself toward her and tried to frame a plea for forgiveness anyway. "I don't know why I—"

With languid grace her hand came out from behind her back. The knife flashed up in a killing arc, and that was when Dannel finally noticed the hole burned in her suit, still smoking, just between her breasts.

"Your *mother?*" Melantha Jhirl said incredulously as they hung helpless in the emptiness beyond the ship.

"She can hear everything we say," Royd replied.

"But at this point it no longer makes any difference. Rojan must have done something very foolish, very threatening. Now she is determined to kill you all."

"She, she, what do you mean?" D'Branin's voice was puzzled. "Royd, surely you do not tell us that your mother is still alive. You said she died even before you were born."

"She did, Karoly," Royd said. "I did not lie to you."

"No," Melantha said. "I didn't think so. But you did not tell us the whole truth either."

Royd nodded. "Mother is dead, but her—her spirit still lives, and animates my *Nightflyer*." He sighed. "Perhaps it would be more fitting to say her *Nightflyer*. My control has been tenuous at best."

"Royd," d'Branin said, "spirits do not exist. They are not real. There is no survival after death. My *volcryn* are more real than any ghosts."

"I don't believe in ghosts either," said Melantha curtly.

"Call it what you will, then," Royd said. "My term is as good as any. The reality is unchanged by the terminology. My mother, or some part of my mother, lives in the *Nightflyer*, and she is killing all of you as she has killed others before."

"Royd, you do not make sense," d'Branin said.

"Quiet, Karoly. Let the captain explain."

"Yes," Royd said. "The *Nightflyer* is very—very advanced, you know. Automated, self-repairing, large. It had to be, if mother were to be freed from the necessity of crew. It was built on Newholme, you will recall. I have never been there, but I understand that Newholme's technology is quite sophisticated. Avalon could not duplicate this ship, I suspect. There are few worlds that could."

"The point, captain?"

"The point—the point is the computers, Melantha. They had to be extraordinary. They are; believe me, they are. Crystal-matrix cores, lasergrid data retrieval, full sensory extension, and other—features."

"Are you trying to tell us that the *Nightflyer* is an Artificial Intelligence? Lommie Thorne suspected as much."

"She was wrong," Royd said. "My ship is not an Artificial Intelligence; not as I understand it. But it is something close. Mother had a capacity for personality impress built in. She filled the central crystal with her own memories, desires, quirks, her loves and her—her hates. That was why she could trust the computer with my education, you see? She knew it would raise me as she herself would, had she the patience. She programmed it in certain other ways as well."

"And you cannot deprogram, my friend?" Karoly asked.

Royd's voice was despairing. "I have *tried*, Karoly. But I am a weak hand at systems work, and the programs are very complicated, the machines very sophisticated. At least three times I have eradicated her, only to have her surface once again. She is a phantom program, and I cannot track her. She comes and goes as she will. A ghost, do you see? Her memories and her personality are so intertwined with the programs that run the *Nightflyer* that I cannot get rid of her without destroying the central crystal, wiping the entire system. But that would leave me helpless. I could never reprogram, and with the computers down, the entire ship would fail—drives, life support, everything. I would have to leave the *Nightflyer*, and that would kill me."

"You should have told us, my friend," Karoly d'Branin said. "On Avalon we have many cyberneticists, some very great minds. We might have aided you. We could have provided expert help. Lommie Thorne might have helped you."

"Karoly, I have *had* expert help. Twice I have

brought systems specialists on board. The first one told me what I have just told you; that it was impossible without wiping the programs completely. The second had trained on Newholme. She thought she might be able to help me. Mother killed her."

"You are still holding something back," Melantha Jhirl said. "I understand how your cybernetic ghost can open and close airlocks at will and arrange other accidents of that nature. But how do you explain what she did to Thale Lasamer?"

"Ultimately I must bear the guilt," Royd replied. "My loneliness led me to a grievous error. I thought I could safeguard you, even with a telepath among you. I have carried other riders safely. I watch them constantly, warn them away from dangerous acts. If mother attempts to interfere, I countermand her directly from the master control console. That usually works. Not always. Usually. Before this trip she had killed only five times, and the first three died when I was quite young. That was how I learned about her, about her presence in my ship. That party included a telepath too.

"I should have known better, Karoly. My hunger for life has doomed you all to death. I overestimated my own abilities, and underestimated her fear of exposure. She strikes out when she is threatened, and telepaths are always a threat. They sense her, you see. A malign, looming presence, they tell me, something cool and hostile and inhuman."

"Yes," Karoly d'Branin said, "yes, that was what Thale said. An alien; he was certain of it."

"No doubt she feels alien to a telepath used to the familiar contours of organic minds. Hers is not a human brain, after all. What it is I cannot say—a complex of crystallized memories, a hellish network of interlocking programs, a meld of circuitry and spirit. Yes, I can understand why she might feel alien."

"You still haven't explained how a computer program could explode a man's skull," Melantha said.

"You wear the answer between your breasts, Melantha."

"My whisperjewel?" she said, puzzled. She felt it then, beneath her vacuum suit and her clothing; a touch of cold, a vague hint of eroticism that made her shiver. It was as if his mention had been enough to make the gem come alive.

"I was not familiar with whisperjewels until you told me of yours," Royd said, "but the principle is the same. Esper-etched, you said. Then you know that psionic power can be stored. The central core of my computer is resonant crystal, many times larger than your tiny jewel. I think mother impressed it as she lay dying."

"Only an esper can etch a whisperjewel," Melantha said.

"You never asked the *why* of it, either of you," Royd said. "You never asked why mother hated people so. She was born gifted, you see. On Avalon she might have been a class one, tested and trained and honored, her talent nurtured and rewarded. I think she might have been very famous. She might have been stronger than a class one, but perhaps it is only after death that she acquired such power, linked as she is to the *Nightflyer*.

"The point is moot. She was not born on Avalon. On Vess, her ability was seen as a curse, something alien and fearful. So they cured her of it. They used drugs and electroshock and hypnotraining that made her violently ill whenever she tried to use her talent. They used other less savory methods as well. She never lost her power, of course; only the ability to use it effectively, to control it with her conscious mind. It remained part of her, suppressed, erratic, a source of shame and pain, surfacing violently in times of great emotional stress. And half a decade of institutional care almost drove her insane. No wonder she hated people."

"What was her talent? Telepathy?"

"No. Oh, some rudimentary ability, perhaps. I have read that all psi talents have several latent abilities in addition to their one developed strength. But mother could not read minds. She had some empathy, although her cure had twisted it curiously, so that the emotions she felt literally sickened her. But her major strength, the talent they took five years to shatter and destroy, was teke."

Melantha Jhirl swore. "Of *course* she hated gravity! Telekinesis under weightlessness is—"

"Yes," Royd finished. "Keeping the *Nightflyer* under gravity tortures me, but it limits mother."

In the silence that followed that comment, each of them looked down the dark cylinder of the driveroom. Karoly d'Branin moved awkwardly on his sled. "Dannel and Lindran have not returned," he said.

"They are probably dead," Royd said dispassionately.

"What will we do, then? We must plan. We cannot wait here indefinitely."

"The first question is what *I* can do," Royd Eris replied. "I have talked freely, you'll note. You deserved to know. We have passed the point where ignorance was a protection. Obviously things have gone too far. There have been too many deaths and you have been witness to all of them. Mother cannot allow you to return to Avalon alive."

"True," said Melantha. "But what shall she do with you? Is your own status in doubt, captain?"

"The crux of the problem," Royd admitted. "You are still three moves ahead, Melantha. I wonder if it will suffice. Your opponent is four ahead in this game, and most of your pawns are already captured. I fear checkmate is imminent."

"Unless I can persuade my opponent's king to desert, no?"

She could see Royd's wan smile. "She would probably kill me too if I choose to side with you. She does not need me."

Karoly d'Branin was slow to grasp the point. "But —but what else could—"

"My sled has a laser. Yours do not. I could kill you both, right now, and thereby earn my way back into the *Nightflyer*'s good graces."

Across the three meters that lay between their sleds, Melantha's eyes met Royd's. Her hands rested easily on the thruster controls. "You could try, captain. Remember, the improved model isn't easy to kill."

"I would not kill you, Melantha Jhirl," Royd said seriously. "I have lived sixty-eight standard years and I have never lived at all. I am tired, and you tell grand gorgeous lies. Will you really touch me?"

"Yes."

"I risk a lot for that touch. Yet in a way it is no risk at all. If we lose we will all die together. If we win, well, I shall die anyway when they destroy the *Nightflyer*, either that or live as a freak in an orbital hospital, and I would prefer death."

"We will build you a new ship, captain," Melantha promised.

"Liar," Royd replied. But his tone was cheerful. "No matter. I have not had much of a life anyway. Death does not frighten me. If we win, you must tell me about your *volcryn* once again, Karoly. And you, Melantha, you must play chess with me, and find a way to touch me, and . . ."

"And sex with you?" she finished, smiling.

"If you would," he said quietly. He shrugged. "Well, mother has heard all of this. Doubtless she will listen carefully to any plans we might make, so there is no sense making them. Now there is no chance

that the control lock will admit me, since it is keyed
directly into the ship's computer. So we must follow
the others through the driveroom, and enter through
the main lock, and take what small chances we are
given. If I can reach my console and restore gravity,
perhaps we can win. If not—"

He was interrupted by a low groan.

For an instant Melantha thought the *Nightflyer*
was wailing at them again, and she was surprised
that it was so stupid as to try the same tactic twice.
Then the groan sounded once more, and in the back
of Karoly d'Branin's sled, the forgotten fourth member of their company struggled against the bonds
that held her down. D'Branin hastened to free her,
and Agatha Marij-Black tried to rise to her feet and
almost floated off the sled, until d'Branin caught her
hand and pulled her back. "Are you well?" he asked.
"Can you hear me? Have you pain?"

Imprisoned beneath a transparent faceplate, wide
frightened eyes flicked rapidly from Karoly to Melantha to Royd and then to the broken *Nightflyer*.
Melantha wondered whether the woman was insane
and started to caution d'Branin, when Marij-Black
spoke.

"The *volcryn!*" was all she said. "Oh. The *volcryn!*"

Around the mouth of the driveroom, the ring of
nuclear engines took on a faint glow. Melantha Jhirl
heard Royd suck in his breath sharply. She gave the
thruster controls of her sled a violent twist. "Hurry,"
she said loudly. "The *Nightflyer* is preparing to
move."

A third of the way down the long barrel of the
driveroom, Royd pulled abreast of her, stiff and
menacing in his black, bulky armor. Side by side
they sailed past the cylindrical stardrives and the
cyberwebs; ahead, dimly lit, was the main airlock and
its ghastly sentinel.

"When we reach the lock, jump over to my sled," Royd said. "I want to stay armed and mounted, and the chamber is not large enough for two sleds."

Melantha Jhirl risked a quick glance behind her. "Karoly," she called. "Where are you?"

"Outside, my love, my friend," the answer came. "I cannot come. Forgive me."

"We have to stay together!"

"No," d'Branin said, "no, I could not risk it, not when we are so close. It would be so tragic, so futile, Melantha. To come so close and fail. Death I do not mind, but I must see them first, finally, after all these years."

"My mother is going to move the ship," Royd cut in. "Karoly, you will be left behind, lost."

"I will wait," d'Branin replied. "My *volcryn* come, and I must wait for them."

Then the time for conversation was gone, for the airlock was almost upon them. Both sleds slowed and stopped, and Royd Eris reached out and began the cycle while Melantha Jhirl moved to the rear of his huge oval worksled. When the outer door moved aside, they glided through into the lock chamber.

"When the inner door opens, it will begin," Royd told her evenly. "The permanent furnishings are either built in or welded or bolted into place, but the things that your team brought on board are not. Mother will use those things as weapons. And beware of doors, airlocks, any equipment tied into the *Nightflyer*'s computer. Need I warn you not to unseal your suit?"

"Hardly," she replied.

Royd lowered the sled a little, and its grapplers made a metallic sound as they touched against the floor of the chamber.

The inner door hissed open, and Royd applied his thrusters.

Inside Dannel and Lindran waited, swimming in a

haze of blood. Dannel had been slit from crotch
to throat and his intestines moved like a nest of pale,
angry snakes. Lindran still held the knife. They swam
closer, moving with a grace they had never possessed
in life.

Royd lifted his foremost grapplers and smashed
them to the side as he surged forward. Dannel
caromed off a bulkhead, leaving a wide wet mark
where he struck, and more of his guts came sliding
out. Lindran lost control of the knife. Royd accelerated past them, driving up the corridor through
the cloud of blood.

"I'll watch behind," Melantha said. She turned
and put her back to his. Already the two corpses were
safely behind them. The knife was floating uselessly
in the air. She started to tell Royd that they were all
right when the blade abruptly shifted and came after
them, gripped by some invisible force.

"*Swerve!*" she cried.

The sled shot wildly to one side. The knife missed
by a full meter and glanced ringingly off a bulkhead.

But it did not drop. It came at them again.

The lounge loomed ahead. Dark.

"The door is too narrow," Royd said. "We will have
to abandon—" As he spoke, they hit; he wedged the
sled squarely into the door frame, and the sudden
impact jarred them loose.

For a moment Melantha floated clumsily in the
corridor, her head whirling, trying to sort up from
down. The knife slashed at her, opening her suit and
her shoulder clear through to the bone. She felt sharp
pain and the warm flush of bleeding. "Damn," she
shrieked. The knife came around again, spraying
droplets of blood.

Melantha's hand darted out and caught it.

She muttered something under her breath and
wrenched the blade free of the hand that had been
gripping it.

Royd had regained the controls of his sled and seemed intent on some manipulation. Beyond him, in the dimness of the lounge, Melantha glimpsed a dark semihuman form rise into view.

"*Royd!*" she warned. The thing activated its small laser. The pencil beam caught Royd square in the chest.

He touched his own firing stud. The sled's heavy-duty laser came alive, a shaft of sudden brilliance. It cindered Christopheris's weapon and burned off his right arm and part of his chest. The beam hung in the air, throbbing, and smoked against the far bulkhead.

Royd made some adjustments and began cutting a hole. "We'll be through in five minutes or less," he said curtly.

"Are you all right?" Melantha asked.

"I'm uninjured," he replied. "My suit is better armored than yours, and his laser was a low-powered toy."

Melantha turned her attention back to the corridor.

The linguists were pulling themselves toward her, one on each side of the passage, to come at her from two directions at once. She flexed her muscles. Her shoulder stabbed and screamed. Otherwise she felt strong, almost reckless. "The corpses are coming after us again," she told Royd. "I'm going to take them."

"Is that wise?" he asked. "There are two of them."

"I'm an improved model," Melantha said, "and they're dead." She kicked herself free of the sled and sailed toward Dannel in a high, graceful trajectory. He raised his hands to block her. She slapped them aside, bent one arm back and heard it snap, and drove her knife deep into his throat before she realized what a useless gesture that was. Blood oozed from his neck in a spreading cloud, but he continued to flail at her. His teeth snapped grotesquely.

Melantha withdrew her blade, seized him, and with all her considerable strength threw him bodily down the corridor. He tumbled, spinning wildly, and vanished into the haze of his own blood.

Melantha flew in the opposite direction, revolving lazily.

Lindran's hands caught her from behind.

Nails scrabbled against her faceplate until they began to bleed, leaving red streaks on the plastic.

Melantha whirled to face her attacker, grabbed a thrashing arm, and flung the woman down the passageway to crash into her struggling companion. The reaction sent her spinning like a top. She spread her arms and stopped herself, dizzy, gulping.

"I'm through," Royd announced.

Melantha turned to see. A smoking, meter-square opening had been cut through one wall of the lounge. Royd killed the laser, gripped both sides of the door frame, and pushed himself toward it.

A piercing blast of sound drilled through her head. She doubled over in agony. Her tongue flicked out and clicked off the comm; then there was blessed silence.

In the lounge it was raining. Kitchen utensils, glasses and plates, pieces of human bodies all lashed violently across the room and glanced harmlessly off Royd's armored form. Melantha, eager to follow, drew back helplessly. That rain of death would cut her to pieces in her lighter, thinner vacuum suit. Royd reached the far wall and vanished into the secret control section of the ship. She was alone.

The *Nightflyer* lurched, and sudden acceleration provided a brief semblance of gravity. Melantha was thrown to one side. Her injured shoulder smashed painfully against the sled.

All up and down the corridor doors were opening. Dannel and Lindran were moving toward her once

*   *   *

The *Nightflyer* was a distant star sparked by its nuclear engines. Blackness and cold enveloped them, and below was the unending emptiness of the Tempter's Veil, but Karoly d'Branin did not feel afraid. He felt strangely transformed.

The void was alive with promise.

"They *are* coming," he whispered. "Even I, who have no psi at all, even I can feel it. The Crey story must be so; even from light-years off they can be sensed. Marvelous!"

Agatha Marij-Black seemed small and shrunken. "The *volcryn*," she muttered. "What good can they do us? I hurt. The ship is gone. D'Branin, my head aches." She made a small, frightened noise. "Thale said that, just after I injected him, before—before—you know. He said that his head hurt. It aches so terribly."

"Quiet, Agatha. Do not be afraid. I am here with you. Wait. Think only of what we shall witness, think only of that!"

"I can sense them," the psipsych said.

D'Branin was eager. "Tell me, then. We have our little sled. We shall go to them. Direct me."

"Yes," she agreed. "Yes. Oh, yes."

Gravity returned: in a flicker, the universe became almost normal.

Melantha fell to the deck, landed easily and rolled, and was on her feet cat-quick.

The objects that had been floating ominously through the open doors along the corridor all came clattering down.

The blood was transformed from a fine mist to a slick covering on the corridor floor.

The two corpses dropped heavily from the air and lay still.

Royd spoke to her from the communicators built into the walls. "I made it," he said.

"I noticed," she replied.

"I'm at the main control console. I have restored the gravity with a manual override, and I'm cutting off as many computer functions as possible. We're still not safe, though. She will try to find a way around me. I'm countermanding her by sheer force, as it were. I cannot afford to overlook anything, and if my attention should lapse, even for a moment . . . Melantha, was your suit breached?"

"Yes. Cut at the shoulder."

"Change into another one. *Immediately.* I think the counterprogramming I'm doing will keep the locks sealed, but I can't take any chances."

Melantha was already running down the corridor toward the cargo hold where the suits and equipment were stored.

"When you have changed," Royd continued, "dump the corpses into the mass conversion unit. You'll find the appropriate hatch near the driveroom airlock, just to the left of the lock controls. Convert any other loose objects that are not indispensible as well; scientific instruments, books, tapes, tableware—"

"Knives," suggested Melantha.

"By all means."

"Is teke still a threat, captain?"

"Mother is vastly weaker in a gravity field," Royd said. "She has to fight it. Even boosted by the *Nightflyer*'s power, she can only move one object at a time, and she has only a fraction of the lifting force she wields under weightless conditions. But the power is still there, remember. Also, it is possible she will find a way to circumvent me and cut out the gravity again. From here I can restore it in an instant, but I don't want any likely weapons lying around even for that brief period of time."

Melantha reached the cargo area. She stripped off her vacuum suit and slipped into another one in record time, wincing at the pain in her shoulder. It was bleeding badly, but she had to ignore it. She gathered up the discarded suit and a double armful of instruments and dumped them into the conversion chamber. Afterward she turned her attention to the bodies. Dannel was no problem. Lindran crawled down the corridor after her as she pushed him through and thrashed weakly when it was her own turn, a grim reminder that the *Nightflyer*'s powers were not all gone. Melantha easily overcame her feeble struggles and forced her through.

Christopheris's burned, ruined body writhed in her grasp and snapped its teeth at her, but Melantha had no real trouble with it. While she was cleaning out the lounge, a kitchen knife came spinning at her head. It came slowly, though, and Melantha just batted it aside, then picked it up and added it to the pile for conversion.

She was working through the cabins, carrying Agatha Marij-Black's abandoned drugs and injection gun under her arm, when she heard Royd cry out.

A moment later a force like a giant invisible hand wrapped itself around her chest and squeezed and pulled her, struggling, to the floor.

Something was moving across the stars.

Dimly and far off, d'Branin could see it, though he could not yet make out details. But it was there, that was unmistakable—some vast shape that blocked off a section of the starscape. It was coming at them dead on.

How he wished he had his team with him now, his computer, his telepath, his experts, his instruments.

He pressed harder on the thrusters and rushed to meet his *volcryn*.

* * *

Pinned to the floor, hurting, Melantha Jhirl risked opening her suit's comm. She had to talk to Royd. "Are you there?" she asked. "What's happen . . . happening?" The pressure was awful, and it was growing steadily worse. She could barely move.

The answer was pained and slow in coming. ". . . outwitted . . . me," Royd's voice managed. ". . . hurts . . . to . . . talk."

"Royd—"

". . . she . . . teked . . . the . . . dial . . . up . . . two . . . gees . . . three . . . higher . . . right . . . here . . . on . . . the . . . board . . . all . . . I . . . have to . . . to do . . . turn it . . . back . . . let me."

Silence. Then, finally, when Melantha was near despair, Royd's voice again. One word:

". . . can't . . ."

Melantha's chest felt as if it were supporting ten times her own weight. She could imagine the agony Royd must be in; Royd, for whom even one gravity was painful and dangerous. Even if the dial was an arm's length away, she knew his feeble musculature would never let him reach it. "Why," she started. Talking was not as hard for her as it seemed to be for him. "Why would . . . she turn *up* the . . . the gravity . . . it . . . weakens her too . . . yes?"

". . . yes . . . but . . . in a . . . a time . . . hour . . . minute . . . my . . . my heart . . . will burst . . . and . . . and then . . . you alone . . . she . . . will . . . kill gravity . . . kill you . . ."

Painfully Melantha reached out her arm and dragged herself half a length down the corridor. "Royd . . . hold on . . . I'm coming . . ." She dragged herself forward again. Agatha's drug kit was still under her arm, impossibly heavy. She eased it down and started to shove it aside. It felt as if weighed a hundred kilos. She reconsidered. Instead she opened its lid.

The ampules were all neatly labeled. She glanced

over them quickly, searching for adrenaline or syn-
thastim, anything that might give her the strength
she needed to reach Royd. She found several stimu-
lants, selected the strongest, and was loading it into
the injection gun with awkward, agonized slowness
when her eyes chanced on the supply of esperon.

Melantha did not know why she hesitated. Esperon
was only one of a half-dozen psionic drugs in the kit,
none of which could do her any good, but something
about seeing it bothered her, reminded her of something she could not quite lay her finger on. She was
trying to sort it out when she heard the noise.

"Royd," she said, "your mother . . . could she move
. . . she couldn't move anything . . . teke it . . . in
this high a gravity . . . could she?"

"Maybe," he answered, ". . . if . . . concentrate . . . all
her . . . power . . . hard . . . maybe possible . . . why?"

"Because," Melantha Jhirl said grimly, "because
something. . . some*one* . . . is cycling through the airlock."

"It is not truly a ship, not as I thought it would
be," Karoly d'Branin was saying. His suit, Academy-
designed, had a built-in encoding device, and he was
recording his comments for posterity, strangely secure in the certainty of his impending death. "The
scale of it is difficult to imagine, difficult to estimate.
Vast, vast. I have nothing but my wrist computer, no
instruments, I cannot make accurate measurements,
but I would say, oh, a hundred kilometers, perhaps
as much as three hundred, across. Not solid mass, of
course, not at all. It is delicate, airy, no ship as we
know ships, no city either. It is—oh, beautiful—it is
crystal and gossamer, alive with its own dim lights, a
vast intricate kind of spiderwebby craft—it reminds
me a bit of the old starsail ships they used once, in
the days before drive, but this great construct, it is
not solid, it cannot be driven by light. It is no ship at

all, really. It is all open to vacuum, it has no sealed
cabins or life-support spheres, none visible to me, unless blocked from my line of sight in some fashion,
and no, I cannot believe that, it is too open, too
fragile. It moves quite rapidly. I would wish for the
instrumentation to measure its speed, but it is enough
to be here. I am taking the sled at right angles to it,
to get clear of its path, but I cannot say that I will
make it. It moves so much faster than we. Not at
light speed, no, far below light speed, but still faster
than the *Nightflyer* and its nuclear engines, I would
guess. Only a guess.

"The *volcryn* craft has no visible means of propulsion. In fact, I wonder how—perhaps it is a light-sail,
laser-launched millenia ago, now torn and rotted by
some unimaginable catastrophe—but no, it is too sym-
metrical, too beautiful—the webbings, the great shimmering veils near the nexus, the beauty of it.

"I must describe it; I must be more accurate, I
know. It is difficult; I grow too excited. It is large, as
I have said, kilometers across. Roughly—let me count
—yes, roughly octagonal in shape. The nexus, the center, is a bright area, a small darkness surrounded by a
much greater area of light, but only the dark portion
seems entirely solid—the lighted areas are translucent.
I can see stars through them, though discolored,
shifted toward the purple. Veils, I call those the veils.
From the nexus and the veils eight long—oh, vastly
long—spurs project, not quite spaced evenly, so it is
not a true geometric octagon—ah, I see better now,
one of the spurs is shifting, oh, very slowly, the veils
are rippling—they are mobile then, those projections,
and the webbing runs from one spur to the next,
around and around, but there are—patterns, odd patterns. It is not at all the simple webbing of a spider.
I cannot quite see order in the patterns, in the traceries
of the webs, but I feel sure the order is there; the
meaning is waiting to be found.

"There are lights. Have I mentioned the lights? The lights are brightest around the center nexus, but they are nowhere very bright, a dim violet. Some visible radiation then, but not much. I would like to take an ultraviolet reading of this craft, but I do not have the instrumentation. The lights move. The veils seem to ripple, and lights can run constantly up and down the length of the spurs, at differing rates of speed, and sometimes other lights can be seen transversing the webbing, moving across the patterns. I do not know what the lights are. Some form of communication, perhaps. I cannot tell whether they emanate from inside the craft or outside. I—oh! There was another light just then. Between the spurs, a brief flash, a starburst. It is gone now, already. It was more intense than the others, indigo. I feel so helpless, so ignorant. But they are beautiful, my *volcryn* . . .

"The myths, they—this is really not much like the legends, not truly. The size, the lights. The *volcryn* have often been linked to lights, but those reports were so vague, they might have meant anything, described anything from a laser propulsion system to simple exterior lighting. I could not know it meant this. Ah, what mystery! The ship is still too far away to see the finer detail. It is so large, I do not think we shall get clear of it. It seems to have turned toward us, I think, yet I may be mistaken. It is only an impression. My instruments! If I only had my instruments. Perhaps the darker area in the center is a craft, a life capsule. The *volcryn* must be inside it. I wish my team were with me, and Thale, poor Thale. He was a class one. We might have made contact, might have communicated with them. The things we would learn! The things they have seen! To think how old this craft is, how ancient the race, how long they have been outbound . . . it fills me with awe. Communication would be such a gift, such an impossible gift, but they are so alien."

"*D'Branin,*" Agatha Marij-Black said in a low, urgent voice. "Can't you feel?"

Karoly d'Branin looked at her as if seeing her for the first time. "Can *you* feel them? You are a three—can you sense them now, strongly?"

"Long ago," the psipsych said, "long ago."

"Can you project? Talk to them, Agatha. Where are they? In the center area? The dark?"

"Yes," she replied, and she laughed. Her laugh was shrill and hysterical, and d'Branin had to recall she was a very sick woman. "Yes, in the center, d'Branin, that's where the pulses come from. Only you're wrong about them. It's not a *them* at all. Your legends are all lies, lies! I wouldn't be surprised if we were the first ever to see your *volcryn,* to come this close. The others, those aliens of yours, they merely *felt,* deep and distantly, sensed a bit of the nature of the *volcryn* in their dreams and visions, and fashioned the rest to suit themselves. Ships, and wars, and a race of eternal travelers, it is all—all—"

"Yes? What do you mean, Agatha, my friend? You do not make sense. I do not understand."

"No," Marij-Black said, "you do not, do you?" Her voice was suddenly gentle. "You cannot feel it, as I can. So clear now. This must be how a one feels, all the time. A one full of esperon."

"What do you feel? *What?*"

"It's not a *them,* Karoly. It's an *it.* Alive, Karoly, and quite mindless, I assure you."

"Mindless?" d'Branin said. "No, you must be wrong; you are not reading correctly. I will accept that it is a single creature if you say so, a single great marvelous star-traveler, but how can it be mindless? You sensed it—its mind, its telepathic emanations. You and the whole of the Crey sensitives and all the others. Perhaps its thoughts are too alien for you to read."

"Perhaps. But what I do read is not so terribly alien at all. Only animal. Its thoughts are slow and dark and strange, hardly thoughts at all, faint. Stirrings cold and distant. The brain must be huge all right, I grant you that, but it can't be devoted to conscious thought."

"What do you mean?"

"The propulsion system, d'Branin. Don't you *feel?* The pulses? They are threatening to rip off the top of my skull. Can't you guess what is driving your damned *volcryn* across the galaxy? And why they avoid gravity wells? Can't you guess how it is moving?"

"No," d'Branin said, but even as he denied it, a dawn of comprehension broke across his face, and he looked away from his companion, back at the swelling immensity of the *volcryn*, its lights moving, its veils a-ripple, as it came on and on, across light-years, light-centuries, across eons.

When he looked at her, he mouthed only a single word. "Teke," he said.

She nodded.

Melantha Jhirl struggled to lift the injection gun and press it against an artery. It gave a single loud hiss, and the drug flooded her system. She lay back and gathered her strength and tried to think. Esperon, esperon—why was that important? It had killed Lasamer, made him a victim of his own latent abilities, multiplied his power and his vulnerability. Psi. It all came back to psi.

The inner door of the airlock opened. The headless corpse came through.

It moved with jerks, unnatural shufflings, never lifting its legs from the floor. It sagged as it moved, half-crushed by the weight upon it. Each shuffle was

crude and sudden; some grim force was literally
yanking one leg forward, then the next. It moved in
slow motion, arms stiff by its sides.

But it moved.

Melantha summoned her own reserves and began
to squirm away from it, never taking her eyes off its
advance.

Her thoughts went round and round, searching for
the piece out of place, the solution to the chess problem, finding nothing.

The corpse was moving faster than she was. Clearly, visibly, it was gaining.

Melantha tried to stand. She got to her knees with
a grunt, her heart pounding. Then one knee. She
tried to force herself up, to lift the impossible burden
on her shoulders as if she were lifting weights. She
was strong, she told herself. She was the improved
model.

But when she put all her weight on one leg, her
muscles would not hold her. She collapsed, awkwardly, and when she smashed against the floor, it was
as if she had fallen from a building. She heard a sharp
snap, and a stab of agony flashed up her arm, her
good arm, the arm she had tried to use to break her
fall. The pain in her shoulder was terrible and intense. She blinked back tears and choked on her
own scream.

The corpse was halfway up the corridor. It must be
walking on two broken legs, she realized. It didn't
care. A force greater than tendons and bone and
muscle was holding it up.

"Melantha . . . heard you . . . are . . . you . . .
Melantha?"

"Quiet," she snarled at Royd. She had no breath to
waste on talk.

Now she used all the disciplines she had ever
learned to will away the pain. She kicked feebly, her
boots scraping for purchase, and she pulled herself

forward with her unbroken arm, ignoring the fire in her shoulder.

The corpse came on and on.

She dragged herself across the threshold of the lounge, worming her way under the crashed sled, hoping it would delay the cadaver. The thing that had been Thale Lasamer was a meter behind her.

In the darkness, in the lounge, where it had all begun, Melantha Jhirl ran out of strength.

Her body shuddered and she collapsed on the damp carpet, and she knew that she could go no further.

On the far side of the door, the corpse stood stiffly. The sled began to shake. Then, with the scrape of metal against metal, it slid backward, moving in tiny sudden increments, jerking itself free and out of the way.

Psi. Melantha wanted to curse it, and cry. Vainly she wished for a psi power of her own, a weapon to blast apart the teke-driven corpse that stalked her. She was improved, she thought despairingly, but not improved enough. Her parents had given her all the genetic gifts they could arrange, but psi was beyond them. The genes were astronomically rare, recessive, and—

—and suddenly it came to her.

"Royd," she said, putting all her remaining will into her words. She was weeping, wet, frightened. "The dial . . . *teke it*. Royd, teke it!"

His reply was faint, troubled. ". . . can't . . . I don't . . . mother . . . only . . . her . . . not me . . . no . . . mother . . ."

"Not mother," she said, desperate. "You always . . . say . . . *mother*. I forgot . . . forgot. Not your mother . . . listen . . . you're a *clone* . . . same genes . . . you have it too . . . power."

"Don't," he said. "Never . . . must be . . . sex-linked."

"No! It *isn't*. I know . . . Promethean, Royd . . .

don't tell a Promethean . . . about genes . . . turn it!"

The sled jumped a third of a meter and listed to the side. A path was clear.

The corpse came forward.

". . . trying," Royd said. "Nothing . . . I *can't!*"

"She *cured* you," Melantha said bitterly. "Better than . . . she . . . was cured . . . prenatal . . . but it's only . . . suppressed . . . you *can!*"

"I . . . don't . . . know . . . how."

The corpse stood above her. Stopped. Its pale-fleshed hands trembled, spasmed, jerked upward. Long painted fingernails. Made claws. Began to rise.

Melantha swore. *"Royd!"*

". . . sorry . . ."

She wept and shook and made a futile fist.

And all at once the gravity was gone. Far, far away, she heard Royd cry out and then fall silent.

"The flashes come more frequently now," Karoly d'Branin dictated, "or perhaps it is simply that I am closer, that I can see them better. Bursts of indigo and deep violet, short and fast-fading. Between the webbing. A field, I think. The flashes are particles of hydrogen, the thin ethereal stuff of the reaches between the stars. They touch the field, between the webbing, the spurs, and shortly flare into the range of visible light. Matter to energy, yes, that is what I guess. My *volcryn* feeds.

"It fills half the universe, comes on and on. We shall not escape it, oh, so sad. Agatha is gone, silent, blood on her faceplate. I can almost see the dark area, almost, almost. I have a strange vision, in the center is a face, small, ratlike without mouth or nose or eyes, yet still a face somehow, and it stares at me. The veils move so sensuously. The webbing looms around us.

"Ah, the light, the light!"

* * *

The corpse bobbed awkwardly into the air, its hands hanging limply before it. Melantha, reeling in the weightlessness, was suddenly and violently sick. She ripped off the helmet, collapsed it, and pushed away from her own nausea, trying to ready herself for the *Nightflyer*'s furious assault.

But the body of Thale Lasamer floated dead and still, and nothing else moved in the darkened lounge. Finally Melantha recovered, and she moved to the corpse, weakly, and pushed it, a small and tentative shove. It sailed across the room.

"Royd?" she said uncertainly.

There was no answer.

She pulled herself through the hole into the control chamber.

And found Royd Eris suspended in his armored suit. She shook him, but he did not stir. Trembling, Melantha Jhirl studied his suit and then began to dismantle it. She touched him.

"Royd," she said, "here. Feel. Royd, here, I'm here, feel it." His suit came apart easily, and she flung the pieces of it away. "Royd, *Royd.*"

Dead. Dead. His heart had given out. She punched it, pummeled it, tried to pound it into new life. It did not beat. Dead. Dead.

Melantha Jhirl moved back from him, blinded by her own tears, edged into the console, glanced down.

Dead. Dead.

But the dial on the gravity grid was set on zero.

"Melantha," said a mellow voice from the walls.

I have held the *Nightflyer*'s crystalline soul within my hands.

It is deep red and multifaceted, large as my head, and icy to the touch. In its scarlet depths, two small sparks of smoky light burn fiercely and sometimes seem to whirl.

I have crawled through the consoles, wound my

way carefully past safeguards and cybernets, taking care to damage nothing, and I have laid rough hands on that great crystal, knowing it is where *she* lives.

And I cannot bring myself to wipe it.

Royd's ghost has asked me not to.

Last night we talked about it once again, over brandy and chess in the lounge. Royd cannot drink, of course, but he sends his specter to smile at me, and he tells me where he wants his pieces moved.

For the thousandth time he offered to take me back to Avalon, or any world of my choice. If only I would go outside and complete the repairs we abandoned so many years ago, so the *Nightflyer* might safely slip into stardrive.

For the thousandth time I refused.

He is stronger now, no doubt. Their genes are the same, after all. Their power is the same. Dying, he too found the strength to impress himself upon the great crystal. The ship is alive with both of them, and frequently they fight. Sometimes she outwits him for a moment, and the *Nightflyer* does odd, erratic things. The gravity goes up or down or off completely. Blankets wrap themselves around my throat when I sleep. Objects come hurtling out of dark corners.

Those times have come less frequently of late, though. When they do come, Royd stops her, or I do. Together, the *Nightflyer* is ours.

Royd claims he is strong enough alone, that he does not really need me, that he can keep her under check. I wonder. Over the chessboard, I still beat him nine games out of ten.

And there are other considerations. Our work, for one. Karoly would be proud of us. The *volcryn* will soon enter the mists of the Tempter's Veil, and we follow close behind. Studying, recording, doing all that old d'Branin would have wanted us to do. It is all in the computer, and on tape and paper as well, should the system ever be wiped. It will be interesting to see how the *volcryn* thrives in the Veil. Matter is so thick there, compared to the thin diet of interstellar hydrogen on which the creature has fed so many endless eons.

We have tried to communicate with it, with no success. I do not believe it is sentient at all. And lately Royd has tried to imitate its ways, gathering all his energies in an attempt to move the *Nightflyer* by teke. Sometimes, oddly, his mother even joins with him in those efforts. So far they have always failed, but we will keep trying.

So goes our work. We know our results will reach humanity. Royd and I have discussed it, and we have a plan. Before I die, when my time is near, I will destroy the central crystal and clear the computers, and afterward I will set course manually for the close vicinity of an inhabited world. The *Nightflyer* will become a true ghost ship then. It will work. I have all the time I need, and I am an improved model.

I will not consider the other option, although it means much to me that Royd suggests it again and again. No doubt I could finish the repairs, and perhaps Royd could control the ship without me, and go on with the work. But that is not important.

I was wrong so many times. The esperon, the monitors, my control of the others; all of them my failures, payment for my *hubris*. Failure hurts. When I finally touched him, for the first and last and only time, his body was still warm. But *he* was gone already. He never felt my touch. I could not keep that promise.

But I can keep my other.

I will not leave him alone with her.

Ever.

AFTERWORD

by Vernor Vinge

WARNING: This afterword gives away secrets from both *Nightflyers* and *True Names*.

There are interesting parallels and contrasts between the two stories in this *Binary Star* (which, considering the careful attentions of our Illustrious Editor, can be no coincidence). The backgrounds, however, are very different. My yarn (*True Names*) is securely stuck in Near Earth Space, almost the world of our present, where the notion of interstellar travel is regarded as fantasy. George's story takes place in an age where interstellar travel is an old—for some an *ancient*—technology. His characters are part of a culture that is itself just one of thousands scattered across thousands of light-years. Such a background is hard to handle (and is frequently *mishandled*). Our Earth has greater variety than can be comprehended. How can an author convincingly write of something millions of times greater?

George R. R. Martin has succeeded in doing just this: his universe is credible. His success is partly due to indirection, partly to hints of things offstage, and partly to insight into the implications of such an expanded reality:

We see constant references to a bewildering variety of races. These are not gratuitous; almost all relate directly to the plot or the outlook of the characters. Even so, the hints and the mysteries are enough to make us realize that there are stories beyond stories here. Apparently the starships in use move at about a thousand times the speed of light, and this (paradoxically to us twentieth-century types) is so *slow* that known cultures are separated by decades of flight time. And beyond these are others, and beyond these. . . . The numbers are right: just count the number of stars in our galaxy and think how many star-spanning empires there would have to be if life is common and stardrives exist. And of course, few of these cultures—even the traveling ones—would be at the same level of development, either technologically or culturally. Some would be dying, some would be like the "classical" Terrans of *Astounding Science Fiction,* sweeping out into interstellar space as though it were some infinite *lebensraum.* There is room for all of them in this one galaxy, and room for wars that would last thousands of years. Sheer numbers as much as flight time would make many existing cultures mere legends to others. But unlike the legends of our twentieth century, these would more often than not be reality somewhere.

George invents new specialties for this new universe: xenomythology, the study of the legends of alien cultures. In many cases the cultures are so old that even their legends were created after they were star traveling and thousands of years ahead of present-day Earth. And in many cases the cultures are themselves so far away that they are half-myth. Karoly d'Branin, the project manager, has studied the "legend of the legends," as ship's captain Royd Eris so well puts it. These are the sorts of images that give his future an underpinning of credibility. (And incidentally, these are the images that make readers like me wish to see such a new reality. There would be greater terrors, greater evil in such a universe—but also greater wonders, greater good. For the educated there could never be the smug twentieth-century attitude that so clearly separates truth and science from myth and magic.)

FINAL WARNING: I really am going to give away much of the endings; here comes a discussion of plot.

One of the principal similarities between *Nightflyers* and *True Names* is the mystery used to drive the action. We both have an individual (George's Royd Eris and my Mailman) whose true identity is unknown. (George has an additional mystery in the *volcryn*.) We both trickle out speculations about the mystery figure: perhaps he is a computer simulation, or an alien invasion, or a master criminal. This gives us opportunity to build up the tension, but also to provide action and incidents that illuminate the backgrounds of our stories. In the end we choose nearly *opposite* solutions to the mystery. Royd Eris turns out to be a man: my Mailman is not. Yet still there are parallels. We both agree that computers can have whatever is meant by "soul," and we both agree that a human soul can be transferred to a computer. The first of these ideas is disbelieved by most present-day computer professionals, even when they discuss hypothetical future machines and programs. (I say most; *I* don't disbelieve.) The second idea, though it has appeared before in science fiction, is thought by most people to be near-fantasy. Time will tell. *True Names* ends at the point where both these ideas have been realized, and where the future becomes unintelligible (not simply unpredictable or unknowable, but even worse, unintelligible and unimaginable). (The future after my story could not become the present of George's. That makes me sad.)

I counted ten characters with "talking parts" in

Nightflyers. Even the "spear carriers" come across as real people, and this makes the last third of the story especially terrifying as we begin to see casualties. Certain of these people I will remember a long time:

I was ready to kill Karoly d'Branin myself after the fifth time he said "My friend . . ." but then I realized that the fellow really is sincere. He is the distracted, *volcryn*-fixated scientist, but he knows he has to play administrator if he is ever going to get close to those mysterious creatures. He tries to substitute goodwill and sincerity for real administrative competence—and almost succeeds.

I have a soft part in my heart for Lommie Thorne. There are many people like her even in our own time; I don't think outsiders realize just how many. Computers are so interesting and programming is such a malleable art form that it is possible to become completely lost in the machines and to prefer them over reality.

And, of course, Melantha Jhirl is my favorite. I am a sucker for superior types who continue to fight no matter what the odds. One difference between science fiction and mainstream literature is that we have *heroes.* Melantha is such. She is not perfect; her arrogance is completely real even if good-natured. But in the end she recognizes her failure, and the sacrifice she makes proves that she is indeed "an improved model."

TRUE NAMES

In the once upon a time days of the First Age of Magic, the prudent sorcerer regarded his own true name as his most valued possession but also the greatest threat to his continued good health, for—the stories go—once an enemy, even a weak unskilled enemy, learned the sorcerer's true name, then routine and widely known spells could destroy or enslave even the most powerful. As times passed, and we graduated to the Age of Reason and thence to the first and second industrial revolutions, such notions were discredited. Now it seems that the Wheel has turned full circle (even if there never really was a First Age) and we are back to worrying about true names again:

The first hint Mr. Slippery had that his own True Name might be known—and, for that matter, known to the Great Enemy—came with the appearance of two black Lincolns humming up the long dirt driveway that stretched through the dripping pine forest down to Road 29. Roger Pollack was in his garden weeding, had been there nearly the whole morning, enjoying the barely perceptible drizzle and the overcast, and trying to find the initiative to go inside and do work that actually makes money. He looked up the moment the intruders turned, wheels squealing, into his driveway. Thirty seconds passed, and the cars came out of the third-generation forest to pull up beside and behind Pollack's Honda. Four heavy-set men and a hard-looking female piled out, started purposefully across his well-tended cabbage patch, crushing tender young plants with a disregard which told Roger that this was no social call.

Pollack looked wildly around, considered making a break for the woods, but the others had spread out and he was grabbed and frog-marched back to his house. (Fortunately the door had been left unlocked. Roger had the feeling that they might have knocked it down rather than ask him for the key.) He was shoved abruptly into a chair. Two of the heaviest and least collegiate-looking of his visitors stood on either side of him. Pollack's protests—now just being voiced—brought no response. The woman and an older man poked around among his sets. "Hey, I remember this, Al: It's the script for *1965*. See?" The woman spoke as she flipped through the holo-scenes that decorated the interior wall.

The older man nodded. "I told you. He's written more popular games than any three men and even more than some agencies. Roger Pollack is something of a genius."

They're novels, damn you, not games! Old irritation flashed unbidden into Roger's mind. Aloud: "Yeah, but most of my fans aren't as persistent as you all."

"Most of your fans don't know that you are a criminal, Mr. Pollack."

"Criminal? I'm no criminal—but I do know my rights. You FBI types must identify yourselves, give me a phone call, and—"

The woman smiled for the first time. It was not a nice smile. She was about thirty-five, hatchet-faced,

her hair drawn back in the single braid favored by
military types. Even so it could have been a nicer
smile. Pollack felt a chill start up his spine. "Perhaps that would be true, if we *were* the FBI or if
you were *not* the scum you are. But this is a Welfare Department bust, Pollack, and you are suspected
—putting it kindly—of interference with the instru-
mentalities of National and individual survival."

She sounded like something out of one of those
asinine scripts he occasionally had to work on for
government contracts. Only now there was nothing
to laugh about, and the cold between his shoulder-
blades spread. Outside the drizzle had become a misty
rain sweeping across the Northern California forests.
Normally he found that rain a comfort, but now it
just added to the gloom. Still, if there was any chance
he could wriggle out of this, it would be worth the
effort. "Okay, so you have license to hassle innocents,
but sooner or later you're going discover that I am
innocent and then you'll find out what hostile media
coverage can really be like." *And thank God I backed
up my files last night. With luck, all they'll find is
some out-of-date stock-market schemes.*

"You're no innocent, Pollack. An *honest* citizen
is content with an ordinary data set like yours there."
She pointed across the living room at the forty-by-
fifty-centimeter data set. It was the great-grandchild
of the old CRTs. With color and twenty-line-per-
millimeter resolution, it was the standard of government offices and the more conservative industries.
There was a visible layer of dust on Pollack's model.
The femcop moved quickly across the living room
and poked into the drawers under the picture window.
Her maroon business suit revealed a thin and angular
figure. "An *honest* citizen would settle for a standard
processor and a few thousand megabytes of fast storage." With some superior intuition she pulled open
the center drawer—right under the marijuana plants

—to reveal at least five hundred cubic centimeters of optical memory, neatly racked and threaded through to the next drawer which held correspondingly powerful CPUs. Even so, it was nothing compared to the gear he had buried under the house.

She drifted out into the kitchen and was back in a moment. The house was a typical airdropped bungalow, small and easy to search. Pollack had spent most of his money on the land and his . . . hobbies. "And finally," she said, a note of triumph in her voice, "an *honest* citizen does not need one of these!" She had finally spotted the Other World gate. She waved the electrodes in Pollack's face.

"Look, in spite of what you may want, all this is still legal. In fact, that gadget is scarcely more powerful than an ordinary games interface." That should be a good explanation, considering that he was a novelist.

The older man spoke almost apologetically, "I'm afraid Virginia has a tendency to play cat and mouse, Mr. Pollack. You see, we know that in the Other World you are Mr. Slippery."

"Oh."

There was a long silence. Even "Virginia" kept her mouth shut. This had been, of course, Roger Pollack's great fear. They had discovered Mr. Slippery's True Name and it was Roger Andrew Pollack TIN/SSAN 0959-34-2861, and no amount of evasion, tricky programming, or robot sources could ever again protect him from them. "How did you find out?"

A third cop, a technician type, spoke up. "It wasn't easy. We wanted to get our hands on someone who was really good, not a trivial vandal—what your Coven would call a lesser warlock." The younger man seemed to know the jargon, but you could pick that up just by watching the daily paper. "For the last three months, DoW has been trying to find the

identity of someone of the caliber of yourself or
Robin Hood, or Erythrina, or the Slimey Limey. We
were having no luck at all until we turned the
problem around and began watching artists and
novelists. We figured at least a fraction of them must
be attracted to vandal activities. And they would
have the talent to be good at it. Your participation
novels are the best in the world." There was genuine
admiration in his voice. *One meets fans in the oddest
places,* "so you were one of the first people we looked
at. Once we suspected you, it was just a matter of
time before we had the evidence."

It was what he had always worried about. A successful warlock cannot afford to be successful in the
real world. He had been greedy; he loved both realms
too much.

The older cop continued the technician's almost
diffident approach. "In any case, Mr. Pollack, I think
you realize that if the Federal government wants to
concentrate all its resources on the apprehension of a
single vandal, we can do it. The vandals' power comes
from their numbers rather than their power as individuals."

Pollack repressed a smile. That was a common belief—or faith—within government. He had snooped
on enough secret memos to realize that the Feds really
believed it, but it was very far from true. He was not
nearly as clever as someone like Erythrina. He could
only devote fifteen or twenty hours a week to SIG
activities. Some of the others must be on welfare, so
complete was their presence on the Other Plane.
The cops had nailed him simply because he was a
relatively easy catch.

"So you have something besides jail planned for
me?"

"Mr. Pollack, have you ever heard of the Mailman?"

"You mean on the Other Plane?"

"Certainly. He has had no notoriety in the, uh, real world as yet."

For the moment there was no use lying. They must know that no member of a SIG or coven would ever give his True Name to another member. There was no way he could betray any of the others—*he hoped*.

"Yeah, he's the weirdest of the werebots."

"Werebots?"

"Were-robots, like werewolves—get it? They don't really mesh with coven imagery. They want some new mythos, and this notion that they are humans who can turn into machines seems to suit them. It's too dry for me. This Mailman, for instance, never uses real time communication. If you want anything from him, you usually have to wait a day or two for each response— just like the old-time hardcopy mail service."

"That's the fellow. How impressed are you by him?"

"Oh, we've been aware of him for a couple years, but he's so slow that for a long time we thought he was some clown on a simple data set. Lately, though, he's pulled some really—" Pollack stopped short, re- membering just who he was gossiping with.

"—some really tuppin stunts, eh, Pollack?" The femcop **"Virginia" was back in the conversa**tion. She pulled up one of the roller chairs, till her knees were almost touching his, and stabbed a finger at his chest. "You may not know just how tuppin. You vandals have caused Social Security Records enormous prob- lems, and Robin Hood cut IRS revenues by three percent last year. You and your friends are a greater threat than any foreign enemy. Yet you're nothing compared to this Mailman."

Pollack was rocked back. It must be that he had seen only a small fraction of the Mailman's japes. "You're actually scared of him," he said mildly.

Virginia's face began to take on the color of her suit. Before she could reply, the older cop spoke. "Yes,

we are scared. We can scarcely cope with the Robin
Hoods and the Mr. Slipperys of the world. Fortunately, most vandals are interested in personal gain or
in proving their cleverness. They realize that if they
cause too much trouble, they could no doubt be identified. I suspect that tens of thousands of cases of Welfare and Tax fraud are undetected, committed by
little people with simple equipment who succeed because they don't steal much—perhaps just their own
income tax liability—and don't wish the notoriety
which you, uh, warlocks go after. If it weren't for
their petty individualism, they would be a greater
threat than the nuclear terrorists.

"But the Mailman is different: he appears to be
ideologically motivated. He is *very* knowledgeable,
very powerful. Vandalism is not enough for him; he
wants control . . ." The Feds had no idea how long it
had been going on, at least a year. It never would have
been discovered but for a few departments in the
Federal Screw Standards Commission, which kept
their principal copy records on paper. Discrepancies
showed up between those records and the decisions
rendered in the name of the FSSC. Inquiries were
made; computer records were found at variance with
the hardcopy. More inquiries. By luck more than anything else, the investigators discovered that decision
modules as well as data were different from the hardcopy backups. For thirty years government had depended on automated central planning, shifting more
and more from legal descriptions of decision algorithms to program representations that could work
directly with data bases to allocate resources, suggest
legislation, outline military strategy.

The take-over had been subtle, and its extent was
unknown. That was the horror of it. It was not even
clear just what groups within the Nation (or without)
were benefitting from the changed interpretations of
Federal law and resource allocation. Only the decision

modules in the older departments could be directly checked, and some thirty percent of them showed tampering. ". . . and that percentage scares us as much as anything, Mr. Pollack. It would take a large team of technicians and lawyers *months* to successfully make just the changes that we have detected."

"What about the military?" Pollack thought of the Finger of God installations and the thousands of missiles pointed at virtually every country on Earth. If Mr. Slippery had ever desired to take over the world, that is what he would have gone for. To hell with pussy-footing around with Social Security checks.

"No. No penetration there. In fact, it was his attempt to infiltrate—" the older cop glanced hesitantly at Virginia, and Pollack realized who was the boss of this operation, "—NSA that revealed the culprit to be the Mailman. Before that it was anonymous, totally without the ego-flaunting we see in big-time vandals. But the military and NSA have their own systems. Impractical though that is, it paid off this time." Pollack nodded. The SIG steered clear of the military, and especially of NSA.

"But if he was able to slide through DoW and Department of Justice defenses so easy, you really don't know how much a matter of luck it was that he didn't also succeed with his first try on NSA. . . . I think I understand now. You need help. You hope to get some member of the Coven to work on this from the inside."

"It's not a *hope*, Pollack," said Virginia. "It's a certainty. Forget about going to jail. Oh, we could put you away forever on the basis of some of Mr. Slippery's pranks. But even if we don't do that, we can take away your license to operate. You know what that means."

It was not a question, but Pollack knew the answer nevertheless: ninety-eight percent of the jobs in modern society involved some use of a data set. Without

a license, he was virtually unemployable—and that left
Welfare, the prospect of sitting in some urbapt count-
ing flowers on the wall. Virginia must have seen the
defeat in his eyes. "Frankly, I am not as confident as
Ray that you are all that sharp. But you are the best
we could catch. NSA thinks we have a chance of finding the Mailman's true identity if we can get an agent
into your coven. We want you to continue to attend
coven meetings, but now your chief goal is not mis-
chief but the gathering of information about the Mailman. You are to recruit any help you can without revealing that you are working for the government—you
might even make up the story that you suspect the
Mailman of being a government plot. (I'm sure you
see he has some of the characteristics of a Federal
agent working off a conventional data set.) Above all,
you are to remain alert to contact from us, and give
us your instant cooperation in anything we require of
you. Is all this perfectly clear, Mr. Pollack?"

He found it difficult to meet her gaze. He had never
really been exposed to extortion before. There was
something . . . dehumanizing about being used so.
"Yeah," he finally said.

"Good." She stood up, and so did the others. "If
you behave, this is the last time you'll see us in person."

Pollack stood too. "And afterward, if you're . . .
satisfied with my performance?"

Virginia grinned, and he knew he wasn't going to
like her answer. "Afterward, we can come back to considering *your* crimes. If you do a good job, I would
have no objection to your retaining a standard data
set, maybe some of your interactive graphics. But I'll
tell you, if it weren't for the Mailman, nabbing Mr.
Slippery would make my month. There is no way I'd
risk your continuing to abuse the System."

Three minutes later, their sinister black Lincolns
were halfway down the drive, disappearing into the

pines. Pollack stood in the drizzle watching till long after their sound had faded to nothing. He was barely aware of the cold wet across his shoulders and down his back. He looked up suddenly, feeling the rain in his face, wondering if the Feds were so clever that they had taken the day into account: the military's recon satellites could no doubt monitor their cars, but the civilian satellites the SIG had access to could not penetrate these clouds. Even if some other member of the SIG did know Mr. Slippery's True Name, they would not know that the Feds had paid him a visit.

Pollack looked across the yard at his garden. *What a difference an hour can make.*

By late afternoon, the overcast was gone. Sunlight glinted off millions of waterdrop jewels in the trees. Pollack waited till the sun was behind the tree line, till all that was left of its passage was a gold band across the taller trees to the east of his bungalow. Then he sat down before his equipment and prepared to ascend to the Other Plane. What he was undertaking was trickier than anything he had tried before, and he wanted to take as much time as the Feds would tolerate. A week of thought and research would have suited him more, but Virginia and her pals were clearly too impatient for that.

He powered up his processors, settled back in his favorite chair, and carefully attached the Portal's five sucker electrodes to his scalp. For long minutes nothing happened: a certain amount of self-denial—or at least self-hypnosis—was necessary to make the ascent. Some experts recommended drugs or sensory isolation to heighten the user's sensitivity to the faint, ambiguous signals that could be read from the Portal. Pollack, who was certainly more experienced than any of the pop experts, had found that he could make it simply by staring out into the trees and listening to the wind-surf that swept through their upper branches.

And just as a daydreamer forgets his actual sur-
roundings and sees other realities, so Pollack drifted,
detached, his subconscious interpreting the status of
the West Coast communication and data services as a
vague thicket for his conscious mind to inspect, inter-
rogate for the safest path to an intermediate haven.
Like most exurb data-commuters, Pollack rented the
standard optical links: Bell, Boeing, Nippon Electric.
Those, together with the local West Coast data companies, gave him more than enough paths to proceed
with little chance of detection to any accepting processor on Earth. In minutes, he had traced through three
changes of carrier and found a place to do his intermediate computing. The comsats rented processor
time almost as cheaply as ground stations, and an automatic payment transaction (through several dummy
accounts set up over the last several years) gave him
sole control of a large data space within milliseconds
of his request. The whole process was almost at a subconscious level—the proper functioning of numerous
routines he and others had devised over the last four
years. Mr. Slippery (the other name was avoided now,
even in his thoughts) had achieved the fringes of the
Other Plane. He took a quick peek through the eyes
of a low-resolution weather satellite, saw the North
American continent spread out below, the terminator
sweeping through the West, most of the plains clouded
over. One never knew when some apparently irrele-
vant information might help—and though it could all
be done automatically through subconscious access,
Mr. Slippery had always been a romantic about spaceflight.

He rested for a few moments, checking that his in-
direct communication links were working and that
the encryption routines appeared healthy, untampered
with. (Like most folks, honest citizens or warlocks,
he had no trust for the government standard encryption routines, but preferred the schemes that had

leaked out of academia—over NSA's petulant objections—during the last fifteen years.) Protected now against traceback, Mr. Slippery set out for the Coven itself. He quickly picked up the trail, but this was never an easy trip, for the SIG members had no interest in being bothered by the unskilled.

In particular, the traveler must be able to take advantage of subtle sensory indications, and see in them the environment originally imagined by the SIG. The correct path had the aspect of a narrow row of stones cutting through a gray-greenish swamp. The air was cold but very moist. Weird, towering plants dripped audibly onto the faintly iridescent water and the broad lilies. The subconscious knew what the stones represented, handled the chaining of routines from one information net to another, but it was the conscious mind of the skilled traveler that must make the decisions that could lead to the gates of the Coven, or to the symbolic "death" of a dump back to the real world. The basic game was a distant relative of the ancient Adventure that had been played on computer systems for more than forty years, and a nearer relative of the participation novels that are still widely sold. There were two great differences, though. This game was more serious, and was played at a level of complexity impossible without the use of the EEG input/output that the warlocks and the popular data bases called Portals.

There was much misinformation and misunderstanding about the Portals. Oh, responsible data bases like the *LA Times* and the *CBS News* made it clear that there was nothing supernatural about them or about the Other Plane, that the magical jargon was at best a romantic convenience and at worst obscurantism. But even so, their articles often missed the point and were both too conservative and too extravagant. You might think that to convey the full sense imagery of the swamp, some immense bandwidth would be necessary. In fact, that was not so (and if it were, the Feds would have quickly been able to spot warlock and werebot operations). A typical Portal link was around fifty thousand baud, far narrower than even a flat video channel. Mr. Slippery could feel the damp seeping through his leather boots, could feel the sweat starting on his skin even in the cold air, but this was the response of Mr. Slippery's imagination and subconscious to the cues that were actually being presented through the Portal's electrodes. The interpretation could not be arbitrary or he would be dumped back to reality and would never find the Coven; to the traveler on the Other Plane, the detail was there as long as the cues were there. And there is nothing new about this situation. Even a poor writer—if he has a sympathetic reader and an engaging plot—can evoke complete internal imagery with a few dozen words of description. The difference now is that the imagery has interactive significance, just as sensations in the real world do. Ultimately, the magic jargon was perhaps the closest fit in the vocabulary of millenium Man.

The stones were spaced more widely now, and it took all Mr. Slippery's skill to avoid falling into the noisome waters that surrounded him. Fortunately, after another hundred meters or so, the trail rose out of the water, and he was walking on shallow mud. The trees and brush grew in close around him, and large spider webs glistened across the trail and between some of the trees along the side.

Like a yo-yo from some branch high above him, a red-banded spider the size of a man's fist descended into the space right before the traveler's face. "Beware, beware," the tiny voice issued from dripping mandibles. "Beware, beware," the words were repeated, and the creature swung back and forth, nearer and farther from Mr. Slippery's face. He looked carefully at the spider's banded abdomen. There were many species of deathspider here, and each required a different response if a traveler was to survive. Finally he raised the back of his hand and held it level so that the spider could crawl onto it. The creature raced up the damp fabric of his jacket to the open neck. There it whispered something very quietly.

Mr. Slippery listened, then grabbed the animal before it could repeat the message and threw it to the left, at the same time racing off into the tangle of webs and branches on the other side of the trail. Something heavy and wet slapped into the space where he had been, but he was already gone—racing at top speed up the incline that suddenly appeared before him.

He stopped when he reached the crest of the hill. Beyond it, he could see the solemn, massive fortress that was the Coven's haven. It was not more than five hundred meters away, illuminated as the swamp had been by a vague and indistinct light that came only partly from the sky. The trail leading down to it was much more open than the swamp had been, but the traveler proceeded as slowly as before: the sprites the warlocks set to keep eternal guard here had the nasty —though preprogrammed—habit of changing the rules in new and deadly ways.

The trail descended, then began a rocky, winding climb toward the stone and iron gates of the castle. The ground was drier here, the vegetation sparse. Leathery snapping of wings sounded above him, but Mr. Slippery knew better than to look up. Thirty meters from the moat, the heat became more than uncomfortable. He could hear the lava popping and hissing, could see occasional dollops of fire splatter up from the liquid to scorch what vegetation still lived. A pair of glowing eyes set in a coal-black head rose briefly from the moat. A second later, the rest of the creature came surging into view, cascading sparks and lava down upon the traveler. Mr. Slippery raised his hand just so, and the lethal spray separated over his head to land harmlessly on either side of him. He watched with apparent calm as the creature descended ancient stone steps to confront him.

Alan—that was the elemental's favorite name—peered nearsightedly, his head weaving faintly from side to side as he tried to recognize the traveler. "Ah, I do believe we are honored with the presence of Mr. Slippery, is it not so?" he finally said. He smiled, an open grin revealing the glowing interior of his mouth. His breath did not show flame but did have the penetrating heat of an open kiln. He rubbed his clawed hands against his asbestos T-shirt as though anxious to be proved wrong. Away from his magma moat, the dead black of his flesh lightened, trying to contain his body heat. Now he looked almost reptilian.

"Indeed it is. And come to bring my favorite little gifts," Mr. Slippery threw a leaden slug into the air and watched the elemental grab it with his mouth, his eyes slitted with pleasure—melt-in-your-mouth pleasure. They traded conversation, spells, and counterspells for several minutes. Alan's principal job was to determine that the visitor was a known member of the Coven, and he ordinarily did this with little tests of skill (the magma bath he had tried to give Mr. Slippery) and by asking the visitor questions about previous activities within the castle. Alan was a personality simulator, of course. Mr. Slippery was sure that there had never been a living operator behind that toothless, glowing smile. But he was certainly one of the best, probably the product of many hundreds of blocks of psylisp programming, and certainly superior to the little "companionship" programs you can buy nowadays, which generally become repetitive after a few hours of conversation, which don't grow, and which are unable to counter weird responses. Alan had been with the Coven and the castle since before Mr. Slippery had become a member, and no

one would admit to his creation (though Wiley J. was suspected). He hadn't even had a name until this year, when Erythrina had given him that asbestos Alan Turing T-shirt.

Mr. Slippery played the game with good humor, but care. To "die" at the hands of Alan would be a painful experience that would probably wipe a lot of unbacked memory he could ill afford to lose. Such death had claimed many petitioners at this gate, folk who would not soon be seen on this plane again.

Satisfied, Alan waved a clawed fist at the watchers in the tower, and the gate—ceramic bound in wolfram clasps—was rapidly lowered for the visitor. Mr. Slippery walked quickly across, trying to ignore the spitting and bubbling that he heard below him. Alan— now all respectful—waited till he was in the castle courtyard before doing an immense belly-flop back into his magma swimming hole.

Most of the others, with the notable exception of Erythrina, had already arrived. Robin Hood, dressed in green and looking like Errol Flynn, sat across the hall in very close conversation with a remarkably good-looking female (but then they could all be remarkably good-looking here) who seemed unsure whether to project blonde or brunette. By the fireplace, Wiley J. Bastard, the Slimey Limey, and DON.MAC were in animated discussion over a pile of maps. And in the corner, shaded from the fireplace and apparently unused, sat a classic remote printing terminal. Mr. Slippery tried to ignore that teleprinter as he crossed the hall.

"Ah, it's Slip." DON.MAC looked up from the maps and gestured him closer. "Take a look here at what the Limey has been up to."

"Hmm?" Mr. Slippery nodded at the others, then leaned over to study the top map. The margins of the paper were aging vellum, but the "map" itself hung in three dimensions, half sunk into the paper. It was a typical banking defense and cash-flow plot—that is, typical for the SIG. Most banks had no such clever ways of visualizing the automated protection of their assets. (For that matter, Mr. Slippery suspected that most banks still looked wistfully back to the days of credit cards and COBOL.) This was the sort of thing Robin Hood had developed, and it was surprising to see the Limey involved in it. He looked up questioningly. "What's the jape?"

"It's a reg'lar double-slam, Slip. Look at this careful, an' you'll see it's no ord'n'ry protection map. Seems like what you blokes call the Mafia has taken over this banking net in the Maritime states. They must be usin' Portals to do it so slick. Took me a devil of a time to figure out it was them as done it. *Ha ha!* but now that I have . . . look here, you'll see how they've been launderin' funds, embezzlin' from straight accounts.

"They're ever so clever, but not so clever as to know about Slimey." He poked a finger into the map and a trace gleamed red through the maze. "If they're lucky, they'll discover this tap next autumn, when they find themselves maybe three billion dollars short, and not a single sign of where it all disappeared to."

The others nodded. There were many covens and SIGs throughout this plane. Theirs, The Coven, was widely known, had pulled off some of the most publicized pranks of the century. Many of the others were scarcely more than social clubs. But some were old-style criminal organizations which used this plane for their own purely pragmatic and opportunistic reasons. Usually such groups weren't too difficult for the warlocks to victimize, but it was the Slimey Limey who seemed to specialize in doing so.

"But, geez, Slimey, these guys play rough, even rougher than the Great Enemy." That is, the Feds.

"If they ever figure out who you really are, you'll die the True Death for sure."

"I may be slimy, but I ain't crazy. There's no way I could absorb three billion dollars—or even three million—without being discovered. But I played it like Robin over there: the money got spread around three million ordinary accounts here and in Europe, one of which just happens to be mine."

Mr. Slippery's ears perked up. "Three million accounts, you say? Each with a sudden little surplus? I'll bet I could come close to finding your True Name from that much, Slimey."

The Limey made a faffling gesture. "It's actually a wee bit more complicated. Face it, chums, none of you has ever come close to sightin' me, an' you know more than any Mafia."

That was true. They all spent a good deal of their time in this plane trying to determine the others' True Names. It was not an empty game, for the knowledge of another's True Name effectively made him your slave—as Mr. Slippery had already discovered in an unpleasantly firsthand way. So the warlocks constantly probed one another, devised immense programs to sieve government-personnel records for the idiosyncracies that they detected in each other. At first glance, the Limey should have been one of the easiest to discover: he had plenty of mannerisms. His Brit accent was dated and broke down every so often into North American. Of all the warlocks, he was the only one neither handsome nor grotesque. His face was, in fact, so ordinary and real that Mr. Slippery had suspected that it might be his true appearance and had spent several months devising a scheme that searched secret and US and common Europe photo files for just that appearance. It had been for nothing, and they had all eventually reached the conclusion that the Limey must be doubly or triply deceptive.

Wiley J. Bastard grinned, not too impressed. "It's

nice enough, and I agree that the risks are probably small, Slimey. But what do you really get? An ego boost and a little money. But we," he gestured inclusively, "are worth more than that. With a little co-operation, we could be the most powerful people in the real world. Right, DON?"

DON.MAC nodded, smirking. His face was really the only part of him that looked human or had much flexibility of expression—and even it was steely gray. The rest of DON's body was modeled after the standard Plessey-Mercedes all-weather robot.

Mr. Slippery recognized the reference. "So you're working with the Mailman now, too, Wiley?" He glanced briefly at the teleprinter.

"Yup."

"And you still won't give us any clue what it's all about?"

Wiley shook his head. "Not unless you're serious about throwing in with us. But you all know this: DON was the first to work with the Mailman, and he's richer than Croesus now."

DON.MAC nodded again, that silly smile still on his face.

"Hmm." It was easy to get rich. In principal, the Limey could have made three billion dollars off the Mob in his latest caper. The problem was to become that rich and avoid detection and retribution. Even Robin Hood hadn't mastered that trick—but apparently DON and Wiley thought the Mailman had done that and more. After his friendly little chat with Virginia, he was willing to believe it. Mr. Slippery turned to look more closely at the teleprinter. It was humming faintly, and as usual it had a good supply of paper. The paper was torn neatly off at the top, so that the only message visible was the Mailman's asterisk prompt. It was the only way they ever communicated with this most mysterious of their members: type a message on the device, and in an hour or a week the machine would rattle and beat, and a response of up to several thousand words would appear. In the beginning, it had not been very popular—the idea was cute, but the delays made conversation just too damn dull. He could remember seeing meters of Mailman output lying sloppily on the stone floor, mostly unread. But *now*, every one of the Mailman's golden words was eagerly sopped up by his new apprentices, who very carefully removed every piece of output, leaving no clues for the rest of them to work with.

"Ery!" He looked toward the broad stone stairs that led down from the courtyard. It was Erythrina, the Red Witch. She swept down the stairs, her costume shimmering, now revealing, now obscuring. She had a spectacular figure and an excellent sense of design, but of course that was not what was remarkable about her. Erythrina was the sort of person who knew much more than she ever said, even though she always seemed easy to talk to. Some of her adventures—though unadvertised—were in a class with Robin Hood's. Mr. Slippery had known her well for a year; she was certainly the most interesting personality on this plane. She made him wish that all the secrets were unnecessary, that True Names could be traded as openly as phone numbers. What was she really?

Erythrina nodded to Robin Hood, then proceeded down the hall to DON.MAC, who had originally shouted greetings and now continued, "We've just been trying to convince Slimey and Slip that they are wasting their time on pranks when they could have real power and real wealth."

She glanced sharply at Wiley, who seemed strangely irritated that she had been drawn into the conversation. " 'We' meaning you and Wiley and the Mailman?"

Wiley nodded. "I just started working with them last week, Ery," as if to say, *and you can't stop me.*

"You may have something, DON. We all started out as amateurs, doing our best to make the System just a little bit uncomfortable for its bureaucratic masters. But we are experts now. We probably understand the System better than anyone on Earth. That should equate to power." It was the same thing the other two had been saying, but she could make it much more persuasive. Before his encounter with the Feds, he might have bought it (even though he always knew that the day he got serious about Coven activities and went after real gain would also be the day it ceased to be an enjoyable game and became an all-consuming job that would suck time away from the projects that made life entertaining).

Erythrina looked from Mr. Slippery to the Limey and then back. The Limey was an easygoing sort, but just now he was a bit miffed at the way his own pet project had been dismissed. "Not for me, thanky," he said shortly and began to gather up his maps.

She turned her green, faintly oriental eyes upon Mr. Slippery. "How about you, Slip. Have you signed up with the Mailman?"

He hesitated. *Maybe I should.* It seemed clear that the Mailman's confederates were being let in on at least part of his schemes. In a few hours, he might be able to learn enough to get Virginia off his back. And perhaps destroy his friends to boot; it was a hell of a bargain. *God in Heaven, why did they have to get mixed up in this? Don't they realize what the Government will do to them, if they really try to take over, if they ever try to play at being more than vandals?* "Not . . . not yet," he said finally. "I'm awfully tempted, though."

She grinned, regular white teeth flashing against her dark, faintly green face. "I, too. What do you say we talk it over, just the two of us?" She reached out a slim, dark hand to grasp his elbow. "Excuse us, gentlemen; hopefully, when we get back, you'll have a couple of new allies." And Mr. Slippery felt himself gently propelled toward the dark and musty stairs that led to Erythrina's private haunts.

Her torch burned and glowed, but there was no smoke. The flickering yellow lit their path for scant meters ahead. The stairs were steep and gently curving. He had the feeling that they must do a complete circle every few hundred steps: this was an immense spiral cut deep into the heart of the living rock. And it was alive. As the smell of mildew and rot increased, as the dripping from the ceiling grew subtly louder and the puddles in the worn steps deeper, the walls high above their heads took on shapes, and those shapes changed and flowed to follow them. Erythrina protected her part of the castle as thoroughly as the castle itself was guarded against the outside world. Mr. Slippery had no doubt that if she wished, she could trap him permanently here, along with the lizards and the rock sprites. (Of course he could always "escape" simply by falling back into the real world, but until she relented or he saw through her spells, he would not be able to access any other portion of the castle.) Working on some of their projects, he had visited her underground halls, but never anything this deep.

He watched her shapely form preceding him down, down, down. Of all the Coven (with the possible exception of Robin Hood, and of course the Mailman), she was the most powerful. He suspected that she was one of the original founders. If only there were some way of convincing her (without revealing the source of his knowledge) that the Mailman was a threat. If only there was some way of getting her cooperation in nailing down the Mailman's True Name.

Erythrina stopped short and he bumped pleasantly into her. Over her shoulder, a high door ended the passage. She moved her hand in a pattern hidden from Mr. Slippery and muttered some unlocking spell. The door split horizontally, its halves pulling apart with oiled and massive precision. Beyond, he had the impression of spots and lines of red breaking a further darkness.

"Mind your step," she said and hopped over a murky puddle that stood before the high sill of the doorway.

As the door slid shut behind them, Erythrina changed the torch to a single searing spot of white light, like some old-time incandescent bulb. The room was bright-lit now. Comfortable black leather chairs sat on black tile. Red engraving, faintly glowing, was worked into the tile and the obsidian of the walls. In contrast to the stairway, the air was fresh and clean— though still.

She waved him to a chair that faced away from the light, then sat on the edge of a broad desk. The point light glinted off her eyes, making them unreadable. Erythrina's face was slim and fine-boned, almost Asian except for the pointed ears. But the skin was dark, and her long hair had the reddish tones unique to some North American blacks. She was barely smiling now, and Mr. Slippery wished again he had some way of getting her help.

"Slip, I'm scared," she said finally, the smile gone.

You're scared! For a moment, he couldn't quite believe his ears. "The Mailman?" he asked, hoping.

She nodded. "This is the first time in my life I've felt outgunned. I need help. Robin Hood may be the most competent, but he's basically a narcissist; I don't think I could interest him in anything beyond his immediate gratifications. That leaves you and the Limey. And I think there's something special about you. We've done a couple things together," she couldn't help herself, and grinned remembering. "They weren't real impressive, but somehow I have a feeling about you: I think you understand what things up here are silly games and what things are really important. If

you think something is really important, you can be trusted to stick with it even if the going gets a little . . . bloody."

Coming from someone like Ery, the words had special meaning. It was strange, to feel both flattered and frightened. Mr. Slippery stuttered for a moment, inarticulate. "What about Wiley J? Seems to me you have special . . . influence over him."

"You knew . . . ?"

"Suspected."

"Yes, he's my thrall. Has been for almost six months. Poor Wiley turns out to be a life-insurance salesman from Peoria. Like a lot of warlocks, he's rather a Thurberesque fellow in real life: timid, always dreaming of heroic adventures and grandiose thefts. Only nowadays people like that can realize their dreams. . . . Anyway, he doesn't have the background, or the time, or the skill that I do, and I found his True Name. I enjoy the chase more than the extortion, so I haven't leaned on him too hard; now I wish I had. Since he's taken up with the Mailman, he's been giving me the finger. Somehow Wiley thinks that what they have planned will keep him safe even if I give his True Name to the cops!"

"So the Mailman actually has some scheme for winning political power in the real world?"

She smiled. "That's what Wiley thinks. You see, poor Wiley doesn't know that there are more uses for True Names than simple blackmail. I know everything he sends over the data links, everything he has been told by the Mailman."

"So what are they up to?" It was hard to conceal his eagerness. *Perhaps this will be enough to satisfy Virginia and her goons.*

Erythrina seemed frozen for a moment, and he realized that she too must be using the low-altitude satelilte net for preliminary processing: her task had just been handed off from one comsat to a nearer bird. Ordinarily it was easy to disguise the hesitation. She must be truly upset.

And when she finally replied, it wasn't really with an answer. "You know what convinced Wiley that the Mailman could deliver on his promises? It was DON.-MAC—and the revolution in Venezuela. Apparently DON and the Mailman had been working on that for several months before Wiley joined them. It was to be the Mailman's first demonstration that controlling data and information services could be used to take permanent political control of a state. And Venezuela, they claimed, was perfect: it has enormous data-processing facilities—all just a bit obsolete, since they were bought when the country was at the peak of its boom time."

"But that was clearly an internal *coup*. The present leaders are local—"

"Nevertheless, DON is supposedly down there now, the real *Jefe,* for the first time in his life able to live in the physical world the way we do in this plane. If you have your own country, you are no longer small fry that must guard his True Name. You don't have to settle for crumbs."

"You said 'supposedly'."

"Slip, have you noticed anything strange about DON lately?"

Mr. Slippery thought back. DON.MAC had always been the most extreme of the werebots—after the Mailman. He was not an especially talented fellow, but he did go to great lengths to sustain the image that he was both machine and human. His persona was always present in this plane, though at least part of the time it was a simulator—like Alan out in the magma moat. The simulation was fairly good, but no one had yet produced a program that could really pass the Turing test: that is, fool a real human for any extended time. Mr. Slippery remembered the silly smile that seemed pasted on DON's face and the faint-

ly repetitive tone of his lobbying for the Mailman.
"You think the real person behind DON is gone, that
we have a zombie up there?"

"Slip, I think the real DON is *dead,* and I mean the
True Death."

"Maybe he just found the real world more delight-
ful than this, now that he owns such a big hunk of
it?"

"I don't think he owns anything. It's just barely
possible that the Mailman had something to do with
that *coup;* there are a number of coincidences between
what they told Wiley beforehand and what actually
happened. But I've spent a lot of time floating through
the Venezuelan data bases, and I think I'd know if
an outsider were on the scene, directing the new order.

"I think the Mailman is taking us on one at a time,
starting with the weakest, drawing us in far enough
to learn our True Names—and then destroying us. So
far he has only done it to one of us. I've been watching
DON.MAC both directly and automatically since the
coup, and there has never been a real person behind
that facade, not once in two thousand hours. Wiley
is next. The poor slob hasn't even been told yet what
country his kingdom is to be—evidence that the Mailman doesn't really have the power he claims—but even
so, he's ready to do practically anything for the Mailman, and against us.

"Slip, we have *got* to identify this *thing,* this Mailman, before he can get us."

She was even more upset than Virginia and the Feds.
And she was right. For the first time, he felt more
afraid of the Mailman than the government agents. He
held up his hands. "I'm convinced. But what should
we do? You've got the best angle in Wiley. The Mailman doesn't know you've got a tap through him, does
he?"

She shook his head. "Wiley is too chicken to tell
him, and doesn't realize that I can do this with his

True Name. But I'm already doing everything I can with that. I want to pool information, guesses, with you. Between us maybe we can see something new."

"Well for starters, it's obvious that the Mailman's queer communication style—those long time delays—is a ploy. I know that fellow is listening all the time to what's going on in the Coven meeting hall. And he commands a number of sprites in real time." Mr. Slippery remembered the day the Mailman—or at least his teleprinter—had arrived. The image of an American Van Lines truck had pulled up at the edge of the moat, nearly intimidating Alan. The driver and loader were simulators, though good ones. They had answered all of Alan's questions correctly, then hauled the shipping crate down to the meeting hall. They hadn't left till the warlocks signed for the shipment and promised to "wire a wall outlet" for the device. This enemy definitely knew how to arouse the curiosity of his victims. Whoever controlled that printer seemed perfectly capable of normal behavior. *Perhaps it's someone we already know, like in the mysteries where the murderer masquerades as one of the victims. Robin Hood?*

"I know. In fact, he can do many things faster than I. He must control some powerful processors. But you're partly wrong: the living part of him that's behind it all really does operate with at least a one-hour turnaround time. All the quick stuff is programmed."

Mr. Slippery started to protest, then realized that she could be right. "My God, what could that mean? Why would he deliberately saddle himself with that disadvantage?"

Erythrina smiled with some satisfaction. "I'm convinced that if we knew that, we'd have this guy sighted. I agree it's too great a disadvantage to be a simple red herring. I think he must have some time-delay problem to begin with, and—"

"—and he has exaggerated it?" But even if the Mailman were an Australian, the low satellite net made delays so short that he would probably be indistinguishable from a European or a Japanese. There was no place on Earth where . . . *but there are places off Earth!* The mass-transmit satellites were in synchronous orbit 120 milliseconds out. There were about two hundred people there. And further out, at L5, there were at least another four hundred. Some were near-permanent residents. A strange idea, but still a possibility.

"*I* don't think he has exaggerated. Slip, I think the Mailman—not his processors and simulators, you understand—is at least a half-hour out from Earth, probably in the asteroid belt."

She smiled suddenly, and Mr. Slippery realized that his jaw must be resting on his chest. Except for the Joint Mars Recon, no human had been anywhere near that far out. *No human.* Mr. Slippery felt his ordinary, everyday world disintegrating into sheer science fiction. This was ridiculous.

"I know you don't believe; it took me a while to. He's not so obvious that he doesn't add in some time delay to disguise the cyclic variation in our relative positions. But it *is* a consistent explanation for the delay. These last few weeks I've been sniffing around the classified reports on our asteroid probes; there are definitely some mysterious things out there."

"Okay. It's consistent. But you're talking about an interstellar *invasion*. Even if NASA had the funding, it would take them decades to put the smallest interstellar probe together—and decades more for the flight. Trying to invade anyone with those logistics would be impossible. And if these aliens have a decent stardrive, why do they bother with deception? They could just move in and brush us aside."

"Ah, that's the point, Slip. The invasion I'm thinking of doesn't need any "stardrive," and it works fine against any race at exactly our point of development.

Right: most likely interstellar war is a fantastically expensive business, with decade lead times. What better policy for an imperialistic, highly technological race than to lie doggo listening for evidence of younger civilizations? When they detect such, they send only one ship. When it arrives in the victims' solar system, the Computer Age is in full bloom there. We in the Coven know how fragile the present system is; it is only fear of exposure that prevents some warlocks from trying to take over. Just think how appealing our naïveté must be to an older civilization that has thousands of years of experience at managing data systems. Their small crew of agents moves in as close as local military surveillance permits and gradually insinuates itself into the victims' system. They eliminate what sharp individuals they detect in that system— people like us—and then they go after the bureaucracies and the military. In ten or twenty years, another fiefdom is ready for the arrival of the master race."

She lapsed into silence, and for a long moment they stared at each other. It did all hang together with a weird sort of logic. "What can we do, then?"

"That's the question." She shook her head sadly, came across the room to sit beside him. Now that she had said her piece, the fire had gone out of her. For the first time since he had known her, Erythrina looked depressed. "We could just forsake this plane and stay in the real world. The Mailman might still be able to track us down, but we'd be of no more interest to him than anyone else. If we were lucky, we might have years before he takes over." She straightened. "I'll tell you this: if we want to live as warlocks, we have to stop him soon—within days at most. After he gets Wiley, he may drop the con tactics for something more direct.

"If I'm right about the Mailman, then our best bet would be to discover his communication link. That would be his Achilles' heel; there's no way you can hide in the crowd when you're beaming from that far away. We've got to take some real chances now, do things we'd never risk before. I figure that if we work together, maybe we can lessen the risk that either of us is identified."

He nodded. Ordinarily a prudent warlock used only limited bandwidth and so was confined to a kind of linear, personal perception. If they grabbed a few hundred megahertz of comm space, and a bigger share of rented processors, they could manipulate and search files in a way that would boggle Virginia the femcop. Of course, they would be much more easily identifiable. With two of them, though, they might be able to keep it up safely for a brief time, confusing the government and the Mailman with a multiplicity of clues. "Frankly, I don't buy the alien part. But the rest of what you say makes sense, and that's what counts. Like you say, we're going to have to take some chances."

"Right!" She smiled and reached behind his neck to draw his face to hers. She was a very good kisser. (Not everyone was. It was one thing just to look gorgeous, and another to project and respond to the many sensory cues in something as interactive as kissing.) He was just warming to this exercise of their mutual abilities when she broke off. "And the best time to start is right now. The others think we're sealed away down here. If strange things happen during the next few hours, it's less likely the Mailman will suspect *us*." She reached up to catch the light point in her hand. For an instant, blades of harsh white slipped out from between her fingers; then all was dark. He felt faint air motion as her hands moved through another spell. There were words, distorted and unidentifiable. Then the light was back, but as a torch again, and a door—a second door—had opened in the far wall.

He followed her up the passage that stretched

straight and gently rising as far as the torchlight
shone. They were walking a path that could not be—
or at least that no one in the Coven could have believed. The castle was basically a logical structure
"fleshed" out with the sensory cues that allowed the
warlocks to move about it as one would a physical
structure. Its moats and walls were part of that logical
structure, and though they had no physical reality
outside of the varying potentials in whatever processors were running the program, they were proof
against the movement of the equally "unreal" perceptions of the inhabitants of the plane. Erythrina and
Mr. Slippery could have escaped the deep room simply
by falling back into the real world, but in doing so,
they would have left a chain of unclosed processor
links. Their departure would have been detected by
every Coven member, even by Alan, even by the
sprites. An orderly departure scheme, such as represented by this tunnel, could only mean that Erythrina
was far too clever to need his help, or that she had
been one of the original builders of the castle some
four years earlier (lost in the Mists of Time, as the
Limey put it) .

They were wild dogs now, large enough so as to be
not likely to be bothered, small enough to be mistaken
for the amateur users that are seen more and more in
the Other Plane as the price of Portals declines and
the skill of the public increases. Mr. Slippery followed
Erythrina down narrow paths, deeper and deeper into
the swamp that represented commercial and government data space. Occasionally he was aware of sprites
or simulators watching them with hostile eyes from
nests off to the sides of the trail. These were idle creations in many cases—program units designed to infuri-
ate or amuse later visitors to the plane. But many of
them guarded information caches, or peepholes into

other folks' affairs, or meeting places of other SIGs. The Coven might be the most sophisticated group of users on this plane, but they were far from being alone.

The brush got taller, bending over the trail to drip on their backs. But the water was clear here, spread in quiet ponds on either side of their path. Light came from the water itself, a pearly luminescence that shone upward on the trunks of the waterbound trees and sparkled faintly in the droplets of water in their moss and leaves. That light was the representation of the really huge data bases run by the government and the largest companies. It did not correspond to a specific geographical location, but rather to the main East/West net that stretches through selected installations from Honolulu to Oxford, taking advantage of the time zones to spread the user load.

"Just a little bit farther," Erythrina said over her shoulder, speaking in the beast language (encipherment) that they had chosen with their forms.

Minutes later, they shrank into the brush, out of the way of two armored hackers that proceeded implacably up the trail. The pair drove in single file, the impossibly large eight-cylinder engines on their bikes belching fire and smoke and noise. The one bringing up the rear carried an old-style recoilless rifle decorated with swastikas and chrome. Dim fires glowed through their blackened face plates. The two dogs eyed the bikers timidly, as befitted their present disguise, but Mr. Slippery had the feeling he was looking at a couple of amateurs who were imaging beyond their station in life: the bikes' tires didn't always touch the ground, and the tracks they left didn't quite match the texture of the muck. Anyone could put on a heroic image in this plane, or appear as some dreadful monster. The problem was that there were always skilled users who were willing to cut such pretenders down to size—perhaps even to destroy their access. It befitted the less experienced to appear small and inconspicuous, and to stay out of others' way.

(Mr. Slippery had often speculated just how the simple notion of using high-resolution EEGs as input/output devices had caused the development of the "magical world" representation of data space. The Limey and Erythrina argued that sprites, reincarnation, spells, and castles were the natural tools here, more natural than the atomistic twentieth-century notions of data structures, programs, files, and communications protocols. It was, they argued, just more convenient for the mind to use the global ideas of magic as the tokens to manipulate this new environment. They had a point; in fact, it was likely that the governments of the world hadn't caught up to the skills of the better warlocks simply because they refused to indulge in the foolish imaginings of fantasy. Mr. Slippery looked down at the reflection in the pool beside him and saw the huge canine face and lolling tongue looking up at him; he winked at the image. He knew that despite all his friends' high intellectual arguments, there was another reason for the present state of affairs, a reason that went back to the Moon Lander and Adventure games at the "dawn of time": it was simply a hell of a lot of fun to live in a world as malleable as the human imagination.)

Once the riders were out of sight, Erythrina moved back across the path to the edge of the pond and peered long and hard down between the lilies, into the limpid depths. "Okay, let's do some cross-correlation. You take the JPL data base, and I'll take the Harvard Multispectral Patrol. Start with data coming off space probes out to ten AUs. I have a suspicion the easiest way for the Mailman to disguise his transmissions is to play trojan horse with data from a NASA spacecraft."

Mr. Slippery nodded. One way or another, they should resolve her alien invasion theory first.

"It should take me about half an hour to get in place. After that, we can set up for the correlation. Hmmm . . . if something goes wrong, let's agree to meet at Mass Transmit 3," and she gave a password scheme. Clearly that would be an emergency situation. If they weren't back in the castle within three or four hours, the others would certainly guess the existence of her secret exit.

Erythrina tensed, then dived into the water. There was a small splash, and the lillies bobbed gently in the expanding ring waves. Mr. Slippery looked deep, but as expected, there was no further sign of her. He padded around the side of the pool, trying to identify the special glow of the JPL data base.

There was thrashing near one of the larger lilies, one that he recognized as obscuring the NSA connections with the East/West net. A large bullfrog scrambled out of the water onto the pad and turned to look at him. "Aha! Gotcha, you sonofabitch!"

It was Virginia; the voice was the same, even if the body was different. *"Shhhhhh!"* said Mr. Slippery, and looked wildly about for signs of eavesdroppers. There were none, but that did not mean they were safe. He spread his best privacy spell over her and crawled to the point closest to the lily. They sat glaring at each other like some characters out of La Fontaine: The Tale of the Frog and Dog. How dearly he would love to leap across the water and bite off that fat little head. Unfortunately the victory would be a bit temporary. "How did you find me?" Mr. Slippery growled. If people as inexperienced as the Feds could trace him down in his disguise, he was hardly safe from the Mailman.

"You forget," the frog puffed smugly. "We know your Name. It's simple to monitor your home processor and follow your every move."

Mr. Slippery whined deep in his throat. *In thrall to a frog. Even Wiley has done better than that.* "Okay, so you found me. Now what do you want?"

"To let you know that we want results, and to get a progress report."

He lowered his muzzle till his eyes were even with Virginia's. "Heh heh. I'll give you a progress report, but you're not going to like it." And he proceeded to explain Erythrina's theory that the Mailman was an alien invasion.

"Rubbish," spoke the frog afterward. "Sheer fantasy! You're going to have to do better than that, Pol—er, Mister."

He shuddered. She had almost spoken his Name. Was that a calculated threat or was she simply as stupid as she seemed? Nevertheless, he persisted. "Well then, what about Venezuela?" He related the evidence Ery had that the *coup* in that country was the Mailman's work.

This time the frog did not reply. Its eyes glazed over with apparent shock, and he realized that Virginia must be consulting people at the other end. Almost fifteen minutes passed. When the frog's eyes cleared, it was much more subdued. "We'll check on that one. What you say is possible. Just barely possible. If true . . . well, if it's true, this is the biggest threat we've had to face this century."

And you see that I am perhaps the only one who can bail you out. Mr. Slippery relaxed slightly. If they only realized it, they were thralled to him as much as the reverse—at least for the moment. Then he remembered Erythrina's plan to grab as much power as they could for a brief time and try to use that advantage to flush the Mailman out. With the Feds on their side, they could do more than Ery had ever imagined. He said as much to Virginia.

The frog croaked, "*You . . . want . . . us . . . to give you carte blanche in the Federal data system? Maybe* you'd like to be President and Chair of the JCS, to boot?"

"Hey, that's not what I said. I know it's an extraordinary suggestion, but this is an extraordinary situation. And in any case, you know my Name. There's no way I can get around that."

The frog went glassy-eyed again, but this time for only a couple of minutes. "We'll get back to you on that. We've got a lot of checking to do on the rest of your theories before we commit ourselves to anything. Till further notice, though, you're grounded."

"Wait!" What would Ery do when he didn't show? If he wasn't back in the castle in three or four hours, the others would surely know about the secret exit.

The frog was implacable. "I said, you're grounded, Mister. We want you back in the real world immediately. And you'll stay grounded till you hear from us. Got it?"

The dog slumped. "Yeah."

"Okay." The frog clambered heavily to the edge of the sagging lily and dumped itself ungratefully into the water. After a few seconds, Mr. Slippery followed.

Coming back was much like waking from a deep daydream; only here it was the middle of the night.

Roger Pollack stood, stretching, trying to get the kinks out of his muscles. Almost four hours he had been gone, longer than ever before. Normally his concentration began to fail after two or three hours. Since he didn't like the thought of drugging up, this put a definite limit on his endurance in the Other Plane.

Beyond the bungalow's picture window, the pines stood silhouetted against the Milky Way. He cranked open a pane and listened to the night birds trilling out there in the trees. It was near the end of spring; he liked to imagine he could see dim polar twilight to the north. More likely it was just Crescent City. Pollack leaned close to the window and looked high

into the sky, where Mars sat close to Jupiter. It was hard to think of a threat to his own life from as far away as that.

Pollack backed up the spells acquired during this last session, powered down his system, and stumbled off to bed.

The following morning and afternoon seemed the longest of Roger Pollack's life. How would they get in touch with him? Another visit of goons and black Lincolns? What had Erythrina done when he didn't make contact? Was she all right?

And there was just no way of checking. He paced back and forth across his tiny living room, the novel-plots that were his normal work forgotten. *Ah, but there is a way.* He looked at his old data set with dawning recognition. Virginia had said to stay out of the Other Plane. But how could they object to his using a simple data set, no more efficient than millions used by office workers all over the world?

He sat down at the set, scraped the dust from the handpads and screen. He awkwardly entered long-unused call symbols and watched the flow of news across the screen. A few queries and he discovered that no great disasters had occurred overnight, that the insurgency in Indonesia seemed temporarily abated. (Wiley J. was not to be king just yet.) There were no reports of big-time data vandals biting the dust.

Pollack grunted. He had forgotten how tedious it was to see the world through a data set, even with audio entry. In the Other Plane, he could pick up this sort of information in seconds, as casually as an ordinary mortal might glance out the window to see if it is raining. He dumped the last twenty-four hours of the world bulletin board into his home memory space and began checking through it. The bulletin board was ideal for untraceable reception of messages: any-one on Earth could leave a message—indexed by subject, target audience, and source. If a user copied the entire board, and *then* searched it, there was no outside record of exactly what information he was interested in. There were also simple ways to make nearly untraceable entries on the board.

As usual, there were about a dozen messages for Mr. Slippery. Most of them were from fans; the Coven had greater notoriety than any other vandal SIG. A few were for other Mr. Slipperys. With five billion people in the world, that wasn't surprising.

And one of the memos was from the Mailman; that's what it said in the source field. Pollack punched the message up on the screen. It was in caps, with no color or sound. Like all messages directly from the Mailman, it looked as if it came off some incredibly ancient I/O device:

YOU COULD HAVE BEEN RICH. YOU COULD HAVE RULED. INSTEAD YOU CONSPIRED AGAINST ME. I KNOW ABOUT THE SECRET EXIT. I KNOW ABOUT YOUR DOGGY DEPARTURE. YOU AND THE RED ONE ARE DEAD NOW. IF YOU EVER SNEAK BACK ONTO THIS PLANE, IT WILL BE THE TRUE DEATH—I AM THAT CLOSE TO KNOWING YOUR NAMES.
*****WATCH FOR ME IN THE NEWS, SUCKERS*********

Bluff, thought Roger. *He wouldn't be sending out warnings if he has that kind of power*. Still, there was a dropping sensation in his stomach. The Mailman shouldn't have known about the dog disguise. Was he onto Mr. Slippery's connection with the Feds? If so, he might really be able to find Slippery's True Name. And what sort of danger was Ery in? What had she done when he missed the rendezvous at Mass Transmit 3?

A quick search showed no messages from Erythrina. Either she was looking for him in the Other Plane, or she was as thoroughly grounded as he.

He was still stewing on this when the phone rang. He said, "Accept, no video send." His data set cleared to an even gray: the caller was not sending video either.

"You're still there? Good." It was Virginia. Her voice sounded a bit odd, subdued and tense. Perhaps it was just the effect of the scrambling algorithms. He prayed she would not trust that scrambling. He had never bothered to make his phone any more secure than average. (And he had seen the schemes Wiley J. and Robin Hood had devised to decrypt thousands of commercial phone messages in real-time and monitor for key phrases, signaling them when anything interesting was detected. They couldn't use the technique very effectively, since it took an enormous amount of processor space, but the Mailman was probably not so limited.)

Virginia continued, "No names, okay? We checked out what you told us and . . . it looks like you're right. We can't be sure about your theory about *his* origin, but what you said about the international situation was verified." So the Venezuela *coup* had been an outside take-over. "Furthermore, we think *he* has infiltrated us much more than we thought. It may be that the evidence we had of unsuccessful meddling was just a red herring." Pollack recognized the fear in her voice now. Apparently the Feds saw that they were up against something catastrophic. They were caught with their countermeasures down, and their only hope lay with unreliables like Pollack.

"Anyway, we're going ahead with what you suggested. We'll provide you two with the resources you requested. We want you in the Other . . . place as soon as possible. We can talk more there."

"I'm on my way. I'll check with my friend and get

back to you there." He cut the connection without
waiting for a reply. Pollack sat back, trying to savor
this triumph and the near-pleading in the cop's voice.
Somehow, he couldn't. He knew what a hard case she
was; anything that could make her crawl was more
hellish than anything he wanted to face.

His first stop was Mass Transmit 3. Physically, MT3
was a two-thousand-tonne satellite in synchronous
orbit over the Indian Ocean. The Mass Transmits
handled most of the planet's noninteractive communications (and in fact that included a lot of transmission that most people regarded as interactive—
such as human/human and the simpler human/com-
puter conversations). Bandwidth and processor space
was cheaper on the Mass Transmits because of the
240- to 900-millisecond time delays that were involved.

As such, it was a nice out-of-the-way meeting place,
and in the Other Plane it was represented as a five-
meter-wide ledge near the top of a mountain that rose
from the forests and swamps that stood for the lower
satellite layer and the ground-based nets. In the
distance were two similar peaks, clear in pale sky.

Mr. Slippery leaned out into the chill breeze that
swept the face of the mountain and looked down past
the timberline, past the evergreen forests. Through
the unnatural mists that blanketed those realms, he
thought he could see the Coven's castle.

Perhaps he should go there, or down to the swamps.
There was no sign of Erythrina. Only sprites in the
forms of bats and tiny griffins were to be seen here.
They sailed back and forth over him, sometimes soar-
ing far higher, toward the uttermost peak itself.

Mr. Slippery himself was in an extravagant winged
man form, one that subtly projected amateurism, one
that he hoped would pass the inspection of the enemy's eyes and ears. He fluttered clumsily across the

ledge toward a small cave that provided some shelter from the whistling wind. Fine, wind-dropped snow lay in a small bank before the entrance. The insects he found in the cave were no more than what they seemed—amateur transponders.

He turned and started back toward the drop-off; he was going to have to face this alone. But as he passed the snowbank, the wind swirled it up and tiny crystals stung his face and hands and nose. *Trap!* He jumped backward, his fastest escape spell coming to his lips, at the same time cursing himself for not establishing the spell before. The time delay was just too long; the trap lived here at MT3 and could react faster than he. The little snow-devil dragged the crystals up into a swirling column of singing motes that chimed in near-unison. "W-w-wait-t-t!"

The sound matched deep-set recognition patterns; this was Erythrina's work. Three hundred milliseconds passed, and the wind suddenly picked up the rest of the snow and whirled into a more substantial, taller column. Mr. Slippery realized that the trap had been more of an alarm, set to bring Ery if he should be recognized here. But her arrival was so quick that she must already have been at work somewhere in this plane.

"Where have you been-n-n!" The snow-devil's chime was a combination of rage and concern.

Mr. Slippery threw a second spell over the one he recognized she had cast. There was no help for it: he would have to tell her that the Feds had his Name. And with that news, Virginia's confirmation about Venezuela and the Feds' offer to help.

Erythrina didn't respond immediately—and only part of the delay was light lag. Then the swirling snow flecks that represented her gusted up around him. "So you lose no matter how this comes out, eh? I'm sorry, Slip."

Mr. Slippery's wings drooped. "Yeah. But I'm be-

ginning to believe it will be the True Death for us
all if we don't stop the Mailman. He really means
to take over . . . everything. Can you imagine what it
would be like if all the governments' wee megalo-
maniacs got replaced by one big one?"

The usual two-beat pause. The snow-devil seemed
to shudder in on itself. "You're right; we've got to
stop him even if it means working with Sammy Sugar
and the entire DoW." She chuckled, a near-inaudible
chiming. "Even if it means that *they* have to work for
us." She could laugh; the Feds didn't know her Name.
"How did your Federal Friends say we could plug
into their system?" Her form was changing again—
to a solid, winged form, an albino eagle. The only
red she allowed herself was in the eyes, which gleamed
with inner light.

"At the Laurel end of the old arpa net. We'll get
something near carte blanche on that and on the DoJ
domestic intelligence files, but we have to enter
through one physical location and with just the password scheme they specify." He and Erythrina would
have more power than any vandals in history, but
they would be on a short leash, nevertheless.

His wings beat briefly, and he rose into the air.
After the usual pause, the eagle followed. They flew
almost to the mountain's peak, then began the long,
slow glide toward the marshes below, the chill air
whistling around them. In principle, they could have
made the transfer to the Laurel terminus virtually
instantaneously. But it was not mere romanticism that
made them move so cautiously—as many a novice had
discovered the hard way. What appeared to the conscious mind as a search for air currents and clear
lanes through the scattered clouds was a manifestation
of the almost-subconscious working of programs that
gradually transferred processing from rented space on
MT^3 to low satellite and ground-based stations. The

game was tricky and time-consuming, but it made it virtually impossible for others to trace their origin. The greatest danger of detection would probably occur at Laurel, where they would be forced to access the system through a single input device.

The sky glowed momentarily; seconds passed, and an airborne fist slammed into them from behind. The shock wave sent them tumbling tail over wing toward the forests below. Mr. Slippery straightened his chaotic flailing into a head-first dive. Looking back—which was easy to do in his present attitude—he saw the peak that had been MT3 glowing red, steam rising over descending avalanches of lava. Even at this distance, he could see tiny motes swirling above the inferno. (Attackers looking for the prey that had fled?) Had it come just a few seconds earlier, they would have had most of their processing still locked into MT3 and the disaster—whatever it really was— would have knocked them out of this plane. It wouldn't have been the True Death, but it might well have grounded them for days.

On his right, he glimpsed the white eagle in a controlled dive; they had had just enough communications established off MT3 to survive. As they fell deeper into the humid air of the lowlands, Mr. Slippery dipped into the news channels: word was already coming over the *LA Times* of the fluke accident in which the Hokkaido aerospace launching laser had somehow shone on MT3's optics. The laser had shone for microseconds and at reduced power; the damage had been nothing like a Finger of God, say. No one had been hurt, but wideband communications would be down for some time, and several hundred million dollars of information traffic was stalled. There would be investigations and a lot of very irate customers.

It had been no accident, Mr. Slippery was sure.

The Mailman was showing his teeth, revealing infil-
tration no one had suspected. He must guess what his
opponents were up to.

They leveled out a dozen meters above the pine
forest that bordered the swamps. The air around them
was thick and humid, and the faraway mountains
were almost invisible. Clouds had moved in, and a
storm was on the way. They were now securely locked
into the low-level satellite net, but thousands of new
users were clamoring for entry, too. The loss of MT3
would make the Other Plane a turbulent place for
several weeks, as heavy users tried to shift their traffic
here.

He swooped low over the swamp, searching for the
one particular pond with the one particularly large
water lily that marked the only entrance Virginia
would permit them. There! He banked off to the
side, Erythrina following, and looked for signs of the
Mailman or his friends in the mucky clearings that
surrounded the pond.

But there was little purpose in further caution.
Flying about like this, they would be clearly visible
to any ambushers waiting by the pond. *Better to move
fast now that we're committed.* He signaled the red-
eyed eagle, and they dived toward the placid water.
That surface marked the symbolic transition to ob-
servation mode. No longer was he aware of a winged
form or of water coming up and around him. Now he
was interacting directly with the I/O protocols of a
computing center in the vicinity of Laurel, Maryland.
He sensed Ery poking around on her own. This wasn't
the arpa entrance. He slipped "sideways" into an
old-fashioned government office complex. The "feel"
of the 1990-style data sets was unmistakable. He was
fleetingly aware of memos written and edited, reports
hauled in and out of storage. One of the vandals'

favorite sports—and one that even the moderately skilled could indulge in—was to infiltrate one of these office complexes and simulate higher level input to make absurd and impossible demands on the local staff.

This was not the time for such games, and this was still not the entrance. He pulled away from the office complex and searched through some old directories. Arpa went back more than half a century, the first of the serious data nets, now (figuratively) gathering dust. The number was still there, though. He signaled Erythrina, and the two of them presented themselves at the log-in point and provided just the codes that Virginia had given him.

. . . and they were in. They eagerly soaked in the megabytes of password keys and access data that Virginia's people had left there. At the same time, they were aware that this activity was being monitored. The Feds were taking an immense chance leaving this material here, and they were going to do their best to keep a rein on their temporary vandal allies.

In fifteen seconds, they had learned more about the inner workings of the Justice Department and DoW than the Coven had in fifteen months. Mr. Slippery guessed that Erythrina must be busy plotting what she would do with all that data later on. For him, of course, there was no future in it. They drifted out of the arpa "vault" into the larger data spaces that were the Department of Justice files. He could see that there was nothing hidden from them; random archive retrievals were all being honored and with a speed that would have made deception impossible. They had subpoena power and clearances and more.

"Let's go get 'im, Slip." Erythrina's voice seemed hollow and inhuman in this underimaged realm. (How long would it be before the Feds started to make their data perceivable analogically, as on the Other

Plane? It might be a little undignified, but it would revolutionize their operation—which, from the Coven's standpoint, might be quite a bad thing.)

Mr. Slippery "nodded." Now they had more than enough power to undertake the sort of work they had planned. In seconds, they had searched all the locally available files on off-planet transmissions. Then they dove out of the DoJ net, Mr. Slippery to Pasadena and the JPL planetary probe archives, Erythrina to Cambridge and the Harvard Multispectral Patrol.

It should take several hours to survey these records, to determine just what transmissions might be cover for the alien invasion that both the Feds and Erythrina were guessing had begun. But Mr. Slippery had barely started when he noticed that there were dozens of processors within reach that he could just grab with his new Federal powers. He checked carefully to make sure he wasn't upsetting air traffic control or hospital life support, then quietly stole the computing resources of several hundred unknowing users, whose data sets automatically switched to other resources. Now he had more power than he ever would have risked taking in the past. On the other side of the continent, he was aware that Erythrina had done something similar.

In three minutes, they had sifted through five years' transmissions far more thoroughly than they had originally planned.

"No sign of him," he sighed and "looked" at Erythrina. They had found plenty of irregular sources at Harvard, but there was no orbital fit. All transmissions from the NASA probes checked out legitimately.

"Yes." Her face, with its dark skin and slanting eyes, seemed to hover beside him. Apparently with her new power, she could image even here. "But you know, we haven't really done much more than the Feds could—given a couple months of data set work. . . . I know, it's more than we had planned to do. But we've barely used the resources they've opened to us."

It was true. He looked around, feeling suddenly like a small boy let loose in a candy shop: he sensed enormous data bases and the power that would let him use them. Perhaps the cops had not intended them to take advantage of this, but it was obvious that with these powers, they could do a search no enemy could evade. "Okay," he said finally, "let's pig it."

Ery laughed and made a loud snuffling sound. Carefully, quickly, they grabbed noncritical data-processing facilities along all the East/West nets. In seconds, they were the biggest users in North America. The drain would be clear to anyone monitoring the System, though a casual user might notice only increased delays in turnaround. Modern nets are at least as resilient as old-time power nets—but like power nets, they have their elastic limit and their breaking point. So far, at least, he and Erythrina were far short of those.

—but they were experiencing what no human had ever known before, a sensory bandwidth thousands of times normal. For seconds that seemed without end, their minds were filled with a jumble verging on pain, data that was not information and information that was not knowledge. To hear ten million simultaneous phone conversations, to see the continent's entire video output, should have been a white noise. Instead it was a tidal wave of detail rammed through the tiny aperture of their minds. The pain increased, and Mr. Slippery panicked. This could be the True Death, some kind of sensory burnout—

Erythrina's voice was faint against the roar, *"Use everything, not just the inputs!"* And he had just enough sense left to see what she meant. He controlled more than raw data now; if he could master them, the continent's computers could process this avalanche, much the way parts of the human brain preprocess their input. More seconds passed, but now with a sense of time, as he struggled to distribute his very consciousness through the System.

Then it was over, and he had control once more. But things would never be the same: the human that had been Mr. Slippery was an insect wandering in the cathedral his mind had become. There simply was more there than before. No sparrow could fall without his knowledge, via air traffic control; no check could be cashed without his noticing over the bank communication net. More than three hundred million lives swept before what his senses had become.

Around and through him, he felt the other occupant—Erythrina, now equally grown. They looked at each other for an unending fraction of a second, their communication more kinesthetic than verbal. Finally she smiled, the old smile now deep with meanings she could never image before. "Pity the poor Mailman now!"

Again they searched, but now it was through all the civil data bases, a search that could only be dreamed of by mortals. The signs were there, a near invisible system of manipulations hidden among more routine crimes and vandalisms. Someone had been at work within the Venezuelan system, at least at the North American end. The trail was tricky to follow—their enemy seemed to have at least some of their own powers—but they saw it lead back into the labyrinths of the Federal bureaucracy: resources diverted, individuals promoted or transferred, not quite according to the automatic regulations that should govern. These were changes so small they were never guessed at by ordinary employees and only just sensed by the cops. But over the months, they added up to an instability that neither of the two searchers could quite understand except to know that it was planned and that it did the status quo no good.

"He's still too sharp for us, Slip. We're all over the

civil nets and we haven't seen any living sign of him;
yet we know he does heavy processing on Earth or in
low orbit."

"So he's either off North America, or else he has
penetrated the . . . military."

"I bet it's a little of both. The point is, we're going
to have to follow him."

And that meant taking over at least part of the
US military system. Even if that was possible, it certainly went far beyond what Virginia and her friends
had intended. As far as the cops were concerned, it
would mean that the threat against the government
was tripled. So far he hadn't detected any objections
to their searching, but he was aware of Virginia and
her superiors deep in some kind of bunker at Langley, intently watching a whole wall full of monitors,
trying to figure out just what he was up to and if it
was time to pull the plug on him.

Erythrina was aware of his objections almost as fast
as he could bring them to mind. "We don't have any
choice, Slip. We have to take control. The Feds aren't
the only thing watching us. If we don't get the Mailman on this try, he is sure as hell going to get us."

That was easy for her to say. None of her enemies
yet knew her True Name. Mr. Slippery had somehow
to survive *two* enemies. On the other hand, he suspected that the deadlier of those enemies was the
Mailman. "Only one way to go and that's up, huh?
Okay, I'll play."

They settled into a game that was familiar now,
grabbing more and more computing facilities, but
now from common Europe and Asia. At the same
time, they attacked the harder problem—infiltrating
the various North American military nets. Both projects were beyond normal humans or any group of
normal humans, but by now their powers were greater
than any single civil entity in the world.

The foreign data centers yielded easily, scarcely

more than minutes' work. The military was a different
story. The Feds had spent many years and hundreds
of billions of dollars to make the military command
and control system secure. But they had not counted
on the attack from all directions that they faced now;
in moments more, the two searchers found themselves
on the inside of the NSA control system—

—and under attack! Impressions of a dozen sleek,
deadly forms converging on them, and sudden loss of
control over many of the processors he depended on.
He and Erythrina flailed out wildly, clumsy giants
hacking at fast-moving hawks. There was imagery
here, as detailed as on the Other Plane. They were
fighting people with some of the skills the warlocks
had developed—and a lot more power. But it was
still an uneven contest. He and Erythrina had too
much experience and too much sheer processing mass
behind them. One by one, the fighters flashed into
incandescent destruction.

He realized almost instantly that these were not
the Mailman's tools. They were powerful, but they
fought as only moderately skilled warlocks might. In
fact, they had encountered the most secret defense
the government had for its military command and
control. The civilian bureaucracies had stuck with
obsolete data sets and old-fashioned dp languages, but
the cutting edge of the military is always more willing
to experiment. They had developed something like
the warlocks' system. Perhaps they didn't use magical
jargon to describe their computer/human symbiosis,
but the techniques and the attitudes were the same.
These swift-moving fighters flew against a background
imagery that was like an olive drab Other Plane.

Compared to his present power, they were nothing.
Even as he and Erythrina swept the defenders out of
the "sky," he could feel his consciousness expanding
further as more and more of the military system was
absorbed into their pattern. Every piece of space junk

out to one million kilometers floated in crystal detail
before his attention; in a fraction of a second he sorted
through it all, searching for some evidence of alien
intelligence. No sign of the Mailman.

The military and diplomatic communications of the
preceding fifty years showed before the light of their
minds. At the same time as they surveyed the satellite
data, Mr. Slippery and Erythrina swept through these
bureaucratic communications, looking carefully but
with flickering speed at every requisition for toilet
paper, every "declaration" of secret war, every travel
voucher, every one of the trillions of pieces of "paper"
that made it possible for the machinery of state to
creak forward. And here the signs were much clearer:
large sections were subtly changed, giving the same
feeling the eye's blind spot gives, the feeling that
nothing is really obscured but that some things are
simply gone. Some of the distortions were immense.
Under their microscopic yet global scrutiny, it was
obvious that all of Venezuela, large parts of Alaska,
and most of the economic base for the low satellite
net were all controlled by some single interest that
had little connection with the proper owners. Who
their enemy was was still a mystery, but his works
loomed larger and larger around them.

In a distant corner of what his mind had become,
tiny insects buzzed with homicidal fury, tiny insects
who knew Mr. Slippery's True Name. They knew
what he and Erythrina had done, and right now they
were more scared of the two warlocks than they had
ever been of the Mailman. As he and Ery continued
their search, he listened to the signals coming from
the Langley command post, followed the helicopter
gunships that were dispatched toward a single rural
bungalow in Northern California—and changed their
encrypted commands so that the sortie dumped its
load of death on an uninhabited stretch of the Pacific.

Still with but a tiny fraction of his attention, Mr.

Slippery noticed that Virginia—actually her superiors, who had long since taken over the operation—knew of this defense. They were still receiving real-time pictures from military satellites.

He signaled a pause to Erythrina. For a few seconds, she would work alone while he dealt with these persistent antagonists. He felt like a man attacked by several puppies: they were annoying and could cause substantial damage unless he took more trouble than they were worth. They had to be stopped without causing themselves injury.

He should freeze the West Coast military and any launch complexes that could reach his body. Beyond that, it would be a good idea to block recon satellite transmission of the California area. And of course, he'd better deal with the Finger of God installations that were above the California horizon. Already he felt one of those heavy lasers, sweeping along in its ten-thousand-kilometer orbit, go into aiming mode and begin charging. He still had plenty of time—at least two or three seconds—before the weapons laser reached its lowest discharge threshold. Still, this was the most immediate threat. Mr. Slippery sent a tendril of consciousness into the tiny processor aboard the Finger of God satellite—

—and withdrew, bloodied. *Someone was already there.* Not Erythrina and not the little military warlocks. *Someone* too great for even him to overpower.

"Ery! I've found him!" It came out a scream. The laser's bore was centered on a spot thousands of kilometers below, a tiny house that in less than a second would become an expanding ball of plasma at the end of a columnar explosion descending through the atmosphere.

Over and over in that last second, Mr. Slippery threw himself against the barrier he felt around the tiny military processor—with no success. He traced its control to the lower statellite net, to bigger processors that were equally shielded. Now he had a feel for the nature of his opponent. It was not the direct imagery he was used to on the Other Plane; this was more like fighting blindfolded. He could sense the other's style. The enemy was not revealing any more of himself than was necessary to keep control of the Finger of God for another few hundred milliseconds.

Mr. Slippery slashed, trying to cut the enemy's communications. But his opponent was strong, much stronger—he now realized—than himself. He was vaguely aware of the other's connections to the computing power in those blind-spot areas he and Erythrina had discovered. But for all that power, he was almost the enemy's equal. There was something missing from the other, some critical element of imagination or originality. If Erythrina would only come, they might be able to stop him. Milliseconds separated him from the True Death. He looked desperately around. *Where is she?*

Military Status announced the discharge of an Orbital Weapons Laser. He cowered even as his quickened perceptions counted the microseconds that remained till his certain destruction, even as he noticed a ball of glowing plasma expanding about what had been a Finger of God—*the Finger that had been aimed at him!*

He could see now what had happened. While he and the other had been fighting, Erythrina had commandeered another of the weapons satellites, one already very near discharge threshold, and destroyed the threat to him.

Even as he realized this, the enemy was on him again, this time attacking conventionally, trying to destroy Mr. Slippery's communications and processing space. But now that enemy had to fight both Erythrina and Mr. Slippery. The other's lack of imagination and creativity was beginning to tell, and even with his greater strength, they could feel him slowly,

slowly losing resources to his weaker opponents. There was something familiar about this enemy, something Mr. Slippery was sure he could see, given time.

Abruptly the enemy pulled away. For a long moment, they held each others' sole attention, like cats waiting for the smallest sign of weakness to launch back into combat—only here the new attack could come from any of ten thousand different directions, from any of the communications nodes that formed their bodies and their minds.

From beside him, he felt Erythrina move forward, as though to lock the other in her green-eyed gaze. "You know who we have here, Slip?" He could tell that all her concentration was on this enemy, that she almost vibrated with the effort. "This is our old friend DON.MAC grown up to super size, and doing his best to disguise himself."

The other seemed to tense and move even further in upon himself. But after a moment, he began imaging. There stood DON.MAC, his face and Plessey-Mercedes body the same as ever. DON.MAC, the first of the Mailman's converts, the one Erythrina was sure had been killed and replaced with a simulator. "And all the time he's been the Mailman. The last person we would suspect, the Mailman's first victim."

DON rolled forward half a meter, his motors keening, his hydraulic fists raised. But he did not deny what Mr. Slippery said. After a moment he seemed to relax. "You are very . . . clever. But then, you two have had help; I never thought you and the cops would cooperate. That was the one combination that had any chance against the 'Mailman.' " He smiled, a familiar automatic twitch. "But don't you see? It's a combination with lethal genes. We three have much more in common than you and the government.

"Look around you. If we were warlocks before, we are gods now. Look!" Without letting the center of their attention wander, the two followed his gaze. As before, the myriad aspects of the lives of billions spread out before them. But now, many things were changed. In their struggle, the three had usurped virtually all of the connected processing power of the human race. Video and phone communications were frozen. The public data bases had lasted long enough to notice that something had gone terribly, terribly wrong. Their last headlines, generated a second before the climax of the battle, were huge banners announcing GREATEST DATA OUTAGE OF ALL TIME. Nearly a billion people watched blank data sets, feeling more panicked than any simple power blackout could ever make them. Already the accumulation of lost data and work time would cause a major recession.

"They are lucky the old arms race is over, or else independent military units would probably have already started a war. Even if we hand back control this instant, it would take them more than a year to get their affairs in order." DON.MAC smirked, the same expression they had seen the day before when he was bragging to the Limey. "There have been few deaths yet. Hospitals and aircraft have some stand-alone capability."

Even so . . . Mr. Slippery could see thousands of aircraft stacked up over major airports from London to Christchurch. Local computing could never coordinate the safe landing of them all before some ran out of fuel.

"*We* caused all that—with just the fallout of our battle," continued DON. "If we chose to do them harm, I have no doubt we could exterminate the human race." He detonated three warheads in their silos in Utah just to emphasize his point. With dozens of video eyes, in orbit and on the ground, Mr. Slippery and Erythrina watched the destruction sweep across the launch sites. "Consider: how are we different from the gods of myth? And like the gods of myth, we can rule and prosper, just so long as we don't fight among ourselves." He looked expectantly from Mr. Slippery to Erythrina. There was a frown on the Red One's dark face; she seemed to be concentrating on their opponent just as fiercely as ever.

DON.MAC turned back to Mr. Slippery. "Slip, you especially should see that we have no choice but to cooperate. *They know your True Name.* Of the three of us, your life is the most fragile, depending on protecting your body from a government that now considers you a traitor. You would have died a dozen times over during the last thousand seconds if you hadn't used your new powers.

"And you can't go back. Even if you play Boy Scout, destroy me, and return all obedient—even then they will kill you. They know how dangerous you are, perhaps even more dangerous than I. They can't afford to let you exist."

And megalomania aside, that made perfect and chilling sense. As they were talking, a fraction of Mr. Slippery's attention was devoted to confusing and obstructing the small infantry group that had been air-dropped into the Arcata region just before the government lost all control. Their superiors had realized how easily he could countermand their orders, and so the troops were instructed to ignore all outside direction until they had destroyed a certain Roger Pollack. Fortunately they were depending on city directories and orbit-fed street maps, and he had been keeping them going in circles for some time now. It was a nuisance, and sooner or later he would have to decide on a more permanent solution.

But what was a simple nuisance in his present state would be near-instant death if he returned to his normal self. He looked at Erythrina. Was there any way around DON's arguments?

Her eyes were almost shut, and the frown had deepened. He sensed that more and more of her resources were involved in some pattern analysis. He wondered if she had even heard what DON.MAC said. But after a moment her eyes came open, and she looked at the two of them. There was triumph in that look. "You know, Slip, I don't think I have ever been fooled by a personality simulator, at least not for more than a few minutes."

Mr. Slippery nodded, puzzled by this sudden change in topic. "Sure. If you talk to a simulator long enough, you eventually begin to notice little inflexibilities. I don't think we'll ever be able to write a program that could pass the Turing test."

"Yes, little inflexibilities, a certain lack of imagination. It always seems to be the tipoff. Of course DON here has always pretended to be a program, so it was hard to tell. But I was sure that for the last few months there has been no living being behind his mask . . .

". . . and furthermore, I don't think there is any-body there even now." Mr. Slippery's attention snapped back to DON.MAC. The other smirked at the accusation. Somehow it was not the right reaction. Mr. Slippery remembered the strange, artificial flavor of DON's combat style. In this short an encounter, there could be no really hard evidence for her theory. She was using her intuition and whatever deep analysis she had been doing these last few seconds.

"But that means we still haven't found the Mail-man."

"Right. This is just his best tool. I'll bet the Mail-man simply used the pattern he stole from the mur-dered DON.MAC as the basis for this automatic de-fense system we've been fighting. The Mailman's time lag is a very real thing, not a red herring at all. Some-how it is the whole secret of who he really is.

"In any case, it makes our present situation a lot easier." She smiled at DON.MAC as though he were a real person. Usually it was easier to behave that way toward simulators; in this case, there was a good deal of triumph in her smile. "You almost won for your master, DON. You almost had us convinced. But now that we know what we are dealing with, it will be easy to—"

Her image flicked out of existence, and Mr. Slippery felt DON grab for the resources Ery controlled. All through near-Earth space, they fought for the weapon systems she had held till an instant before.

And alone, Mr. Slippery could not win. Slowly, slowly, he felt himself bending before the other's force, like some wrestler whose bones were breaking one by one under a murderous opponent. It was all he could do to prevent the DON construct from blasting his home; and to do that, he had to give up progressively more computing power.

Erythrina was gone, gone as though she had never been. Or was she? He gave a sliver of his attention to a search, a sliver that was still many times more powerful than any mere warlock. That tiny piece of consciousness quickly noticed a power failure in southern Rhode Island. Many power failures had developed during the last few minutes, consequent to the data failure. But this one was strange. In addition to power, comm lines were down and even his intervention could not bring them to life. It was about as thoroughly blacked out as a place could be. This could scarcely be an accident.

. . . and there was a voice, barely telephone quality and almost lost in the mass of other data he was processing. *Erythrina!* She had, via some incredibly tortuous detour, retained a communication path to the outside.

His gaze swept the blackened-out Providence suburb. It consisted of new urbapts, perhaps one hundred thousand units in all. Somewhere in there lived the human that was Erythrina. While she had been concentrating on DON.MAC, he must have been working equally hard to find her True Name. Even now, DON did not know precisely who she was, only enough to black out the area she lived in.

It was getting hard to think; DON.MAC was systematically dismantling him. The lethal intent was clear: as soon as Mr. Slippery was sufficiently reduced, the Orbital Lasers would be turned on his body, and then on Erythrina's. And then the Mailman's faithful servant would have a planetary kingdom to turn over to his mysterious master.

He listened to the tiny voice that still leaked out of Providence. It didn't make too much sense. She sounded hysterical, panicked. He was surprised that she could speak at all; she had just suffered—in losing all her computer connections—something roughly analogous to a massive stroke. To her, the world was now seen through a keyhole, incomplete, unknown and dark.

"There is a chance; we still have a chance," the voice went on, hurried and slurred. "An old military communication tower north of here. Damn. I don't know the number or grid, but I can see it from where I'm sitting. With it you could punch through to the roof antenna . . . has plenty of bandwith, and I've got some battery power here . . . but *hurry*."

She didn't have to tell him that; he was the guy who was being eaten alive. He was almost immobilized now, the other's attack squeezing and stifling where it could not cut and tear. He spasmed against DON's strength and briefly contacted the comm towers north of Providence. Only one of them was in line of sight with the blacked-out area. Its steerable antenna was very, very narrow beam.

"Ery, I'm going to need your house number, maybe even your antenna id."

A second passed, two—a hellish eon for Mr. Slippery. In effect, he had asked her for her True Name—

he who was already known to the Feds. Once he returned to the real world, there would be no way he
could mask this information from them. He could
imagine her thoughts: never again to be free. In her
place, he would have paused too, but—

"*Ery!* It's the True Death for both of us if you
don't. He's got me!"

This time she barely hesitated. "D-Debby Charteris,
4448 Grosvenor Row. Cut off like this, I don't know
the antenna id. Is my name and house enough?"

"Yes. Get ready!"

Even before he spoke, he had already matched the
name with an antenna rental and aligned the military
antenna on it. Return contact came as he turned his
attention back to DON.MAC. With luck, the enemy
was not aware of their conversation. Now he must be
distracted.

Mr. Slippery surged against the other, breaking communications nodes that served them both. DON shuddered, reorganizing around the resources that were
left, then moved in on Mr. Slippery again. Since DON
had greater strength to begin with, the maneuver had
cost Mr. Slippery proportionately more. The enemy
had been momentarily thrown off balance, but now
the end would come very quickly.

The spaces around him, once so rich with detail and
colors beyond color, were fading now, replaced by the
sensations of his true body straining with animal fear
in its little house in California. Contact with the
greater world was almost gone. He was scarcely aware
of it when DON turned the Finger of God back upon
him—

Consciousness, the superhuman consciousness of before, returned almost unsensed, unrecognized till
awareness brought surprise. Like a strangling victim
back from oblivion, Mr. Slippery looked around
dazedly, not quite realizing that the struggle continued.

But now the roles were reversed. DON.MAC had been caught by surprise, in the act of finishing off what he thought was his only remaining enemy. Erythrina had used that surprise to good advantage, coming in upon her opponent from a Japanese data center, destroying much of DON's higher reasoning centers before the other was even aware of her. Large, unclaimed processing units lay all about, and as DON and Erythrina continued their struggle, Mr. Slippery quietly absorbed everything in reach.

Even now, DON could have won against either one of them alone, but when Mr. Slippery threw himself back into the battle, they had the advantage. DON.-MAC sensed this too, and with a brazenness that was either mindless or genius, returned to his original appeal. "There is still time! The Mailman will still forgive you."

Mr. Slippery and Erythrina ripped at their enemy from both sides, disconnecting vast blocks of communications, processing and data resources. They denied the Mass Transmits to him, and one by one put the low-level satellites out of synch with his data accesses. DON was confined to land lines, tied into a single military net that stretched from Washington to Denver. He was flailing, randomly using whatever instruments of destruction were still available. All across the midsection of the US, silo missiles detonated, ABM lasers swept back and forth across the sky. The world had been stopped short by the beginning of their struggle, but the ending could tear it to pieces.

The damage to Mr. Slippery and Erythrina was slight, the risk that the random strokes would seriously damage them small. They ignored occasional slashing losses and concentrated single-mindedly on dismantling DON.MAC. They discovered the object code for the simulator that was DON, and zeroed it. DON—or his creator—was clever and had planted many copies, and a new one awakened every time they destroyed the running copy. But as the minutes passed, the simulator found itself with less and less to work with. Now it was barely more than it had been back in the Coven.

"*Fools!* The Mailman is your natural ally. The Feds will *kill* you! Don't you underst—"

The voice stopped in midshriek, as Erythrina zeroed the currently running simulator. No other took up the task. There was a silence, an . . . absence . . . throughout. Erythrina glanced at Mr. Slippery, and the two continued their search through the enemy's territory. This data space was big, and there could be many more copies of DON hidden in it. But without the resources they presently held, the simulator could have no power. It was clear to both of them that no effective ambush could be hidden in these unmoving ruins.

And they had complete copies of DON.MAC to study. It was easy to trace the exact extent of his infection of the system. The two moved systematically, changing what they found so that it would behave as its original programmers had intended. Their work was so thorough that the Feds might never realize just how extensively the Mailman and his henchman had infiltrated them, just how close he had come to total control.

Most of the areas they searched were only slightly altered and required only small changes. But deep within the military net, there were hundreds of trillions of bytes of program that seemed to have no intelligible function yet were clearly connected with DON's activities. It was apparently object code, but it was so huge and so ill organized that even they couldn't decide if it was more than hash now. There was no possibility that it had any legitimate function; after a few moments' consideration, they randomized it.

At last it was over. Mr. Slippery and Erythrina stood

alone. They controlled all connected processing facilities in near-Earth space. There was no place within that volume that any further enemies could be lurking. And there was no evidence that there had ever been interferencee from beyond.

It was the first time since they had reached this level that they had been able to survey the world without fear. (He scarcely noticed the continuing, pitiful attempts of the American military to kill his real body.) Mr. Slippery looked around him, using all his millions of perceptors. The Earth floated serene. Viewed in the visible, it looked like a thousand pictures he had seen as a human. But in the ultraviolet, he could follow its hydrogen aura out many thousands of kilometers. And the high-energy detectors on satellites at all levels perceived the radiation belts in thousands of energy levels, oscillating in the solar wind. Across the oceans of the world, he could feel the warmth of the currents, see just how fast they were moving. And all the while, he monitored the millions of tiny voices that were now coming back to life as he and Erythrina carefully set the human race's communication system back on its feet and gently prodded it into function. Every ship in the seas, every aircraft now making for safe landing, every one of the loans, the payments, the meals of an entire race registered clearly on some part of his consciousness. With perception came power; almost everything he saw, he could alter, destroy, or enhance. By the analogical rules of the covens, there was only one valid word for themselves in their present state: they were gods.

" . . . we could rule," Erythrina's voice was hushed, self-frightened. "It might be tricky at first, assuring our bodies protection, but we could rule."

"There's still the Mailman—"

She seemed to wave a hand, dismissingly. "Maybe, maybe not. It's true we still are no closer to knowing who he is, but we do know that we have destroyed all

his processing power. We would have plenty of warning if he ever tries to reinsinuate himself into the System." She stared at him intently, and it wasn't until some time later that he recognized the faint clues in her behavior and realized that she was holding something back.

What she said was all so clearly true; for as long as their bodies lived, they could rule. And what DON.- MAC had said also seemed true: they were the greatest threat the "forces of law and order" had ever faced, and that included the Mailman. How could the Feds afford to let them be free, how could they even afford to let them *live,* if the two of them gave up the power they had now? But—"A lot of people would have to die if we took over. There are enough independent military entities left on Earth that we'd have to use a good deal of nuclear blackmail, at least at first."

"Yeah," her voice was even smaller than before, and the image of her face was downcast. "During the last few seconds I've done some simulating on that. We'd have to take out four, maybe six, major cities. If there are any command centers hidden from us, it could be a lot worse than that. And we'd have to develop our own human secret-police forces as folks began to operate outside our system. . . . Damn. We'd end up being worse than the human-based government."

She saw the same conclusion in his face and grinned lopsidedly. "You can't do it and neither can I. So the State wins again."

He nodded, "reached" out to touch her briefly. They took one last glorious minute to soak in the higher reality. Then, silently, they parted, each to seek his own way downward.

It was not an instantaneous descent to ordinary humanity. Mr. Slippery was careful to prepare a safe exit. He created a complex set of misdirections for the army unit that was trying to close in on his physical body; it would take them several hours to find him, far longer than necessary for the government to call them off. He set up preliminary negotiations with the Federal programs that had been doing their best to knock him out of power, telling them of his determination to surrender if granted safe passage and safety for his body. In a matter of seconds he would be talking to humans again, perhaps even Virginia, but by then a lot of the basic ground rules would be automatically in operation.

As per their temporary agreements, he closed off first one and then another of the capabilities that he had so recently acquired. It was like stopping one's ears, then blinding one's eyes, but somehow much worse since his very ability to think was being deliberately given up. He was like some lobotomy patient (victim) who only vaguely realizes now what he has lost. Behind him the Federal forces were doing their best to close off the areas he had left, to protect themselves from any change of heart he might have.

Far away now, he could sense Erythrina going through a similar procedure, but more slowly. That was strange; he couldn't be sure with his present faculties, but somehow it seemed that she was deliberately lagging behind and doing something more complicated than was strictly necessary to return safely to normal humanity. And then he remembered that strange look she had given him while saying that they had not figured out who the Mailman was.

One could rule as easily as two!

The panic was sudden and overwhelming, all the more terrible for the feeling of being betrayed by one so trusted. He struck out against the barriers he had so recently allowed to close in about him, but it was too late. He was already weaker than the Feds. Mr. Slippery looked helplessly back into the gathering dimness, and saw . . .

. . . Ery coming down toward the real world with him, giving up the advantage she had held all alone.

Whatever problems had slowed her must have had nothing to do with treachery. And somehow his feeling of relief went beyond the mere fact of death avoided—Ery was still what he had always thought her.

He was seeing a lot of Virginia lately, though of course not socially. Her crew had set up offices in Arcata, and twice a week she and one of her goons would come up to the house. No doubt it was one of the few government operations carried out face-to-face. She or her superiors seemed to realize that anything done over the phone might be subject to trickery. (Which was true, of course. Given several weeks to himself, Pollack could have put together a robot phone connection and—using false ids and priority permits—been on a plane to Djakarta.)

There were a lot of superficial similarities between these meetings and that first encounter the previous spring:

Pollack stepped to the door and watched the black Lincoln pulling up the drive. As always, the vehicle came right into the carport. As always, the driver got out quickly, eyes flickering coldly across Pollack. As always, Virginia moved with military precision (in fact, he had discovered, she had been promoted out of the Army to her present job in DoW intelligence). The two walked purposefully toward the bungalow, ignoring the summer sunlight and the deep wet green of the lawn and pines. He held the door open for them, and they entered with silent arrogance. As always.

He smiled to himself. In one sense nothing had changed. They still had the power of life and death over him. They could still cut him off from everything he loved. But in another sense . . .

"Got an easy one for you today, Pollack," she said as she put her briefcase on the coffee table and enabled its data set. "But I don't think you're going to like it."

"Oh?" He sat down and watched her expectantly.

"The last couple of months, we've had you destroying what remains of the Mailman and getting the National program and data bases back in operation."

Behind everything, there still stood the threat of the Mailman. Ten weeks after the battle—the War, as Virginia called it—the public didn't know any more than that there had been a massive vandalism of the System. Like most major wars, this had left ruination in everyone's camp. The US government and the economy of the entire world had slid far toward chaos in the months after that battle. (In fact, without his work and Erythrina's, he doubted if the US bureaucracies could have survived the ruination of the Mailman War. He didn't know whether this made them the saviors or the betrayers of America.) But what of the enemy? His power was almost certainly destroyed. In the last three weeks Mr. Slippery had found only one copy of the program kernel that had been DON.-MAC, and that had been in nonexecutable form. But the man—or the beings—behind the Mailman was just as anonymous as ever. In that, Virginia, the government, and Pollack were just as ignorant as the general public.

"Now," Virginia continued, "we've got some smaller problems—mopping-up action, you might call it. For nearly two decades, we've had to live with the tuppin vandalism of irresponsible individuals who put their petty self-interest ahead of the public's. Now that we've got you, we intend to put a stop to that:

"We want the True Names of all abusers currently on the System, in particular the members of this so-called coven you used to be a part of."

He had known that the demand would eventually come, but the knowledge made this moment no less unpleasant. "I'm sorry, I can't."

"Can't? Or won't? See here, Pollack, the price of your freedom is that you play things our way. You've broken enough laws to justify putting you away for-ever. And we both know that you are so dangerous that you *ought* to be put away. There are people who feel even more strongly than that, Pollack, people who are not as soft in the head as I am. They simply want you and your girl friend in Providence safely dead." The speech was delivered with characteristic flat blunt-ness, but she didn't quite meet his eyes as she spoke. Ever since he had returned from the battle, there had been a faint diffidence behind her bluster.

She covered it well, but it was clear to Pollack that she didn't know if she should fear him or respect him —or both. In any case, she seemed to recognize a basic mystery in him; she had more imagination than he had originally thought. It was a bit amusing, for there was very little special about Roger Pollack, the man. He went from day to day feeling a husk of what he had once been and trying to imagine what he could barely remember.

Roger smiled almost sympathetically. "I can't *and* I won't, Virginia. And I don't think you will harm me for it—Let me finish. The only thing that frightens your bosses more than Erythrina and me is the pos-sibility that there may be other unknown persons—maybe even the Mailman, back from wherever he has disappeared to—who might be equally powerful. She and I are your only real experts on this type of sub-version. I bet that even if they could, your people wouldn't train their own clean-cut, braided types as replacements for us. The more paranoid a security organization is, the less likely it is to trust anyone with this sort of power. Mr. Slippery and Erythrina are the known factors, the experts who turned back from the brink. Our restraint was the only thing that stood between the Powers That Be and the Powers That Would Be."

Virginia was speechless for a moment, and Pollack could see that this was the crux of her changed attitude toward him. All her life she had been taught that the individual is corrupted by power: she boggled at the notion that he had been offered mastery of all mankind—and had refused it.

Finally she smiled, a quick smile that was gone almost before he noticed it. "Okay. I'll pass on what you say. You may be right. The vandals are a long-range threat to our basic American freedoms, but day to day, they are a mere annoyance. My superiors—the Department of Welfare—are probably willing to fight them as we have in the past. They'll tolerate your, uh, disobedience *in this single matter* as long as you and Erythrina loyally protect us against the superhuman threats."

Pollack felt a great sense of relief. He had been so afraid DoW would be willing to destroy him for this refusal. And since the Feds would never be free of their fear of the Mailman, he and Debby Charteris—Erythrina—would never be forced to betray their friends.

"But," continued the cop, "that doesn't mean you get to ignore the covens. The most likely place for superhuman threats to resurface is from within them. The vandals are the people with the most real experience on the System—even the Army is beginning to see that. And if a superhuman type originates outside the covens, we figure his ego will still make him show off to them, just as with the Mailman.

"In addition to your other jobs, we want you to spend a couple of hours a week with each of the major covens. You'll be one of the 'boys'—only now you're under responsible control, watching for any sign of Mailman-type influence."

"I'll get to see Ery again!"

"No. That rule still stands. And you should be grateful. I don't think we could tolerate your existence if there weren't two of you. With only one in the Other Plane at a time, we'll always have a weapon in reserve. And as long as we can keep you from meeting there, we can keep you from scheming against us. This is serious, Roger: if we catch you two or your surrogates playing around in the Other Plane, it will be the end."

"Hmm."

She looked hard at him for a moment, then appeared to take that for acquiescence. The next half-hour was devoted to the details of this week's assignments. (It would have been easier to feed him all this when he was in the Other Plane, but Virginia— or at least DoW—seemed wedded to the past.) He was to continue the work on Social Security Records and the surveillance of the South American data nets. There was an enormous amount of work to be done, at least with the limited powers the Feds were willing to give him. It would likely be October before the welfare machinery was working properly again. But that would be in time for the elections.

Then, late in the week, they wanted him to visit the Coven. Roger knew he would count the hours; it had been so long.

Virginia was her usual self, intense and all business, until she and her driver were ready to leave. Standing in the carport, she said almost shyly, "I ran your *Anne Boleyn* last week . . . It's really very good."

"You sound surprised."

"No. I mean yes, maybe I was. Actually I've run it several times, usually with the viewpoint character set to Anne. There seems to be a lot more depth to it than other participation games I've read. I've got the feeling that if I am clever enough, someday I'll stop Henry and keep my head!"

Pollack grinned. He could imagine Virginia, the hard-eyed cop, reading *Anne* to study the psychology of her client-prisoner—then gradually getting caught up in the action of the novel. "It is possible."

In fact, it was possible she might turn into a rather nice human being someday.

But by the time Pollack was starting back up the walk to his house, Virginia was no longer on his mind. He was going back to the Coven!

A chill mist that was almost rain blew across the hillside and obscured the far distance in shifting patches. But even from here, on the ridge above the swamp, the castle looked different: heavy, stronger, darker.

Mr. Slippery started down the familiar slope. The frog on his shoulder seemed to sense his unease and its clawlets bit tighter into the leather of his jacket. Its beady yellow eyes turned this way and that, recording everything. (Altogether, that frog was much improved —almost out of amateur status nowadays.)

The traps were different. In just the ten weeks since the War, the Coven had changed them more than in the previous two years. Every so often, he shook the gathering droplets of water from his face and peered more closely at a brush or boulder by the side of the path. His advance was slow, circuitous, and interrupted by invocations of voice and hand.

Finally he stood before the towers. A figure of black and glowing red climbed out of the magma moat to meet him. Even Alan had changed: he no longer had his asbestos T-shirt, and there was no humor in his sparring with the visitor. Mr. Slippery had to stare upward to look directly at his massive head. The elemental splashed molten rock down on them, and the frog scampered between his neck and collar, its skin cold and slimy against his own. The passwords were different, the questioning more hostile, but Mr. Slippery was a match for the tests and in a matter of minutes Alan retreated sullenly to his steaming pool, and the drawbridge was lowered for their entrance.

* * *

The hall was almost the same as before: perhaps a bit drier, more brightly lit. There were certainly more people. And they were all looking up at him as he stood in the entranceway. Mr. Slippery gave his traveling jacket and hat to a liveried servant and started down the steps, trying to recognize the faces, trying to understand the tension and hostility that hung in the air.

"Slimey!" The Limey stepped forward from the crowd, a familiar grin splitting his bearded face.

"Slip! Is that really you?" (Not entirely a rhetorical question, under the circumstances.)

Mr. Slippery nodded, and after a moment, the other did, too. The Limey almost ran across the space that separated them, stuck out his hand, and clapped the other on the shoulder. "Come on, come on! We have rather a lot to talk about!"

As if on cue, the others turned back to their conversations and ignored the two friends as they walked to one of the sitting rooms that opened off the main hall. Mr. Slippery felt like a man returning to his old school ten years after graduation. Almost all the faces were different, and he had the feeling that he could never belong here again. But this was only ten weeks, not ten years.

The Slimey Limey shut the heavy door, and the sounds from the main room were muted. He waved Slip to a chair and made a show of mixing them some drinks.

"They're all simulators, aren't they?" Slip said quietly.

"Uh?" The Limey broke off his stream of chatter and shook his head glumly. "Not all. I've recruited four or five apprentices. They do their best to make the place look thriving and occupied. You may have noticed various improvements in our security."

"It looks stronger, but it's more appearance than fact."

Slimey shrugged. "I really didn't expect it to fool the likes of you."

Mr. Slippery leaned forward. "Who's left from the old group, Slimey?"

"DON's gone. The Mailman is gone. Wiley J. Bastard shows up a couple of times a month, but he's not much fun anymore. I think Erythrina's still on the System, but she hasn't come by. I thought you were gone until today."

"What about Robin Hood?"

"Gone."

That accounted for all the top talents. Virginia the Frog hadn't been giving away all that much when she excused him from betraying the Coven. Slip wondered if there was any hint of smugness in the frog's fixed and lipless smile.

"What happened?"

The other sighed. "There's a depression on down in the real world, in case you hadn't noticed; and it's being blamed on us vandals.

"—I know, that could scarce explain Robin's disappearance, only the lesser ones. Slip, I think most of our old friends are either dead—Truly Dead—or very frightened that if they come back into this Plane, they will become Truly Dead."

This felt very much like history repeating itself. "How do you mean?"

The Limey leaned forward. "Slip, it's quite obvious the government's feeding us lies about what caused the depression. They say it was a combination of programming errors and the work of 'vandals.' We know that can't be true. No ordinary vandals could cause that sort of damage. Right after the crash, I looked at what was left of the Feds' data bases. Whatever ripped things up was more powerful than any vandal. . . .

And I've spoken with—p'raps I should say interrogated
—Wiley. I think what we see in the real world and on
this plane is in fact the wreckage of a bloody major
war."

"Between?"

"Creatures as far above me as I am above a chimp.
The names we know them by are the Mailman, Erythrina . . . and just possibly Mr. Slippery."

"Me?" Slip tensed and sent out probes along the
communications links which he perceived had created
the image before him. Even though on a leash, Mr.
Slippery was far more powerful than any normal warlock, and it should have been easy to measure the
power of this potential opponent. But the Limey was
a diffuse, almost nebulous presence. Slip couldn't tell
if he were facing an opponent in the same class as himself; in fact, he had no clear idea of the other's
strength, which was even more ominous.

The Limey didn't seem to notice. "That's what I
thought. Now I doubt it. I wager you were used—like
Wiley and possibly DON—by the other combatants.
And I see that now you're in *someone's* thrall." His
finger stabbed at the yellow-eyed frog on Mr. Slippery's shoulder, and a sparkle of whiskey flew into the
creature's face. Virginia—or whoever was controlling
the beast—didn't know what to do, and the frog froze
momentarily, then recovered its wits and emitted a
pale burst of flame.

The Limey laughed. "But it's no one very competent. The Feds is my guess. What happened? Did
they sight your True Name, or did you just sell out?"

"The creature's my familiar, Slimey. We all have our
apprentices. If you really believe we're the Feds, why
did you let us in?"

The other shrugged. "Because there are enemies and
enemies, Slip. Beforetime, we called the government
the Great Enemy. Now I'd say they are just one in a
pantheon of nasties. Those of us who survived the

crash are a lot tougher, a lot less frivolous. We don't
think of this as all a wry game anymore. And we're
teaching our apprentices a lot more systematically. It's
not near so much fun. Now when we talk of traitors
in the Coven, we mean real, life-and-death treachery.

"But it's necessary. When it comes to it, if we little
people don't protect ourselves, we're going to be eaten
up by the government or . . . certain other creatures
I fear even more."

The frog shifted restively on Mr. Slippery's shoulder, and he could imagine Virginia getting ready to
deliver some speech on the virtue of obeying the laws
of society in order to reap its protection. He reached
across to pat its cold and pimply back; now was not
the time for such debate.

"You had one of the straightest heads around here,
Slip. Even if you aren't one of us anymore, I don't
reckon you're an absolute enemy. You and your . . .
friend may have certain interests in common with us.
There are things you should know about—if you don't
already. An' p'raps there'll be times you'll help us
similarly."

Slip felt the Federal tether loosen. Virginia must
have convinced her superiors that there was actually
help to be had here. "Okay. You're right. There was
a war. The Mailman was the enemy. He lost and now
we're trying to put things back together."

"Ah, that's just it, old man. *I don't think the war is
over.* True, all that remains of the Mailman's con-
structs are 'craterfields' spread through the government's program space. But something like him is still
very much alive." He saw the disbelief in Mr. Slippery's face. "I know, you an' your friends are more
powerful than any of us. But there are many of us—
not just in the Coven—and we have learned a lot these
past ten weeks. There are signs, so light and fickle you
might call 'em atmosphere, that tell us something like

the Mailman is still alive. It doesn't quite have the
texture of the Mailman, but it's there."

Mr. Slippery nodded. He didn't need any special
explanations of the feeling. *Damn! If I weren't on a
leash, I would have seen all this weeks ago, instead of
finding it out secondhand.* He thought back to those
last minutes of their descent from godhood and felt a
chill. He knew what he must ask now, and he had a
bad feeling about what the answer might be. Somehow he had to prevent Virginia from hearing that
answer. It would be a great risk, but he still had a few
tricks he didn't think DoW knew of. He probed back
along the links that went to Arcata and D.C., feeling
the interconnections and the redundancy checks. If
he was lucky, he would not have to alter more than a
few hundred bits of the information that would flow
down to them in the next few seconds. "So who do you
think is behind it?"

"For a while, I thought it might be you. Now I've
seen you and, uh, done some tests, I know you're more
powerful than in the old days and probably more
powerful than I am now, but you're no superman."

"Maybe I'm in disguise."

"Maybe, but I doubt it." The Limey was coming
closer to the critical words that must be disguised.
Slip began to alter the redundancy bits transmitted
through the construct of the frog. He would have to
fake the record both before and after those words if
the deception was to escape detection completely.
"No, there's a certain style to this presence. A style
that reminds me of our old friend, REorbyitnh
rHionoad." The name he said, and the name Mr.
Slippery heard, was "Erythrina." The name blended
imperceptibly in its place, the name the frog heard,
and reported, was "Robin Hood."

"Hmm, possible. He always seemed to be power
hungry." The Limey's eyebrows went up fractionally
at the pronoun "he." Besides, Robin had been a

fantastically clever vandal, not a power grabber.
Slimey's eyes flickered toward the frog, and Mr. Slippery prayed that he would play along. "Do you really think this is as great a threat as the Mailman?"

"Who knows? The presence isn't as widespread as the Mailman's, and since the crash no more of us have disappeared. Also, I'm not sure that . . . he . . . is the only such creature left. Perhaps the original Mailman is still around."

And you can't decide who it is that I'm really trying to fool, can you?

The discussion continued for another half-hour, a weird three-way fencing match with just two active players. On the one hand, he and the Limey were trying to communicate past the frog, and on the other, the Slimey Limey was trying to decide if perhaps Slip was the real enemy and the frog a potential ally. The hell of it was, Mr. Slippery wasn't sure himself of the answer to that puzzle.

Slimey walked him out to the drawbridge. For a few moments, they stood on the graven ceramic plating and spoke. Below them, Alan paddled back and forth, looking up at them uneasily. The mist was a light rain now, and a constant sizzling came from the molten rock.

Finally Slip said, "You're right in a way, Slimey. I am someone's thrall. But I will look for Robin Hood. If you're right, you've got a couple of new allies. If he's too strong for us, this might be the last you see of me."

The Slimey Limey nodded, and Slip hoped he had gotten the real message: He would take on Ery all by himself.

"Well then, let's hope this ain't good-bye, old man."

Slip walked back down into the valley, aware of the Limey's not unsympathetic gaze on his back.

How to find her, how to speak with her? And survive the experience, that is. Virginia had forbidden

him—literally on pain of death—from meeting with
Ery on this plane. Even if he could do so, it would
be a deadly risk for other reasons. What had Ery been
doing in those minutes she dallied, when she had
fooled him into descending back to the human plane
before her? At the time, he had feared it was a be-
trayal. Yet he had lived and had forgotten the mystery. Now he wondered again. It was impossible for
him to understand the complexity of those minutes.
Perhaps she had weakened herself at the beginning to
gull him into starting the descent, and perhaps then
she hadn't been quite strong enough to take over.
Was that possible? And now she was slowly, secretly
building back her powers, just as the Mailman had
done? He didn't want to believe it, and he knew if
Virginia heard his suspicions, the Feds would kill her
immediately. There would be no trial, no deep investigation.

Somehow he must get past Virginia and confront
Ery—confront her in such a way that he could destroy
her if she were a new Mailman. *And there is a way!*
He almost laughed: it was absurd and absurdly simply, and it was the only thing that might work. All
eyes were on this plane, where magic and power
flowed easily to the participants. He would attack
from beneath, from the lowly magicless real world!

But there was one final act of magic he must slip
past Virginia, something absolutely necessary for a
real world confrontation with Erythrina.

He had reached the far ridge and was starting down
the hillside that led to the swamps. Even preoccupied,
he had given the right signs flawlessly. The guardian
sprites were not nearly so vigilant toward contructs
moving away from the castle. As the wet brush closed
in about them, the familiar red and black spider—or
its cousin—swung down from above.

"Beware, beware," came the tiny voice. From the
flecks of gold across its abdomen, he knew the right

response: left hand up and flick the spider away. Instead Slip raised his right hand and struck at the creature.

The spider hoisted itself upward, screeching faintly, then dropped toward Slip's neck—to land squarely on the frog. A free-for-all erupted as the two scrambled across the back of his neck, pale flame jousting against venom. Even as he moved to save the frog, Mr. Slippery melted part of his attention into a data line that fed a sporting goods store in Montreal. An order was placed and later that day a certain very special package would be in the mail to the Boston International Rail Terminal.

Slip made a great show of dispatching the spider, and as the frog settled back on his shoulder, he saw that he had probably fooled Virginia. That he had expected. Fooling Ery would be much the deadlier, chancier thing.

If this afternoon were typical, then July in Providence must be a close approximation to Hell. Roger Pollack left the tube as it passed the urbapt block and had to walk nearly four hundred meters to get to the tower he sought. His shirt was soaked with sweat from just below the belt line right up to his neck. The contents of the package he had picked up at the airport train station sat heavily in his right coat pocket, tapping against his hip with every step, reminding him that this was high noon in more ways than one.

Pollack quickly crossed the blazing concrete plaza and walked along the edge of the shadow that was all the tower cast in the noon day sun. All around him the locals swarmed, all ages, seemingly unfazed by the still, moist, hot air. Apparently you could get used to practically anything.

Even an urbapt in summer in Providence. Pollack had expected the buildings to be more depressing. Workers who had any resources became data com-

muters and lived outside the cities. Of course, some
of the people here were data-set users too and so could
be characterized as data commuters. Many of them
worked as far away from home as any exurb dweller.
The difference was that they made so little money
(when they had a job at all) that they were forced to
take advantage of the economies of scale the urbapts
provided.

Pollack saw the elevator ahead but had to detour
around a number of children playing something like
stickball in the plaza. The elevator was only half-full,
so a wave from him was all it took to keep it grounded
till he could get aboard.

No one followed him on, and the faces around him
were disinterested and entirely ordinary. Pollack was
not fooled. He hadn't violated the letter of Virginia's
law; he wasn't trying to see Erythrina on the data net.
But he was going to see Debby Charteris, which came
close to being the same thing. He imagined the Feds
debating with themselves, finally deciding it would be
safe to let the two godlings get together if it were on
this plane where the *State* was still the ultimate, all-
knowing god. He and Debby would be observed. Even
so, he would somehow discover if she were the threat
the Limey saw. If not, the Feds would never know of
his suspicions. But if Ery had betrayed them all and
meant to set herself up in place of—or in league with—
the Mailman, then in the next few minutes one of
them would die.

The express slid to a stop with a deceptive gentle-
ness that barely gave a feeling of lightness. Pollack
paid and got off.

Floor 25 was mainly shopping mall. He would have
to find the stairs to the residential apts between Floors
25 and 35. Pollack drifted through the mall. He was
beginning to feel better about the whole thing. *I'm
still alive, aren't I?* If Ery had really become what the

Limey and Slip feared, then he probably would have had a little "accident" before now. All the way across the continent he sat with his guts frozen, thinking how easy it would be for someone with the Mailman's power to destroy an air transport, even without resorting to the military's lasers. A tiny change in navigation or traffic-control directions, and any number of fatal incidents could be arranged. But nothing had happened, which meant that either Ery was innocent or that she hadn't noticed him. (And that second possibility was unlikely if she were a new Mailman. One impression that remained stronger than any other from his short time as godling was the omniscience of it all.)

It turned out the stairs were on the other side of the mall, marked by a battered sign reminiscent of old-time highway markers: FOOTS > 26–30. The place wasn't really too bad, he supposed, eyeing the stained but durable carpet that covered the stairs. And the hallways coming off each landing reminded him of the old motels he had known as a child, before the turn of the century. There was very little trash visible, the people moving around him weren't poorly dressed, and there was only the faintest spice of disinfectant in the air. Apt module 28355, where Debbie Charteris lived, might be high-class. It did have an exterior view, he knew that. Maybe Erythrina—Debbie —*liked* living with all these other people. Surely, now that the government was so interested in her, she could move anywhere she wished.

But when he reached it, he found floor 28 no different from the others he had seen: carpeted hallway stretching away forever beneath dim lights that showed identical module doorways dwindling in perspective. What was Debbie/Erythrina like that she would choose to live here?

"Hold it." Three teenagers stepped from behind the

slant of the stairs. Pollack's hand edged toward his
coat pocket. He had heard of the gangs. These three
looked like heavies, but they were well and conserva-
tively dressed, and the small one actually had his hair
in a braid. They wanted very much to be thought part
of the establishment.

The short one flashed something silver at him.
"Building Police." And Pollack remembered the news
stories about Federal Urban Support paying young-
sters for urbapt security: "A project that saves money
and staff, while at the same time giving our urban
youth an opportunity for responsible citizenship."

Pollack swallowed. Best to treat them like real cops.
He showed them his id. "I'm from out of state. I'm
just visiting."

The other two closed in, and the short one laughed.
"That's sure. Fact, Mr. Pollack, Sammy's little gadget
says you're in violation of Building Ordinance." The
one on Pollack's left waved a faintly buzzing cylinder
across Pollack's jacket, then pushed a hand into the
jacket and withdrew Pollack's pistol, a lightweight
ceramic slug-gun perfect for hunting hikes—and which
should have been perfect for getting past a building's
weapon detectors.

Sammy smiled down at the weapon, and the short
one continued, "Thing you didn't know, Mr. Pollack,
is Federal law requires a metal tag in the butt of these
cram guns. Makes 'em easy to detect." Until the tag
was removed. Pollack suspected that somehow this
incident might never be reported.

The three stepped back, leaving the way clear for
Pollack. "That's all? I can go?"

The young cop grinned. "Sure. You're out-of-
towner. How could you know?"

Pollack continued down the hall. The others did
not follow. Pollack was fleetingly surprised: maybe
the FUS project actually worked. Before the turn of

the century, goons like those three would have at least robbed him. Instead they behaved something like real cops.

Or maybe—and he almost stumbled at this new thought—*they all work for Ery now.* That might be the first symptom of conquest: the new god would simply become the government. And he—the last threat to the new order—was being granted one last audience with the victor.

Pollack straightened and walked on more quickly. There was no turning back now, and he was damned if he would show any more fear. Besides, he thought with a sudden surge of relief, it was out of his control now. If Ery was a monster, there was nothing he could do about it; he would not have to try to kill her. If she were not, then his own survival would be proof, and he need think of no complicated tests of her innocence.

He was almost hurrying now. He had always wanted to know what the human being beyond Erythrina was like; sooner or later he would have had to do this anyway. Weeks ago he had looked through all the official directories for the state of Rhode Island, but there wasn't much to find: Linda and Deborah Charteris lived at 28355 Place on 4448 Grosvenor Row. The public directory didn't even show their "interests and occupations."

28313, 315, 317. . . .

His mind had gone in circles, generating all the things Debby Charteris might turn out to be. She would not be the exotic beauty she projected in the Other Plane. That was too much to hope for; but the other possibilities vied in his mind. He had lived with each, trying to believe that he could accept whatever turned out to be the case:

Most likely, she was a perfectly ordinary looking person who lived in an urbapt to save enough money to buy high-quality processing equipment and rent

dense comm lines. Maybe she wasn't good-looking, and
that was why the directory listing was relatively secre-
tive.

Almost as likely, she was massively handicapped.
He had seen that fairly often among the warlocks
whose True Names he knew. They had extra medical
welfare and used all their free money for equipment
that worked around whatever their problem might be
—paraplegia, quadriplegia, multiple sense loss. As
such, they were perfectly competitive on the job mar-
ket, yet old prejudices often kept them out of normal
society. Many of these types retreated into the Other
Plane, where one could completely control one's appearance.

And then, since the beginning of time, there had
been the people who simply did not like reality, who
wanted another world, and if given half a chance
would live there forever. Pollack suspected that some
of the best warlocks might be of this type. Such people
were content to live in an urbapt, to spend all their
money on processing and life-support equipment, to
spend days at a time in the Other Plane, never moving, never exercising their real world bodies. They
grew more and more adept, more and more knowledgeable—while their bodies slowly wasted. Pollack
could imagine such a person becoming an evil thing
and taking over the Mailman's role. It would be like
a spider sitting in its web, its victims all humanity.
He remembered Ery's contemptuous attitude on learning he never used drugs to maintain concentration
and so stay longer in the Other Plane. He shuddered.

And there, finally, and yet too soon, the numbers
28355 stood on the wall before him, the faint hall light
glistening off their bronze finish. For a long moment,
he balanced between the fear and the wish. Finally
he reached forward and tapped the door buzzer.

Fifteen seconds passed. There was no one nearby in
the hall. From the corner of his eye, he could see the

"cops" lounging by the stairs. About a hundred meters the other way, an argument was going on. The contenders rounded the faraway corner and their voices quieted, leaving him in near silence.

There was a click, and a small section of the door became transparent, a window (more likely a holo) on the interior of the apt. And the person beyond that view would be either Deborah or Linda Charteris.

"Yes?" The voice was faint, cracking with age. Pollack saw a woman barely tall enough to come up to the pickup on the other side. Her hair was white, visibly thin on top, especially from the angle he was viewing.

"I'm . . . I'm looking for Deborah Charteris."

"My granddaughter. She's out shopping. Downstairs in the mall, I think." The head bobbed, a faintly distracted nod.

"Oh. Can you tell me—" *Deborah, Debby.* It suddenly struck him what an old-fashioned name that was, more the name of a grandmother than a granddaughter. He took a quick step to the door and looked down through the pane so that he could see most of the other's body. The woman wore an old-fashioned skirt and blouse combination of some brilliant red material.

Pollack pushed his hand against the immovable plastic of the door. "Ery, please. Let me in."

The pane blanked as he spoke, but after a moment the door slowly opened. "Okay." Her voice was tired, defeated. Not the voice of a god boasting victory.

The interior was decorated cheaply and with what might have been good taste except for the garish excesses of red on red. Pollack remembered reading somewhere that as you age, color sensitivity decreases. This room might seem only mildly bright to the person Erythrina had turned out to be.

The woman walked slowly across the tiny apt and gestured for him to sit. She was frail, her back curved in a permanent stoop, her every step considered yet somehow tremulous. Under the apt's window, he noticed an elaborate GE processor system. Pollack sat and found himself looking slightly upward into her face.

"Slip—or maybe I should call you Roger here—you always were a bit of a romantic fool." She paused for breath, or perhaps her mind wandered. "I was beginning to think you had more sense than to come out here, that you could leave well enough alone."

"You . . . you mean, you didn't know I was coming?" The knowledge was a great loosening in his chest.

"Not until you were in the building." She turned and sat carefully upon the sofa.

"I had to see who you really are," and that was certainly the truth. "After this spring, there is no one the likes of us in the whole world."

Her face cracked in a little smile. "And now you see how different we are. I had hoped you never would and that someday they would let us back together on the Other Plane. . . . But in the end, it doesn't really matter." She paused, brushed at her temple, and frowned as though forgetting something, or remembering something else.

"I never did look much like the Erythrina you know. I was never tall, of course, and my hair was never red. But I didn't spend my whole life selling life insurance in Peoria, like poor Wiley."

"You . . . you must go all the way back to the beginning of computing."

She smiled again, and nodded just so, a mannerism Pollack had often seen on the Other Plane. "Almost, almost. Out of high school, I was a keypunch operator. You know what a keypunch is?"

He nodded hesitantly, visions of some sort of machine press in his mind.

"It was a dead-end job, and in those days they'd

keep you in it forever if you didn't get out under your own power. I got out of it and into college quick as I could, but at least I can say I was in the business during the stone age. After college, I never looked back; there was always so much happening. In the Nasty Nineties, I was on the design of the ABM and FoG control programs. The whole team, the whole of DoD for that matter, was trying to program the thing with procedural languages; it would take 'em a thousand years and a couple of wars to do it that way, and they were beginning to realize as much. I was responsible for getting them away from CRTs, for getting into really interactive EEG programming—what they call portal programming nowadays. Sometimes ... sometimes when my ego needs a little help, I like to think that if I had never been born, hundreds of millions more would have died back then, and our cities would be glassy ponds today.

"... And along the way there was a marriage ..." her voice trailed off again, and she sat smiling at memories Pollack could not see.

He looked around the apt. Except for the processor and a fairly complete kitchenette, there was no special luxury. What money she had must go into her equipment, and perhaps in getting a room with a real exterior view. Beyond the rising towers of the Grosvenor complex, he could see the nest of comm towers that had been their last-second salvation that spring. When he looked back at her, he saw that she was watching him with an intent and faintly amused expression that was very familiar.

"I'll bet you wonder how anyone so daydreamy could be the Erythrina you knew in the Other Plane."

"Why, no," he lied. "You seem perfectly lucid to me."

"Lucid, yes. I am still that, thank God. But I know —and no one has to tell me—that I can't support a train of thought like I could before. These last two or three years, I've found that my mind can wander, can drop into reminiscence, at the most inconvenient times. I've had one stroke, and about all 'the miracles of modern medicine' can do for me is predict that it will not be the last one.

"But in the Other Plane, I can compensate. It's easy for the EEG to detect failure of attention. I've written a package that keeps a thirty-second backup; when distraction is detected, it forces attention and reloads my short-term memory. Most of the time, this gives me better concentration than I've ever had in my life. And when there is a really serious wandering of attention, the package can interpolate for a number of seconds. You may have noticed that, though perhaps you mistook it for poor communications coordination."

She reached a thin, blue-veined hand toward him. He took it in his own. It felt so light and dry, but it returned his squeeze. "It really is me—Ery—inside, Slip."

He nodded, feeling a lump in his throat.

"When I was a kid, there was this song, something about us all being aging children. And it's so very, very true. Inside I still feel like a youngster. But on this plane, no one else can see . . ."

"But I know, Ery. We knew each other on the Other Plane, and I know what you truly are. Both of us are so much more there than we could ever be here." This was all true: even with the restrictions they put on him now, he had a hard time understanding all he did on the Other Plane. What he had become since the spring was almost a fuzzy dream to him when he was down in the physical world. Sometimes he felt like a fish trying to imagine what a man in an airplane might be feeling. He never spoke of it like this to Virginia and her friends: they would be sure he had finally gone crazy. It was far beyond what he had known as a warlock. And what they had been

those brief minutes last spring had been equally far
beyond that.

"Yes, I think you do know me, Slip. And we'll
be . . . friends as long as this body lasts. And when I'm
gone—"

"I'll remember; I'll always remember you, Ery."

She smiled and squeezed his hand again. "Thanks.
But that's not what I was getting at. . . ." Her gaze
drifted off again. "I figured out who the Mailman was
and I wanted to tell you."

Pollack could imagine Virginia and the other DoW
eavesdroppers hunkering down closer to their spy
equipment. "I hoped you knew something." He went
on to tell her about the Slimey Limey's detection of
Mailman-like operations still on the System. He spoke
carefully, knowing that he had two audiences.

Ery—even now he couldn't think of her as Debby—
nodded. "I've been watching the Coven. They've
grown, these last months. I think they take themselves
more seriously now. In the old days, they never would
have noticed what the Limey warned you about. But
it's not the Mailman he saw, Slip."

"How can you be sure, Ery? We never killed more
than his service programs and his simulators—like
DON.MAC. We never found his True Name. We
don't even know if he's human or some science-
fictional alien."

"You're wrong, Slip. I know what the Limey saw,
and I know who the Mailman is—or was," she spoke
quietly, but with certainty. "It turns out the Mailman
was the greatest cliché of the Computer Age, maybe
of the entire Age of Science."

"Huh?"

"You've seen plenty of personality simulators in
the Other Plane. DON.MAC—at least as he was re-
written by the Mailman—was good enough to fool
normal warlocks. Even Alan, the Coven's elemental,
shows plenty of human emotion and cunning." Pol-

lack thought of the new Alan, so ferocious and intimidating. The Turing T-shirt was beneath his dignity now. "Even so, Slip, I don't think you've ever believed you could be permanently fooled by a simulation, have you?"

"Wait. Are you trying to tell me that the Mailman was just another simulator? That the time lag was just to obscure the fact that he was a simulator? That's ridiculous. You know his powers were more than human, almost as great as ours became."

"But do you think you could ever be fooled?"

"Frankly, no. If you talk to one of those things long enough, they display a repetitiveness, an inflexibility that's a giveaway. I don't know; maybe someday there'll be programs that can pass the Turing test. But whatever it is that makes a person a person is terribly complicated. Simulation is the wrong way to get at it, because being a person is more than symptoms. A program that was a person would use enormous data bases, and if the processors running it were the sort we have now, you certainly couldn't expect real-time interaction with the outside world." And Pollack suddenly had a glimmer of what she was thinking.

"That's the critical point, Slip: *if you want real-time interaction*. But the Mailman—the sentient, conversational part—never did operate real time. We thought the lag was a communications delay that showed the operator was off-planet, but really he was here all the time. It just took him hours of processing time to sustain seconds of self-awareness."

Pollack opened his mouth, but nothing came out. It went against all his intuition, almost against what religion he had, but it might just barely be possible. The Mailman had controlled immense resources. All his quick time reactions could have been the work of ordinary programs and simulators like DON.MAC. The only evidence they had for his humanity were those teleprinter conversations where his responses were spread over hours.

"Okay, for the sake of argument, let's say it's possible. Someone, somewhere had to write the original Mailman. Who was that?"

"Who would you guess? The government, of course. About ten years ago. It was an NSA team trying to automate system protection. Some brilliant people, but they could never really get it off the ground. They wrote a developmental kernel that by itself was not especially effective or aware. It was designed to live within large systems and gradually grow in power and awareness, *independent* of what policies or mistakes the operators of the system might make.

"The program managers saw the Frankenstein analogy—or at least they saw a threat to their personal power—and quashed the project. In any case, it was very expensive. The program executed slowly and gobbled incredible data space."

"And you're saying that someone conveniently left a copy running all unknown?"

She seemed to miss the sarcasm. "It's not that unlikely. Research types are fairly careless—outside of their immediate focus. When I was in FoG, we lost thousands of megabytes 'between the cracks' of our data bases. And back then, that was a lot of memory. The development kernel is not very large. My guess is a copy was left in the system. Remember, the kernel was designed to live untended if it ever started executing. Over the years it slowly grew—both because of its natural tendencies and because of the increased power of the nets it lived in."

Pollack sat back on the sofa. Her voice was tiny and frail, so unlike the warm, rich tones he remembered from the Other Plane. But she spoke with the same authority.

Debby's—Erythrina's—pale eyes stared off beyond the walls of the apt, dreaming. "You know, they are right to be afraid," she said finally. "Their world is ending. Even without us, there would still be the Limey, the Coven—and someday most of the human race."

Damn. Pollack was momentarily tongue-tied, trying desperately to think of something to mollify the threat implicit in Ery's words. *Doesn't she understand that DoW would never let us talk unbugged? Doesn't she know how trigger-happy scared the top Feds must be by now?*

But before he could say anything, Ery glanced at him, saw the consternation in his face, and smiled. The tiny hand patted his. "Don't worry, Slip. The Feds are listening, but what they're hearing is tearful chitchat—you overcome to find me what I am, and me trying to console the both of us. They will never know what I really tell you here. They will never know about that gun the local boys took off you."

"What?"

"You see, I lied a little. I know why you really came. I know you thought that *I* might be the new monster. But I don't want to lie to you anymore. You risked your life to find out the truth, when you could have just told the Feds what you guessed." She went on, taking advantage of his stupefied silence. "Did you ever wonder what I did in those last minutes this spring, after we surrendered—when I lagged behind you in the Other Plane?

"It's true, we really did destroy the Mailman; that's what all that unintelligible data space we plowed up was. I'm sure there are copies of the kernel hidden here and there, like little cancers in the System, but we can control them one by one as they appear.

"I guessed what had happened when I saw all that space, and I had plenty of time to study what was left, even to trace back to the original research project. Poor little Mailman, like the monsters of fiction— he was only doing what he had been designed to do.

He was taking over the System, protecting it from everyone—even its owners. I suspect he would have announced himself in the end and used some sort of nuclear blackmail to bring the rest of the world into line. But even though his programs had been running for several years, he had only had fifteen or twenty hours of human type self-awareness when we did him in. His personality programs were that slow. He never attained the level of consciousness you and I had on the System.

"But he really was self-aware, and that was the triumph of it all. And in those few minutes, I figured out how I could adapt the basic kernel to accept any input personality. . . . That is what I really wanted to tell you."

"Then what the Limey saw was—"

She nodded. "Me . . ."

She was grinning now, an open though conspiratorial grin that was very familiar. "When Bertrand Russell was very old, and probably as dotty as I am now, he talked of spreading his interests and attention out to the greater world and away from his own body, so that when that body died he would scarcely notice it, his whole consciousness would be so diluted through the outside world.

"For him, it was wishful thinking, of course. But not for me. My kernel is out there in the System. Every time I'm there, I transfer a little more of myself. The kernel is growing into a true Erythrina, who is also truly me. When this body dies," she squeezed his hand with hers, "when this body dies, *I* will still be, and you can still talk to me."

"Like the Mailman?"

"Slow like the Mailman. At least till I design faster processors. . . .

". . . So in a way, I am everything you and the Limey were afraid of. *You* could probably still stop me, Slip." And he sensed that she was awaiting his judgment, the last judgment any mere human would ever be allowed to levy upon her.

Slip shook his head and smiled at her, thinking of the slow-moving guardian angel that she would become. *Every race must arrive at this point in its history,* he suddenly realized. A few years or decades in which its future slavery or greatness rests on the goodwill of one or two persons. It could have been the Mailman. Thank God it was Ery instead.

And beyond those years or decades . . . for an instant, Pollack came near to understanding things that had once been obvious. Processors kept getting faster, memories larger. What now took a planet's resources would someday be possessed by everyone. Including himself.

Beyond those years or decades . . . were millennia. And Ery.

AFTERWORD

by George R. R. Martin

Arthur C. Clarke's Third Law says, "Any sufficiently advanced technology is indistinguishable from magic." That simple statement has been fodder for innumerable SF writers, the germ of countless stories. Most of those stories have not been terribly interesting, chiefly because they fail to go beyond the most obvious and shallow implications of Clarke's Third Law. Thus we have seen a good many stories in which the time-traveler uses a butane lighter and a Saturday Night Special to set himself up among the primitives as a god or sorcerer, and a good many others in which the vast, arbitrary, supernatural powers of the aliens were supposed to be creditable because, early on, someone had muttered something about how advanced their technology must be. The television show "Star Trek" fed us both plots over and over again. They ought to have paid Clarke royalties for sketching out the territory.

It is rather a pity that so many of the writers who have chosen to explore this magic/technology interface have done so in such unoriginal, derivative ways, for there are wilder and more colorful pathways to be taken on this dark road that wanders from "hard" science fiction to "high" fantasy.

The relationship of the two genres (or are they one?) has always been intriguing. They are alike and yet unalike, siblings who have grown up to affect very different life-styles.

In one sense, science fiction is but a form of fantasy; fantasy for our modern, materialistic, technological age. Alexei and Cory Panshin set forth and expanded on this theory in a brilliant and insightful series of columns in *Fantastic* in the early 1970s. Traditional fantasy, once a major and respected current in the mainstream of literature, lost its power when the Age of Reason and the Industrial Revolution destroyed belief in so many of its old symbols and devices; ghosts and vampires and magic spells, sorcerers and things that go bump in the night, all were banished by the machines. Yet the emotional needs once filled by fantasy remained. Literature was left half-complete. Thus science fiction. Certainly science is the magic and religion of our century. Most of us have a superficial and limited understanding of scientific principles and modern technology, if that. But we see the effects, we use the machines, and we believe. We have *faith* in our doctors, our TV repairmen, and our pocket calculators, just as the people of another age had faith in their priests, shamans, and alchemists. Thus many of the old plots and devices of fantasy have resurfaced, rendered more potent and believable by modern, "scientific" dress.

Yet, in another sense, science fiction and fantasy have been very much opposed. Brian Aldiss, in his SF history *Billion Year Spree*, speaks of a "dreaming pole" and a "thinking pole," useful terminology. A good deal of fantasy has always clustered about the dreaming pole; through it run dark rivers of mysticism, irrationality, awe and wonder and fear, emotions

grim and strong and primal. Much SF, in contrast, has
been written beneath the shadow of the thinking pole,
a better-lit and more optimistic place where rule the
spirits of cool rationality and logic and reason and
scientific inquiry, where wonders exist to be understood and not marveled at or feared.

So there are really two fundamental differences between science fiction and fantasy. The furniture is different; one gives us flying carpets and demons and
magic swords, the other offers aircars and aliens and
disintegrators. But beyond that, there exists a great
fundamental difference in the basic philosophies of the
two related genres.

This gives rise to some intriguing paradoxes. SF
and fantasy are often bracketed together, edited by a
single person in a publishing house, pressed between
the covers of the same magazines, honored by the same
awards. And certainly a good many readers who enjoy
one also cherish the other. Yet you have only to attend
a few SF conventions to realize that there are also SF
readers who want nothing to do with fantasy, and
fantasy aficionados who loath SF. And alongside the
magazines like *The Magazine of Fantasy & Science
Fiction* exist "pure" SF journals like *Analog*, whose
readers brook no ghosts mingling with their aliens,
thank you.

I think that those who totally love one form to the
exclusion of the other are much the losers for that.
For human beings are neither animals nor disembodied intellect, but rather creatures of both mind
and body, capable of both logic and mysticism, of
rational thought and irrational fear. The strongest,
greatest, longest-lasting stories are those which appeal
to both sides of our natures. The pure-bred forms of
both SF and fantasy tend to sterility—hard SF offers
us empty little intellectual puzzles without discernible
human emotion, while fantasy breeds incestuously in
the shadows of Tolkien and Howard.

For a long time, the most interesting work has been done in the middle, between the two poles, where dreams and thought can mesh together. The wedding of SF and fantasy produces endless varieties, each different, and difficult to categorize, but possessed of a certain hybrid vigor. Thus arise such paradoxes as H. P. Lovecraft, who used SF devices like extraterrestrials in the philosophic service of fantasy at its darkest and most primal, and the Harold Shea fantasies of de Camp and Pratt, where gods and magic become as logical and demystified as a wiring diagram.

Vernor Vinge's splendid novella, *True Names*, and my own *Nightflyers*, offered cheek-to-jowl in this volume of *Binary Stars*, represent two more writers setting out into the broad land between the poles, breeding SF with fantasy and playing games with Clarke's Third Law. When I first read *True Names*, I was sucked right into the story and had no time to reflect on any of it, which is as it should be with any work of fiction. On second reading, however, I was bemused and intrigued by the ways my own story and Vinge's meshed with each other, the likenesses and contrasts providing an interesting study in the manifold possibilities that arise when magic meets technology, possibilities much richer and more varied than those tired and obvious applications of Clarke's Law that I mentioned at the beginning of this essay. There are more things under heaven and earth, Captain Kirk, than are dreamt of aboard the *Enterprise*.

Certain similarities are striking. More striking for me, perhaps, since I wrote *Nightflyers* long before I knew it would be half of a *Binary Star* or had any inkling of my partner (I also wrote it well before I saw the film *Alien*, by the way). The parallels are therefore extraordinary. The key roles of computers, of course. The endings, each suggesting a cybernetic possibility for life after death. The basic plot structures, both of which embody both a struggle and a mystery. Who is the enemy? Is it one of the Coven? Is it one of the passengers on the *Nightflyer*? Who is the Mailman, really? Who or what killed Thale Lasamer? Both stories even offer up a false answer; Royd Eris and DON.MAC. There are even certain resonances between Erythrina and Melantha Jhirl. Both novellas are, to my way of thinking, fundamentally science fiction, despite heavy borrowings from fantasy.

But the differences are fascinating as well. Vernor Vinge sets his tale solidly in the here-and-now, the day after tomorrow, but most of the action takes place in the Other Plane (a lovely and original idea, by the way, and a wonderfully logical extrapolation of trends underway right now among cyberneticists, games fanatics, and role-players). Though it is reached by means of computers, the Other Plane is a quintessentially *fantasy* landscape. Here there be demons and castles, smoking mountains and spider-haunted swamps through which strange creatures prowl. The setting, the furniture, the very terms invoked are from high fantasy; the story is the story of great wizards at war. And true names, as in pure fantasy, are keys to victory and defeat.

Nightflyers, on the other hand, brims with the trappings of hard science fiction. Here the setting is a starship in deep space, off to find a mysterious race of aliens. The cast of characters are all scientists and scholars, not amateur wizards, and the only magic powers invoked are the science-fictional ones of psionics.

Nonetheless, *True Names* is *harder* science fiction, to my mind. For all its borrowings from fantasy's terminology, *True Names* is a relentlessly worked out and logical tale, with every bit of magic solidly anchored in technology. Mr. Slippery, Erythrina, the Slimey Limey, and all the rest are grand and potent necromancers, yet they are also human beings with computer consoles, and neither they nor the reader is ever unaware of that fact. It is almost possible to read Vinge's novella twice, picking and choosing among the images, so one time it takes shape as a fantasy epic, the next as the hardest of cybernetic extrapolations. The double texture deepens and enriches the story. But, with everyone aware that the fantasy images are facade, it is easy to see that the hybrid Vinge has produced partakes of the spirit of SF, though it may be dressed as a wizard.

As for my own story, it too is a hybrid, but of a different sort. It may wear a space suit, but the spirit within has the grinning skeletal face of the horror story, the darkest and least rational aspect of fantasy.

The Coven and the Other Plane in *True Names* are both striking and real. In a way, it's rather a shame that the novella ends so thoroughly; it would be fun to see Vinge return and use the setting again for other stories. Clearly there are hundreds there, waiting to be told. Reading over *True Names* with *Nightflyers* in the back of my mind, I couldn't keep from speculating how Lommie Thorne or Royd's mother might manifest themselves were they to jump from my story to his, a sure sign that I'd been hooked by his concept. I can only hope the dark corridors of the *Nightflyer*—and particularly its lounge—are as real and intriguing. Both stories, I hope, suggest and illuminate the variety of plots and textures and settings and characters and moods available to the writer who dares to cross genre lines. The heart and soul of good fiction is to get the reader wondering about *what will happen next*. In high fantasy and hard SF, far too often, what happens next is predictable, mostly because we've seen it happen so many times before.

But between lies a land wide and varied and largely unexplored, which might just be the richest part of the whole continent of imaginative fiction.

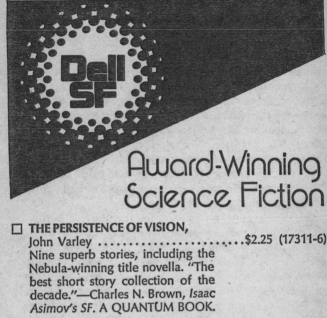